A
Travelling
Lark

Diana Reynolds

For all my loves.

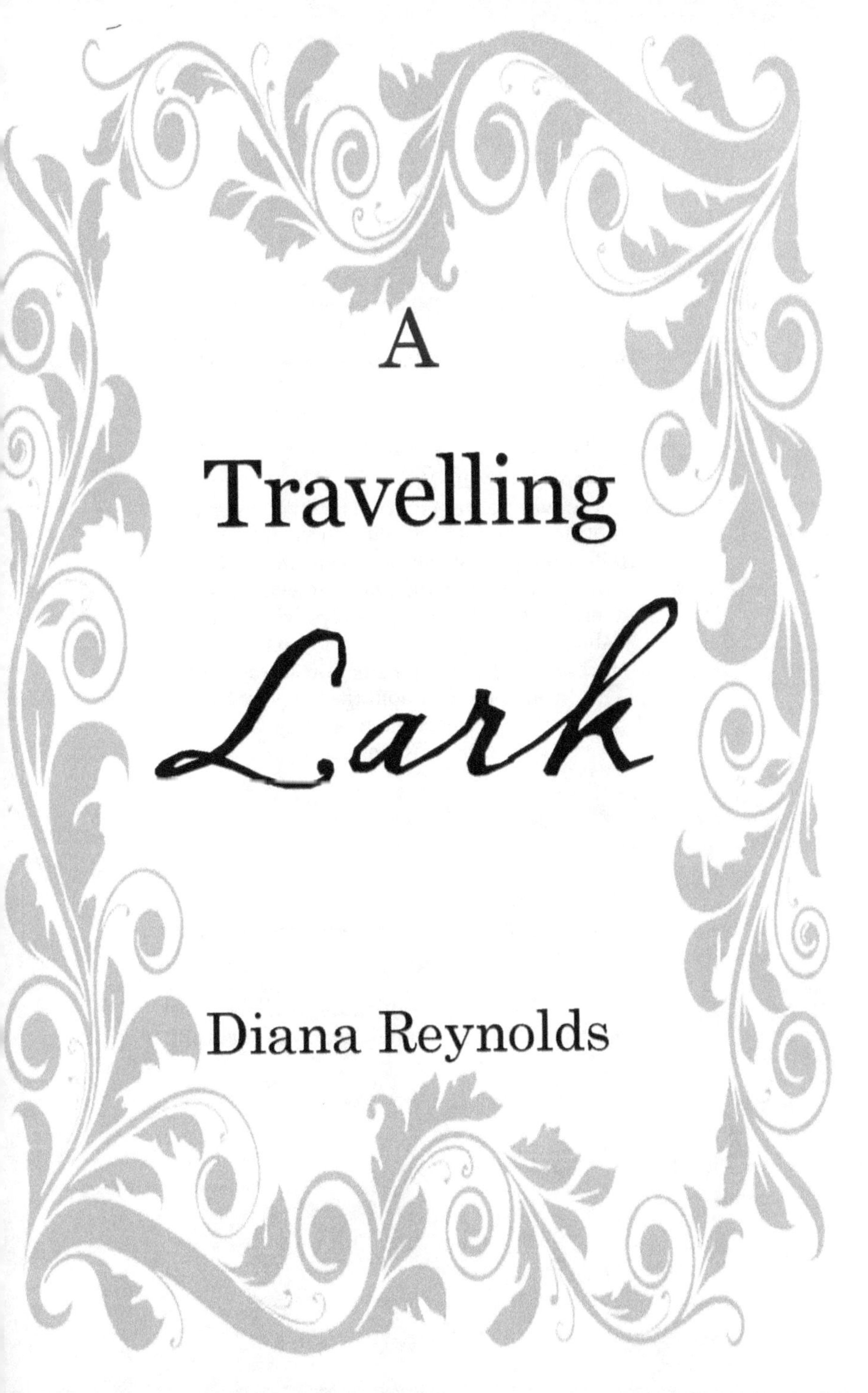

A Travelling *Lark*

Diana Reynolds

A Travelling Lark

Design & text
© Copyright Diana Reynolds 2016

The moral right of the author has been asserted.

Printed by Ingram Spark/Lightning Source Australia

ISBN: 978-0-9942485-8-9
Catalogue Listing National Library of Australia

Lark:

http://www.urbandictionary.com/define.php?term=lark

noun
1. a merry, carefree adventure with the objective of sexual satisfaction

The artist's experience lies so unbelievably close to the sexual, to its pain and its pleasure, that the two phenomena are really just different forms of one and the same longing and bliss.

Rainer Maria Rilke (1875 - 1926)

The creative effort is a lot like sex. It's not so much the equipment you have as what is in your mind. The real excitement and beauty is in what we think and feel and what we do about it.

Kelly Borsheim

1

'Lark,' Martin rolls his tongue in a purr on the 'r' in my name. He dabs my nose with a light kiss before shifting away to take photos with Skippy near other spring tourists, who climbed the clattering stairs to see the view of Paris before us.

Weeks before at the airport boarding lounge, Mum thrust Skippy into my hands while kissing me goodbye. He's a small stuffed toy kangaroo from one of the Sydney airport stores, about fifteen centimetres high. We include Skippy in our tourist photos to send across the ether home – a tacky joke I know Mum and my friends appreciate. You know; kangaroo larger than the Eiffel Tower, that kind of thing.

The warm Parisian breeze curls about us up there amongst the creepy old gargoyles, leaping like fruit bats from the parapets of Notre Dame Cathedral.

'What type of architecture is it and how old?'

Martin is a history professor so he's the best person to ask and he doesn't mansplain, something I like about him.

'French Gothic, begun in 1163, but not completed until 1345.' He rubs his hand across the stonework. 'Notre Dame has been vandalised, damaged and restored several times since.'

Martin's so happy, I look at him, take a tender, slow eyeful. He doesn't realise I'm barely taking in what he's saying. I drink in his profile like a thirsting dingo lapping at a waterhole – I even feel parched despite having just taken a long swig from my water bottle. I gaze at the periwinkle blue sky with swallows flitting about, ordered French architecture spread like a crochet rug around the Eiffel Tower, itself constructed from crochet hooks. Yet my heart's in my mouth. Kaboom, kaboom - it tastes large and metallic as I try to swallow.

I zip and unzip my bag, such uncertainty flitting from my fingertips. He doesn't notice my fixed grin as he turns his phone my way for a picture. He's still free. I slide out my own phone to take a photo of him, for Before, knowing After, all will be irrevocably changed. Hope flutters like a zephyr driven flower, like a multitude of Catholic prayers folded into the cathedral stonework as I capture his image. I hesitate to tell him my big news. This one is not a momentary skydive or a thrilling bungy jump, but a far more incontrovertible leap. How do other women do it I wonder? Big breath, here goes.

'Martin.'

'Look, there's Sacre Coeur.' He points, repositions Skippy on the wall and clicks away.

'Martin, I'm pregnant.' I whisper and the breeze lifts my secret away.

Louder. 'Martin... I'm pregnant.'

My news reaches him, there's a glaze of incomprehension. No smile. Oh. I slide my phone away. Finger the zip.

'What? How do you know? How pregnant?' A frown.

'A test yesterday, a few weeks I think.'

'You're kidding right?'

I shake my head. An inward cringe.

He looks down then, 'What bad timing.' Sucks in a breath. 'When?'

'Maybe before we left, I don't know. I've bled a little since we've been here, but hardly much. You know, peri-menopause... we talked about that.' Unzip, zip.

Another sharp inhalation. 'Cigarette, I need one,' says Martin, a reformed smoker, already drawing imagined smoke through tightened lips.

Hope wavers, gargoyles chitter. I'm terrified.

We look at each other, surprised and searching. The breadth of Paris about us spirals in like water down the plughole. He looks at my waist. Reaches out, but stops short of touching. Earlier this morning I cradled his weight as he thrust into me at Guil and Jordy's place where we're staying. Dazed, I lift my wrist to my nose and sniff our come blooming in my skin.

'Holy shit Lark,' he says, lifting dark sunglasses to rub his eyes.

His elbow nudges Skippy and the toy pirouettes and falls past the safety mesh, plummeting over the edge. We watch as it somersaults through the air to the square below, hitting two copulating pigeons. Kaboom! A fluster of feathers and flight. A small girl in day-glo shorts and singlet detaches from a family group. She picks Skippy up, gives the busy square a surreptitious gaze and with a hug, carries him away. Kangaroos are a rare species to find in Paris.

I gaze at Martin, stricken. Some strange symbolism has transpired; losing Skippy and gaining our newly discovered embryo. I'm thirty eight. I want to keep the baby, aware I am already swirling in a soup of biological instinct that is colouring my choices.

I look again at Martin savaging a quick on his finger with a glassy stare. Of course babies have been discussed. Well, having babies later. Sometime in the powder puff future when we have the perfect everything. House, car, job security, school zoning. But thirty eight is already old and double income, no kids is a seductive lifestyle that doesn't always lead to the right time or right situation to have kids.

Contraception's been an ad hoc, shifting responsibility between us but mostly left up to me. I run my tongue over my dingo teeth, instinct alert for discord. We thought we were safe before we left. Such a manic time trying to finalise everything before departure. We've done the rhythm method for a fair while. Finally it's somersaulted us, kaboom! Into an unchartered billabong.

2

Martin and Lark arrived a month before at Gare Du Nord, Paris, on a brutal no sleep Qantas flight which changed at Hong Kong to an Air France connection. Relief sex in the tiny toilet next to the smoking compartment with swarthy men lounging and staring from a haze of Gauloise smoke. Planned since the beginning of the year, they intend staying six months to see the sights of Europe.

They work their way through the jungle of trains, taking Line 5, changing at Republic to Line 11, Port des Lilas. Dragging heavy suitcases to Saint Fargeau in the early afternoon where Guil picks them up. All the shadows seem to slant the wrong way to Lark. By then she's cross eyed with tiredness and outrage. After all it's the middle of the night in Sydney and she has only had snatches of sleep for two days.

'Ello, bonjour mes cherie's.' Guil gives them both generous câlins et bisous, hugs and kisses, one for each cheek. His goatee tickles. It has a patch of white in it and he reminds Lark of a ringtail possum with his moist protruding eyes darting about. 'Your flight est trés bon?'

He takes Lark's suitcase to tug along the footpath, minding the little dog shits everywhere with a local's eye. Lark's French is almost non existent but Martin is pretty fluent. He laughs and tells Guil about the flight. They walk past shops, a Carrefour supermarché and up a tree lined street to the apartment Guil shares with Jordy and their tiny eight month old daughter Celeste. When they get out of the elevator Jordy greets them at the door with the baby holding her leg. More câlins et bisous.

'Halloo, halloo, so good to see you,' says Jordy grinning.

We smell rank, but the good friends that they are, they pretend not to notice. Guil carries his own nicotine cloud with him anyway and naturellement, lights up again as soon as he settles his lanky frame onto the lounge. Lark is happy to see her old friend Jordy who she shared a flat with in Sydney for a few years before they paired off with boyfriends.

'This is Celeste.' Celeste stares up at Martin and Lark and hides behind her mother.

'We'll get wine to celebrate your safe arrival, yes?'

That's Guil who indulges in any vice he can. He works in a stressful animation job which is his excuse, according to Jordy. He rubs his hands together and a discussion about French and Australian wine ensues with Martin. Surreal, Lark floats along, listening to them. Might as well be discussing earth samples from the Paleozoic age, she rolls her eyes in half crazed sleep deprivation

'Hello Celeste,' Lark says, trying for normality as she drifts down to the tiny girl now sitting on Jordy's lap. 'This is Skippy.' She fishes a small stuffed kangaroo out of her handbag and shows it to Celeste, who takes the toy, examines it and drops it.

'These are my friends Lark and Martin,' Jordy says to Celeste. 'They're going to stay in your room Celeste and you can sleep with us.'

Celeste writhes, 'duh. duh.'

Jordy puts her down on the floor. The baby picks up Skippy, stuffing the tail in her gummy mouth. She skirts the couch holding on, dropping down to a pile of toys on the floor.

'Ow is Australie,' asks Guil. 'Bondi Beach, always sunny. The Opera 'ouse?'

Jordy laughs and shakes her golden ponytail. 'Ah the

French believe this is what Australia is. Kangaroos are hopping everywhere in the streets and bush.'

We all laugh.

'We think of Paris as the Eiffel Tower and the French Revolution with many angry Gallic souls,' Lark says.

'Such narrow generalisations!' says Martin, who pops out with more educated opinions sometimes. He works full time as a history professor at Sydney University after all. 'So much has changed...' he murmurs to himself.

'Hmm, like a cartoon snapshot for our brains to file, yes?' says Guil from the kitchen, not hearing Martin. He is already finding wineglasses although its only 4pm. 'I'll take you both for a touristic ride to see Paris later on.'

'Wow its good to see you Jordy,' Lark says, hugging her friend.

Jordy has been living in Paris for three years. They often chat on Facebook or email or skype each other. Jordy tries hard but hasn't quite fitted in to Parisian life.

Lark smothers a yawn which her friend catches. 'Would you both like to shower? I'll start making something to eat.'

'Uh, kill for a shower,' moans Lark.

'I'll put our suitcases away in Celeste's room.' Martin heaves them up and manhandles them down the hall.

'But 'ow can you drink much if it is stronger in alcohol content?' Lark hears Guil ask when she emerges. She's feeling shower-awake and cleansed of stale in-flight aeroplane grime. Guil and Martin drink wine as they chat. The aftermath of a joint lingers in the smoke emanating from another cigarette between Guil's lips. Lark helps Jordy in the kitchen while Celeste crashes around the tiny lounge room in her walker frame. Jordy is vegetarian so its jasmine rice and veggies. She hasn't adapted to the traditional meaty French diet. After flight food, Jordy's cooking is heaven.

Three bottles of wine and a few joints later, Guil takes Lark and Martin for a ride in his low slung, pump up Peugeot. Into Paris to see the sights, he slaloms through the traffic, careening here and there like all the other drivers. Martin nudges Lark awake at every marvel and she falls asleep in between. The Eiffel Tower,

Arche De Triomphe, Place de la Concorde, Île de la Cité, Place de la Bastille and many others pass in a daze. Lark remembers little; a blur of lights, traffic and golden bridges, a big arch. Guil chain smokes and chatters to Martin, who has been here before. Both are pretty are pretty stoned and rather drunk. Unable to resist, the pull of the Australian night tugs Lark's eyelids down, down. The sights of Paris and the backseat disappear in a wave of fatigue.

At the flat again, Guil insists on a joint and more wine. Martin stays up while Lark stumbles to Celeste's room and crashes.

She wakes disorientated and bemused by the pile of soft toys pyramiding in a corner of the little room. There are swirls of pastel colours painted on the walls she hadn't noticed the night before. Its lunchtime by the travel clock propped on the suitcase. She sniffs. The room has the unmistakable aroma of baby – a mixture of sweetness overlaying talc and poo. Martin slumbers on while she dresses and tries on new sandals she bought in Sydney for the trip, finding they don't fit now.

'Probably my feet swelled on the flight,' she thinks, tiptoeing out and closing the door.

In the kitchen Jordy is feeding pumpkin puree to Celeste.

Lark still looks wasted from the journey, thinks Jordy, who is a regular inmate of the parent cycle of tiredness, so she easily detects it in others.

'It's good to rest after the flight but you'll have to get over your jetlag,' she says to Lark, hovering the spoon into Celeste's mouth.

Celeste spits the mashed food out and grizzles. She's had enough and wants to get out of her clip-on baby chair.

Lark notices Jordy's tight expression. She wonders if feeding Celeste is challenging. Jordy puts the baby spoon down, tests the breast milk filled baby bottle she's warmed in the microwave, screws on the silicone teat lid and gives the bottle to Celeste, who sucks with immediate pleasure.

'I breastfeed and do solids, but sometimes Celeste doesn't want her puree and still wants more breast milk. I express it using my breast pump.' Jordy shrugs, 'it's a rhythm thing.'

Lark frowns, not at all sure what Jordy is talking about. Breast did she say really say, pump? What is that? She gets up, 'I'll make us some tea,' she says, too tired to ask what Jordy is on about. She clatters about in the kitchen, with Jordy directing her to where things are.

'There's some salad and baguette if you're hungry,' says Jordy. 'Help yourself.'

Celeste is drowsy after her bottle; it falls from her mouth to the floor. 'I'll just put her down for a nap and we can talk.'

'Guil?' Lark asks.

'At work.'

While Jordy sings Celeste to sleep, Lark eats the remains of the salad, sipping her tea.

'So how is it here? Your apartment is really nice, though quite small,' says Lark, when Jordy returns.

'I miss the beach and my family,' says Jordy, warming her tea up again in the microwave. 'Yes our flat seems very small by Aussie standards but is actually large for Paris. Neighbours are good and don't complain about Celeste's noise. Many children grow up in apartments here and learn to be quiet – eventually,' she smiles.

'And Guil adores you,' says Lark.

It's a repeated line that hangs suspended between them across the internet.

'Yes and I love him to bits and now we have Celeste. So here I am. I've change my stripes to blue, white and red. 'Allons enfants de la Patrie, Le jour de gloire est arrivé!' She begins to sing the French national anthem and then laughs.

'And you are happy with Martin?'

'Yes, we are happy, very busy with our careers and our apartment and Purzia, my cat - my baby. Remember Paul? So glad I finished with him, he gobbled up my twenties and was never going to commit himself.'

'We all knew. Told you too, but you didn't listen.' Jordy tore off a piece of baguette to nibble.

Between them this is old news converted to myth and memory. Both of them know Lark adored Paul and became a doting live-in girlfriend so he got the trimmings with none of the commitment.

'Are you and Martin going to have any kids?'

'Martin wants to wait a bit and get more stable.' Lark takes her hairbrush from her lap, tugging it through her long dark hair. 'You wrote that Celeste's birth was horrible. Is it really as awful as they say, birth? It scares me.'

'For other women it might not be so bad. My hips are so narrow. At the Paediatric Maternity hospital there was no sympathy from the nurses. The doctor and midwife were such dragons. It was very difficult but they made me persevere for many days before finally giving me an epidural and inducing my baby. Perhaps Celeste's birth would have been awful at home in Sydney, who knows.' Jordy sighs.

Lark has no barometer on birth. She has never experienced it and doesn't move in any mother type circles either. 'Epidural, what's that?'

'A needle into your lower spine that deadens the pain of childbirth,' answers Jordy.

'Uh, sounds barbaric. My mum said it was a noble career to be a good parent,' Lark says, skating over her fear with a homily. She has a vague idea of candles and breathing classes with the husband and pushing, yes the pushing, but not much else. 'At least at home you'd have friends and family to help, right?'

'Yes,' sighs Jordy. It's a sore point still fresh in her mind. 'Put me off having any more babies though. I've taken months to recover.' There is a cry from the bedroom. 'Ah, Celeste never sleeps for long.' She's up and moving towards the hall. 'By the way, I'll come into Celeste's room to get some bags of nappies from time to time, okay? I'll change her in our room. Oh, I've got to get out to the shops for some food, wanna come?'

'Ok, I don't think Martin is up to much yet. I need new sandals too, the ones I bought don't seem to fit.'

Lark clears away the snack and tea things, thrilling at the thought of her first shopping venture in Paris. Paris! The prospect of shoe shopping always perks her up and feeds her fetish. She returns to the bedroom where Martin is stirring. He reaches for her, his cock waking stiff and wanting, but she evades him, whispering ... later.'

Jordy waits with Celeste in her pram by the door. They take the elevator down to the street. Lark pushes the stroller for Jordy, a real novelty, while Celeste scowls back at her.

'There are so many dogshits on the street,' she says, trying to avoid wheeling the pram in it.

'Many Parisians have small dogs in their apartments, which are let out to shit on the streets. There used to be a kind of street sweeper vacuum car called 'Caninette,' cleaning it up but it cost the French a fortune. Now there are fines. It sort of works - if the authorities can catch the owners and their dogs,' says Jordy.

'Same in Sydney, owners have to pick it up. Some dogs even carry their turds in a little kind of doggy backpack.'

'Really?' laughs Jordy, who hasn't been back to Sydney for a few years. 'That's so mad.'

Lark finds sandals that fit with Jordy's help. They buy more food and catch up on gossip along the way. Martin is up and Guil arrives home not long after, announcing that they'll eat out for dinner and meet up with some friends. Martin brings out presents from Australia, a surfing tshirt, rainforest bath oils and a little dress Lark has made from Aboriginal fabric for Celeste. Of course Guil consecrates the gifts with more wine.

The French habit of eating late catches them unawares. Hours later, after another joint and more wine, they make their way to Le Soleil café near Belleville metro station.

The evening is warm. Remi and Adelyn with their baby boy, Benoit, who is a little older that Celeste, have already pulled some tables together in the busy café when they arrive. Francois a tall, brown haired Frenchman who on a point of honour speaks only French, turns up. Marcelle, who is dressed in pink with pink punk hair looks like a galah and her friend Simone saunter in nearly an hour late. These friends of Jordy and Guil all make Martin and Lark feel welcome. Martin has met them all on previous journeys to France and England so they have a lot to talk about. Martin and Lark eat the only vegetarian dish on the menu, Salade de Chèvre Chaud - warm Goat's cheese with a lettuce leaf and vinaigrette. After drinking wine on empty stomachs and eating at ten o'clock, they go to bed tipsy and hungry.

Their plan is to get out and about sightseeing in the city for a few days before hiring a car to go to the country. Guil and Jordy protest and say they can stay as long as they like, such marvellous pals, but a few wine and dope soaked days are enough for Martin and the unfamiliar sound of Celeste crying in the night mixed with a slow recovery from jetlag does Lark's head in a bit.

Martin has organised a great travel itinerary. His previous trips to Europe have been business based, delivering history papers and collaborating with his European counterparts. This will be his first purely holiday travel and it's Lark's first time in Europe. They've planned to go south-east and return to Paris a few days here and there so they don't overload Guil and Jordy and the baby.

'Look at the girls,' Martin says to Lark on the metro on their way to the centre. So many seem young, thin and whilst not always elegantly dressed, embody a casual chic unknown in Sydney.

'Look at the shoes!' Lark answers, knowing he is tantalised by so much sexiness. For her, their clothes and especially, her fashion fetish – shoes, are what grabs her. She doesn't mind at all that he is perving. She thinks some of the women are sumptuous enough to observe from an artistic point of view.

In the city they roam around the Île de la Cité, Pont Neuf, Ile Saint Louis, the Palais de Justice and the art markets in the Place de la Bastille. In the Spring sunshine they hunt down an elusive organic vegetarian cafe and eat their picnic on the Alexander III Bridge with its elegant Art Nouveau lamps and golden statues.

Lark has unearthed Skippy from Celeste's toy pile earlier and they have a heap of fun setting up photos featuring the kangaroo about Paris. They buy fresh food on the way home and eat in, early.

Next day is another set of marvels - they visit the Musée d'Orsay enjoying the exhibits for hours.

'I just can't believe some of the art at the Musée d'Orsay,' says Lark walking hand in hand with Martin along the Seine. 'All those years of looking at shabby prints in art books and then you see the real deal. Wow! The pointillists, Seurat and Signac. I'm just blown away.'

'The sculptures, especially that one by Bourdelle, 'The Herculean Archer,' Martin is alight with inspiration just as Lark is.

'Mmm, Degas. I love the pre-Raphaelites as well.'

'The French Impressionists.' Martin laughs, pulling her into a hug against the stone wall. Lark pushes up his shirt and twirls his nipple, which hardens as they kiss. She feels a corresponding hardness form against her pubic bone and a sharp desire crests. She could melt into sex with Martin right then and there.

'Lark,' Martin purrs. He gives her earlobe a gentle lick, while she plays with his curly brown hair and runs a fingertip over his bottom lip. The excitement of the holiday has already revitalised their lovemaking. Their first two days recovering from jetlag gave them alot of time in bed together; time for sex between interludes of sleep. Lark grinds up against him.

'Woah, girl,' he laughs, moving away. He pulls his shirt down over his erection. Tourists are everywhere enjoying the mild weather. Lark bites her lip and shrugs at the rush of heat to her belly. With her backpack on her lap on the train home, she draws Martin's fingers under her skirt for some mild satisfaction.

Back at the flat, Guil takes them downstairs to the apartment's storage cage and digs out a tent, gas stove, mattresses and sleeping bags. He takes Martin to pick up the hire vehicle – from some arrondisement somewhere – laughs Lark when Jordy asks her. Martin arrives back with a four door Megane sedan. They can drive to Annecy with its beautiful lake in the morning.

3

'**B**right and shiny, Lark has a driving lesson to get used to left-hand drive, nearly steering the car up onto the peopled footpath and into a street lamp.

'Well, it'll take a few goes, it's so weird to drive this way,' she defies Martin, green eyes flaring. She runs her tongue over her pointy dingo teeth.

Though shocked, Martin knows that look and says with careful tact, 'How about I drive for a while Lark? Maybe you can try again somewhere quieter.'

She subsides, pride intact. 'Good idea. I'll be map reader. I'll try again out of Paris.'

Lark's noticed that the speedy French drivers make Australians look like sedate snails on the roads. She's already finds it intimidating as a pedestrian trying to cross at the lights on Paris streets, but a timid driver with a spatial issue, no, she'll relearn her driving skills in a quieter place.

They stock up on fresh food and drinks at the supermarché. With suitcases and mattress rolls in the boot, food in boxes finds a place on the backseat. More kisses goodbye and bon chance from Guil and Jordy. Martin drives them out of Paris into the countryside, a five hour drive on the A6 to Annecy, stopping at a lay-by for lunch and mutually satisfying blowjobs along the way. It's easy for Lark to give Martin head in the sedan, but pushing the passenger seat back and cramming his tall frame into the footwell of the front seat to give Lark a licking is hilarious.

At Annecy, which is on a most exquisite lake, they stay at the local youth hostel, arriving late in the day. After unravelling, they make dinner and go for a stroll and an ice cream, Skippy tucked into Lark's shoulder pack.

'Look at the colour of the lake, it's a milky turquoise,' says Lark, who loves the subtleties of colour.

'I think it's from mineral deposits,' says Martin, 'or perhaps quartz sand?'

They strip to their swimmers and go for a late swim. Looking up at the wooded mountains, some still with spring snow upon them, is a magical sight. They're to begin sleeping separately when they stay at hostels, which seems rather peculiar to Lark, having not slept apart from Martin for a while. The hostel is filled with single bunk-beds, five to a room. It's busy with many young tourists, but its a small concession to make for an economical holiday.

For a couple of days they explore Vieux Annecy, the picturesque Old Annecy. Lark marvels at the medieval Château d'Annecy, cobbled streets and old pastel painted houses with their multitude of geraniums. They go for strolls and swims in the radiant turquoise lake. To actually be here after talking about it for so many months and to see so much history awes her: Australia is so culturally young by comparison.

Holidaying with Martin feels terribly romantic. Both are seriously career driven, he with his teaching and she with her freelance design business so holidays are a rare luxury even at home. Walking arm in arm, Lark ponders the marriage question. Will he ask her? Martin is not a demonstrative man, he's pretty reserved but she knows he loves her. Should she ask him to marry her? Lark isn't a traditionalist at all, but respects that others can be. Martin loves her zany unconventional side; it's a panacea to the orderly nature of his career.

She knows little of his past except that he was in a long

relationship with a woman whom he adored. They separated, she managing to get a low evaluation on their house, so he received far less on their investment than he should have. She took their beloved Schnauzer dog as well. About here in any discussion on the subject, Martin gets tight lipped and goes away to sulk, so Lark wisely hasn't tried to dig any further. He also has a sister and as an only child, Lark sometimes expresses her curiosity, but like so many men, he doesn't keep in touch with the sister or have much to say about her.

'Lives in Canada, partner and no kids,' is all he's said about her. The plaza they stop at is filled with families and tourists who mill about the ice cream bar displaying generous tubs with a large selection of flavours.

'Want an ice cream?' Martin asks. 'I know, double Nocciola.'

'Ah you know me so well, I love hazelnuts,' Lark answers.

She twirls her black hair into a chignon against the mild heat, holding the clip in her mouth as she deliberates over the pros and cons of proposing. Everything to gain and nothing to lose if he says no, though a 'no' might be a dent in their relationship, she decides.

'Martin, will you marry me?' Lark says when he returns with a cone in each hand.

'Eh, what?' Martin looks stunned. Laughs, then sobers. 'You mean it?'

'Yes, I do mean it, will you?'

'Yes Lark, of course I will! But later in the year, after our holiday?' Martin smiles down at her.

'No worries,' she says, thrilled. 'Give me my ice cream before it melts away. You're in pre-marital dreamland.'

'Oh-ah, here.'

Martin hands it to her. She takes his hand and licks the ice cream dripping from his fingers.

With a crooked smile Martin lashes his tongue over his leaking chocolate ice cream before it falls off the cone in the sun. They flirt and joke, an arm about each other while they enjoy the rest of their treat. Of course selfies have to be taken, it's a special moment. They look at the images on their phones, amused by

Skippy squished between their faces in some of the shots.

Over three weeks Martin and Lark drift through the south- east of France, sometimes hostelling, sometimes staying in Guil's tiny two man tent. They feel free from their usual daily grind. Before they left Australia, they decided to limit the amount of communication with home, also a boon. After Annecy they move on to Aix-Les-Bains and drive around lake, stopping for a tour of Hautecombe Abbey. There is a cottage for sale on the lake's edge. It prompts a semi-serious discussion about selling up their Bondi digs and moving here to raise a family. A mix up and near theft at the Geneva hostel leaves them less than impressed. After a night they move on to camp at Nice, Monaco, Cannes and St Tropez. The summer sun pours a golden glamour over the French countryside while they roam and enjoy sightseeing.

Lark realises her periods are late at about Cannes but puts it down to being peri-menopausal. For a while now, her periods have been more erratic. She has friends in their early forties who have, without realising, reached the end of their fertility and accepts this transition. So she takes little notice of the scant spots of blood in her underpants over several days. They are just having too much fun.

Their sex life, always robust, has increased. It could be the abstinence created by sleeping alone in hostels that adds to their passion, or perhaps the new level of commitment between them now they are unofficially engaged. Whatever the case, Lark finds she is insatiable when they make love.

'Perhaps it is a woman thing,' she muses, to be able to let go without reserve when a partner is entirely committed. A woman's psyche needs that paradox to dissolve the boundaries of reserve, an invisible force in place with an uncommitted partner. She plays with these thoughts as a passenger between towns and tourist venues while Martin drives. They stop the sedan a couple of times a day and have desperately comical car sex.

'Just. Move thataway.'

'Oof, Skippy's fallen down the side.'

'Ow, your knee, that's better.'

'Oh Lark, yeah! Ride me honey. Mmm, Martin, Agh!'

While Martin is driving Lark makes up songs and poems, which they amuse themselves with. She's always liked to write, sometimes just a word, a phrase, a poem or paragraph to add detail to a sketch, especially if annotating a creative idea or design.

'This one's the best so far,' says Martin. 'It sums up the essence of being young and sexually charged on the way to the beach.'

'Yeah, we've both been there, done that,' agrees Lark with a cheeky grin, knowing exactly how much of her own truth flavours it. 'Here goes, I've improved the end, wanna hear it?

'Yep. Couldn't get much hornier.'

Bondi

Flyway ramp across Bondi Junction
The need to fuck
Reach out to massage his cock while he drives
Unzipping a fly, open his belt.
Plunging down and giving head
Milking the slick hard
Stripping off my underpants still holding him
We move to the slow lane and
push the driver's seat back a little
I take the wheel and take him into my snatch
A tight squeeze behind the wheel
Being screwed from behind tight and hot
Attention shredding, cars peel away staring
We uncaring
An explosion of come as we slow for the lights.
I dismount and he regains the wheel
I mount the gearstick when we are in third and gyrate there
His fingers finding my slick cunt as he changes gear
I am shoving hard and orgasming down Bondi Road.
We find a park and make love again
In the passenger seat
A squeezy top fuck
Juice running down my legs

Lark Connor

From Saint Tropez they drive on to Barcelona in Spain. It still seemed incredible to Lark that so much different culture could exist hours from each other compared to the same distances in Australia.

'My dream has come true seeing the Gaudi Sagrada Família church, what a crazy genius Gaudi was,' says Lark, smoothing cream on her sunburnt legs and shoulders. 'What hard work it is being a tourist.'

'Yes, and so culturally intense. Do you want a lie down in our palatial chariot to recover madame?'

'Sounds just the thing, I'll just get my negligee.'

They eat late at a Tapas bar and retire to the hostel for the evening, segregated into men's and women's quarters. Up next morning they drive to Toulouse, where Guil told them the best wine comes from. At a small family vineyard they purchase a case of red for him and stow it on the back seat among the boxes of food.

On dusk they pull in to camp at Caravan Loisirs, which is crowded. They find a small corner for the night, set up the tent, cook a stir fry on the gas cooker, chatting to other campers from America and Belgium. They crawl into the tent at ten thirty to make love, rising early to drive to Paris the next day.

4

artin and Lark arrive at the Paris outskirts late, intending to stay a few days to do more sightseeing and shopping before heading off again. Lark has felt moments of queasiness, especially in the car on winding roads. It surprises her; she has never felt car sick in her life. They go out for dinner again with Guil, Jordy and Celeste at Le Soleil café. The thought of Chèvre Chaud and red wine just turns Lark's stomach.

'I've been craving porridge of all things for days but we couldn't find any in the supermarchés,' she tells Jordy.

'Porridge isn't at all French breakfast custom – baguettes and black coffee are the norm,' says Jordy, thinking how different Lark looks to when she arrived from the plane. She glows.

'Old habits die hard. Porridge is such a comfort food for me.' Lark not only wants porridge, but has been ravenously hungry the last couple of weeks, chalking it up to all their extra walking and touristic activities. 'Are there any health-food shops nearby that might have some?'

'Mmm, perhaps we can look around tomorrow. Celeste will enjoy an outing. Have you been well Lark?'

'Feeling great! And you?' asks Lark.

'Oh you know, tired, not enough sleep,' Jordy screws up her eyes and smiles. 'Celeste likes attachment sleeping so much. She hasn't really used her bedroom yet. It does mean that Guil and I don't always get enough sleep.'

'Did Martin tell Guil, when he rang? We're getting married!'

'Oh,' Jordy claps her hands. 'Marvellous news. I'm so happy for you both. When?'

'When we get back home.'

They find pre-packaged muesli but no plain oats, out searching the next day. Even with Jordy translating; the local health food shop staff know of this basic foodstuff but haven't seen it packaged separately. Jordy suggests looking further afield another day. While they travel back home, Lark casually mentions her spotty periods, wondering out loud if she should see a gynaecologist or something.

'We can stop at the chemist on the way home if you want,' suggests Jordy, moving Celeste from one hip to another and manoeuvring her into her stroller when their station draws near. At the chemist Lark is advised to buy a home pregnancy kit. She is taken aback; the possibility of pregnancy hasn't occurred to her. She walks home with Jordy, quiet and bemused, goes to the bathroom and does the test. Martin is out with Guil returning the hire car so this women's business she can't talk to him about.

'It's positive Jordy,' she comes out of the bathroom biting her lip. 'I'm going to do another one. It might be wrong.' She stalks back into the bathroom and repeats the test, showing Jordy the same positive lines on each stick when she emerges.

'Oh my God, oh my God, oh my God!'A chasm of shock opens and Lark hurtles into it. She sits in the kitchen with Jordy, while her friend makes lunch. She takes deep breaths, muttering in wonder. How does she feel? – happy? Scared? Shocked? All of these things.

'How wonderful! Martin will be so happy,' says Jordy, eyeing her dear friend. She knows how this feels. Finding out you are pregnant can be a life changing discovery.

Lark bursts into tears. 'I hope so,' she snuffles, reaching for a tissue. 'We haven't really talked about having a baby much. It will change everything won't it? But we can cope. Millions do,' she says, blowing her nose.

There's a lump in her throat and the shock is sending vast ripples. She tries to pinpoint when she might have conceived but fails. Have to think about it later. It's true that babies haven't been a topic of more than general conversation with Martin but if she's scrupulously honest with herself, she's entertained daydreams about the baby question for a while, but that's all it was, the stuff of imagination. But pregnant now! On their holiday!

'Don't you get sick during pregnancy? Morning sickness?' Lark asks, the thought floating through the shock like a zeppelin in a storm.

'Some women do, some not. It just depends on the pregnancy,' says Jordy, empathising with Lark's feelings. It had been the same for her, not so long ago. 'We'll get you some clay pills for that. I had pretty bad morning sickness and later on had a terrible rash. I couldn't sleep.' Jordy brings plates of salad and rice to the table. 'I also was pregnant a few months ago but I miscarried,' she says quietly as she pulls Celeste onto her knee to begin her lunch. Celeste's little fingers reach for her mother's fork and Jordy hands her a sliver of bread to chew.

'Oh, Jordy, are you alright now?' Lark hadn't known and is pulled out of her own careening thoughts for a moment. Even between close friends some things are not revealed.

'Yes, we are all okay, still recovering. I'm on the pill now and we have our beautiful Celeste.'

Lark wonders how many such skeletons are in womens' closets: babies unborn, miscarried or aborted. For a moment she is horrified by the brevity of the thought, then she is back in the whirlwind of her mind, automatically eating her salad but not tasting it at all. Ignorant as she is that choice is the prerogative of biology, she is determined not to get sick on her holiday. What will Martin think? I so hope he will be happy about it, she thinks.

'Welcome to the world of motherhood Lark,' says Jordy, hugging her across the table. She knows there are so many ideas and habits that will be transformed in the transition to becoming parents and eyes her friend with compassion.

'I'd only be maybe six weeks at the most I think,' says Lark, calculating again as she yanks another tissue from the box.

'With the bleeding you're having, I suggest don't tell many people until three months are up. It might seem harsh to say but you may miscarry before that.'

'Wha?'

No sooner does she start thinking about the possibility of a baby, than she might lose it? What a slippery thing the mind is – shocked at such a gift one moment, yet howling at the idea of losing it the next.

'I had an ectopic pregnancy when I was twenty seven,' Lark says.

'With Paul? Yes I remember that,' says Jordy.

'A termination too,' Lark says in a flat voice.

'To Paul?'

'Yes.' Lark stabs her rice with her fork. 'I absolutely want to keep this baby if I don't miscarry.'

'Yes, I can understand that,' says Jordy. 'You'll tell Martin soon?'

'Tomorrow. I need some time to get my head around this baby idea,' Lark answers, looking at Jordy with a pensive smile. 'The bleeding? Have you any ideas about that?'

'I'm not sure. Just wait and see if it settles. If not you're best seeing a gynaecologist. I can arrange an appointment with mine if you like.'

5

'We agreed not to didn't we, Lark? For a while anyway.' Martin stares at her as if she is someone else. His cold change raises the hairs on her arms despite the balmy breeze on top of Notre Dame Cathedral.

Silently they trudge down the stairs and out onto Place Du Parvis Notre Dame. On the plaza there are hundreds of people, pigeons, buskers and beggars. Skippy is nowhere to be seen. They stop in some patchy shade and put down their backpacks.

Automatically Lark gets out her hat. Her breathing is irregular; adrenalin pumps. 'I know Martin, but I want to keep our baby.'

'I saw blood,' he accuses.

'Not enough apparently. I'm about six weeks I think,' she answers.

'But how could you not know? You said it was safe,' he accuses her again.

'We thought so didn't we?' Lark clenches her fists around her hat, determined to keep the conversation in the realm of the dual culpability that it is. 'Jordy says I might miscarry yet.'

'What, she knows?'

'Yes she took me to the pharmacy.'

'Shit!' Eye rolling from Martin, swearing under his breath.

'Look, just cut with the inquisition Martin. I know it's a shock. It is for me too.' Lark straightens herself and stares at him with the defiance of a cornered animal.

'We can't have a baby, we're not prepared. Not even home. Slumming it in Europe actually. How's that for responsible parenting,' he slices her with razor acidity, voice raised. He moans, 'I need a cigarette.' He examines his fingers and begins biting, ripping his index fingernail with his teeth.

'Keep your voice down Martin, people are looking,' she says.

They're sparring like two red kangaroos. A bite to the head, clawing around their hearts, then a kick in the guts. Viewers fade out around the edges.

'Fuck them.'

She has never seen him so angry. She is seeing a stranger emerge from Martin's usually mild mannered skin. She recalls her own shock and the time it took to accommodate this new enormity yesterday. She's had twenty four hours to take it in. For him it's fresh and raw.

'It takes some time to get used to the idea, it's true.'

Martin glowers at her. He mutters and erupts. 'I don't think I can do kids Lark. We're happy enough without that responsibility.'

'Well dammit, I am not going to have an abortion if that's what you mean.' Lark loses her temper. 'I'm old Martin. Have a good look. Thirty eight and peri-menopausal. It might be my last chance,' she spits, throwing her hat down on the ground.

People around them have slowed to watch: perhaps it's another busking act on the plaza. In her peripheral vision, Lark can see people pointing, mouths together, discussing. Martin and Lark glare at each other; far from being the compatible lovers they were half an hour ago. Suddenly estranged and reeling from it.

'I hoped you'd handle it better than this Martin.'

'Oh shit Lark, what'll we do?' Why now?' Martin tears at his hair, another thought of horror upon him. 'Are you sure its mine?' A drawn in breath. 'No, I didn't mean that.'

'What! Of course the baby's yours, you... you. What are you thinking Martin? That I've been playing around?' Lark shrieks, face blanching. She simply can't believe what he's just said.

'We've been together for three years. We're going to get married. You want to screw up our situation with insane theatrics, crazy comments?'

Hair-trigger choices made in rage: 'I didn't mean... Well, a paternity test'll fix that won't it,' he shouts back.

She throws her hat at him; it lands on the ground. His hands up momentarily, she snarls, 'Don't you dare hit me.' Tears leap to her eyes.

Hands drop and Martin's temper gauge visibly lowers. 'Shit Lark, what'm I saying?' He takes a deep shuddering breath. 'I just don't think we should keep it.'

'IT' is a baby Martin. A baby we created from our loving. I think we're plenty old enough to cope with a baby,' Lark enunciates her words with deadly calm. These ugly minutes are annihilating so many sweet preconceptions about each other, their relationship and their future. They've reeled into unknown territory, full of bleak ringbarked trees.

For a moment they are at an impasse. Applause cuts off any further argument. A group of tourists have formed about them. They point and an American even cheers. Speechless with mortification, Lark bows with an absurdist flourish. The dark humiliation seems fitting. Euros drop in Lark's hat as tourists disperse to go to the next spectacle Paris has to offer.

'A sideshow Martin. Great way to show your acceptance. So out of line.' Bitter, she squats to get out her sunglasses to cover her tears.

Martin stands immobilised. Together they are a tableau of a relationship in tatters, still bound but reeling in shock. 'I'm just not ready Lark,' he says quietly.

'Will you ever be?'

'Fuck, I don't know.'

Lark looks up. A middle aged man is hovering. He notices her looking and steps forward.

'A grand performance,' he says. 'If you can write as well as you can act, I'd be interested in employing you.'

Lark looks at the man like he is from Mars. He has a British accent and thinning hair. There isn't a camera hanging from his rather scrawny sunburnt neck, merely a small wallet clasped in his hand, strap wound about his wrist. He hurries on. Probably not a tourist, flits through Lark's mind as she stares agog.

'My name is Michael Lawson, I live here in Paris, in Gartier Latin, have done for many years. I run a business supplying French and British adult websites and media with articles. I act as an agent for many freelance writers. If you can write your street theatre piece down, I will pay you.' Michael rushes out, beaming down at Lark, with overbright teeth.

More and more surreal. Dali-esque, Lark thinks, but Munch, 'The Scream' on the inside. She gets up, automatically taking the business card he hands her. Behind her Martin, collapses onto a narrow wall, hands clasped between his legs and head down, too self involved to help her, too tormented to deal with this person.

'No, I don't think we can do that,' says Lark gravely. 'Thanks anyway.'

Michael shrugs and smiles undaunted. 'Well, you have my card. Ciao.' He darts away and is lost in the crowds.

Lark turns to Martin, who reaches out for her, grim faced. They hug for a long time; the wash of ill feeling dissipating a little.

'Let's talk about it later,' he says.

That's right, defer, thinks Lark with bitterness. Never confront and resolve. A network of threads unearths itself in her memory and she realises that to put issues off is a repeated habit of Martin's; defer and not deal with relationship stuff. She's just hidden it from herself, hope smoothing over it since they've been together, like a thick coat of sugar icing.

'Alright. But we do have to sort it out Martin.' Steel in her voice, but she doesn't want to fight anymore. They pick up their backpacks and catch the metro over to Sacré-Cœur, tipping the Euros from her hat into the bowl of the first beggar they see.

oliday still fantastic, I love Paris.

Lark presses send on her phone, knowing her mum will boast to her friends about her daughter on holiday overseas. She doesn't know the half of it, thinks Lark, towelling her hair after a shower. The holiday from heaven's become the vacation from hell, she thinks bitterly. Not telling family 'till I'm three months or I've lost the baby, she clenches her teeth at the thought. Martin is being so appalling about it, she can hardly believe it. For days they fight on and off with no resolve. Lark nearly capitulates to having a termination several times. She doesn't want to lose Martin and finds it excruciating to defy him. She realises her generally compliant conditioning has set her up for this; being flexible, easygoing and accommodating in a relationship leads to trouble when an issue needs a stronger stand.

He hardens his stance, researches abortion clinics in Paris and London, telling her that it is legal in Paris up to twelve weeks and in London she could take some tablets that'd set off a miscarriage so there'd be less physical intervention – as long as she is between six and nine weeks.

'Which you are,' Martin says. 'As we're going to London next, why don't we book you in?'

The words hang like a choking web. Indeed Lark's throat closes over and her breathing becomes unsteady at the thought.

'This is awful Martin,' she says, reaching for his hand.

Each day they joust, stabbing and wounding, trying to unseat each other from their points of view. Lark breaks down and agrees; they make up, make love, scramble to repair the damage. She goes through an agony of self examination and subsequent refusal and it all sours between them once again.

Jordy and Guil, having only recently had Celeste, urge her to keep the baby.

'Just hang on Lark, Martin will come round. It's just a big shock, you'll see,' says Jordy. Guil even tries to talk to Martin about it but he clams up and refuses to be drawn, even after several bottles of red wine.

Interspersed with this horror show, Lark is aware that she knows nothing about having babies except vague outdated stories from her mum. The actual birth is like a wedding day, she understands; it is only one moment that is the beginning of a lifetime of parenting. She soberly considers how it would be to become a single parent. She has several girlfriends who are, generally because their marriages have failed. She considers her financial resources, her own and joint. If they split up they'll have to sell the flat at Bondi; painful to consider. What about Purzia, their cat? It dawns on her too - how could she continue to work as a single mum? Living with Celeste and observing Jordy's new habits as a mother is an eye-opener. How fractured a mother's time becomes is particularly apparent. Jordy was once such a party girl, full of irreverent fun and fashion choices. Now her time and energy is almost entirely consumed by Celeste.

'It might be possible to do freelance design work,' says Jordy, when she expresses her concerns to her friend. 'But you're recovering after birth, both you and the baby. Often you're very tired and getting used to a new routine. It may be that your baby has colic or doesn't feed properly.' Jordy thinks for a moment. 'But you could put the baby into infant day care or a mothercraft place if you had too so you could work.'

'I don't know about doing that,' says Lark. Now she thinks about it, she has heard of pregnant women already signing their babies up and passing them onto a day care centre at three months old so they can return to work.

Move home with Mum and her partner? She knows they'd help, but how bizarre would that be at thirty eight? All the time she is looking at Martin and agonising. She loves him and doesn't want to split up, despite that he is being so mean and obstreperous. Their unofficial engagement, a thing from a more insouciant time is not even discussed. Lark mourns it nevertheless.

The night before they are to catch the Eurostar to London, Lark and Martin leave the flat so as not to disturb their friends. They wander the streets, arguing. Martin has made a booking at a London abortion clinic for her.

'You can recover at Jordy's aunt's place for a few days after,' he says. Lark shakes her head slowly with tears sliding down her cheeks , feeling overwhelmed by his determination. The tension is gut-clenching: Lark passes a single clot of blood into the toilet on her return to the apartment.

'Looks like you might be in luck Martin. More blood. I might miscarry yet,' she whispers savagely to him as they bed down on in the baby's room. Intimacy is still a compulsion despite that they both feel they are swimming in a violent sea. They make love with care, he behind her. Afterwards, Martin says nothing, just turns and faces the wall and is soon snoring lightly. Lark stays awake stewing until dawn before managing to sleep.

Waking late, she notices immediately that Martin's suitcase is not under the baby change table next to hers. His keys and wallet and other bits of personal stuff spread about his open backpack aren't there either. Only her stuff, and when she lunges up in a panic, she sees his writing scrawled on a piece of paper beneath her hair brush.

Lark, I am sorry. I have to get away. A few days?
To think about the baby and us. I'll go to London. Will call you,
Love Martin

Lark reads the scrawled words over again and slumps back on the futon, bleak. She cries many times, mutters and swears to herself. Texts and phones Martin. No answer; his phone is switched off. She drags herself to the shower, aware of the silence about her. Nobody else is at home. Once dressed, she makes herself a strong coffee. Jordy and Celeste arrive home at late morning. Straight away its obvious Jordy knows.

She unstraps Celeste from the stroller and puts her on the floor to crawl about. Immediately Jordy hugs her friend awhile as more tears fall.

'He needs to get away and grow up,' is the only thing Jordy says.

'He's got his phone switched off, I can't contact him,' Lark cries.

Later, the bereft clouds part a little and she returns to Celeste's room. On closer inspection she realises what else is missing. Her passport, Eurostar tickets, return ticket to Australia, identifying papers and most of their Euros. Oh shit, they're in Martin's security wallet in his suitcase. She searches fruitlessly through her own case and hand bag, finding only some money, random bits of paper with phone numbers, directions and the business card from the man at Notre Dame. No! How could it get any worse? Why did he leave with her essential things? He can't have been thinking straight at all. Martin is usually so methodical and organised. Bastard, she hisses to herself. She tries his phone again. It's still switched off. He would have to know by now that he has her stuff.

Will he come back with it? He'd better.

'He's taken my passport and tickets Jordy, says Lark. 'We kept them together in his suitcase. All he left was a note.'

'Oh no, what a fool,' says Jordy. 'He mustn't have realised. It'll be easy enough to replace your e-tickets, but your passport, that's much more of a hassle.'

'Did you see him this morning?

'Yes of course. He was very confused. I tried to talk him out of leaving. I knew you wouldn't want that,' Jordy frowns. 'I'll call Aunt Lois; she may be able to get a message to him.' She phones immediately, telling her the problem but Martin hasn't turned up at Edgeware yet. Aunt Lois is a little annoyed. She has been waiting all afternoon for Lark and Martin to arrive.

'He hasn't arrived yet, but I told Lois to pass on the message to contact you immediately.' Jordy says.

Lark sinks into a chair. 'What can I do? I'm trapped. I didn't want this to happen Jordy. I really wanted us to be happy about the baby.' She breaks down again. All Jordy can do is hand her tissues, talking quietly to Celeste to distract her.

'It will be alright Lark, you can stay with us. He just needs time to get used to the idea,' says Jordy. 'Did he say he wants to finish with you in the note?

'No,' says Lark and blows her nose.

'I'll call the Australian Consulate here to see what you can do, but I'm sure he'll be back in a few days. He loves you.'

'How can you be sure of either?' Lark says. 'Certainly not showing it is he.'

Jordy purses her lips. She looks up the phone number, frowning at her friend. 'I can't of course, but I'm sure he'll come back.' She picks up Lark's phone and hands it to her. 'Why don't you check the Australian Passport website while I phone the consulate. They may have some information that might help as well.'

7

week passes and still Martin hasn't returned and continues to be unreachable by phone. Lark fills in the paperwork to cancel her passport and apply for a new one after days in a state of shock. It takes three weeks to get a new passport she is assured. Jordy and Guil are so kind and she begins to find a rhythm of sorts to her time trapped in Paris. Paris! She should be happy – of all the places to be confined! She puts on a brave face and forces herself into its centre every day. She queues in the sun with tourists to the Louvre and Centre Georges Pompidou and many other marvellous places. In front of great works of art, she comes too, vacillating between sorrow and anger. How long she's been staring vacantly at the displays she doesn't know.

She has another two smears of blood in her underpants and vague morning sickness but Jordy's recommended clay pills solve that. Most of her thoughts revolve around Martin's return, mixed with a confined sense of restlessness. She understands the isolation of a new resident now as opposed to a tourist blowing through in their own bubble. Masturbating is a big relief. Her need for sex has grown and without Martin available, it feels necessary to bring herself to a climax at least each day. Her whole sex has become engorged, fecund, lush. Even brushing her fingers ever so lightly across her clitoris sets her off. Is it the same for other pregnant women she wonders?

'What you need is something to do,' says Guil one evening when she mentions her restlessness, but modestly refrains from talking about her horniness. 'You're used to being busy. I know! When I am on holiday, after a few days I must be drawing again. You are the same I think?'

'Maybe,' says Lark, realising she misses her watercolours and her tablet. Sketching on her phone just isn't the same.

Guil rummages in a cupboard and finds her a drawing block and some elderly colouring pencils. 'Here, take them with you and do some drawings around Paris. With that baby arriving in a few months, you might not have time again for a while.'

Lark does as he says, but her efforts are half hearted, She finds herself writing spontaneously with a blunt pencil on the reverse sides of her drawings. Diary entries, memories, poems, arguments, fragments of stories burst from her overloaded mind.

She is sitting and writing once again in Place Du Parvis Notre Dame, her sandwich forgotten and a curtain of dark hair falling from her chignon. She becomes aware of someone hovering nearby, not the general swirl and rabble of passers by. A man observing her.

'Ahem. Will you do your show again today?' he asks, stepping forward when she looks up. Older man, British accent.

Lark frowns over her dark sunglasses. 'Excuse me? What are you talking about?'

'You and your partner did some excellent tragi-comic street theatre here perhaps a fortnight ago? If you recall I talked to you and gave you a business card?'

'Oh, yes, I remember,' says Lark, not remembering at all. 'No we are not performing today.' She puts her head down and begins writing again, hoping he'll leave.

'Michael Lawson,' he says and proffers his hand, with a dazzling smile.

Lark looks up again. After a moment, she shakes his hand.

'Lark Connor.'

'Named for an English Lark?'

'No. An Australian Magpie Lark actually.' She shuts her eyes behind her shades, willing him to go away.

'I can see you've forgotten our previous encounter. I'll repeat what I said then and then leave you be,' says Michael. 'I run a business supplying French and British adult websites, EBook media zines and litmags with articles here in Paris. If you can write your street theatre piece down, I will pay you for it or for any other articles you care to submit. I'm always interested in fresh writers,' that overbright smile again. 'At the risk of being a squeaky wheel, here's my card again.'

'Do you usually approach complete strangers and proposition them like this?' asks Lark, frowning.

'Mmm, occasionally,' Michael said, not fazed at all by her question. 'If I think it might be worthwhile.' He glanced at her pages of scribble with a greedy look.

Seems bizarre to Lark, but hell, everything is pretty crazy. She takes his card again and pushes it into her bag. 'Well perhaps I'll call you when I have written something,' she says, trying to put him off. He salutes and wanders away. A salute thinks Lark, what next!

On the train back to Guil and Jordy's she ponders his offer. Everyday she burns up with all this unresolved emotion. Damn Martin! Doing the touristic thing has lost much of its savour. She is in a limbo. Perhaps writing something might give her a distraction. She turns over the drawings she's done today and knows her artistic muse is too traumatised to be of much use. But writing, she has always scribbled her thoughts and feelings down. Often written small stories with the idea of publishing them, but has been too busy with other pursuits. She fishes out the card and taps the number in on her phone.

'Michael Lawson Agency,' murmurs a young voice, followed by a string of French that Lark can't understand.

'Parlez Anglais s'il vous plait,' says Lark. 'Can I speak to Michael Lawson please?'

'Oui, er yes, un moment.' The phone reconnects.

'Michael Lawson speaking.'

'Hello, it's Lark Connor. You talked to me earlier this afternoon at Notre Dame?'

'Yes the Australian Lark. Of course.'

'What sort of articles do you want? How many words? How much will you pay?'

'I am looking for unusual articles, like your performance Lark. Raw, original pieces from a woman's point of view. Currently I am looking for articles with female perspectives on love, marriage and sex. It sounds unfashionable doesn't it? So the articles need to be something different, something unique that will attract the interest of my clients.'

'Okay,' answers Lark, frowning.

'Up to three thousand words per article. I pay 0.10 € per word up to 30 € for 500 words. For longer articles, up to 600 €, all on approval of course initially based on the first article. If I like what you're writing, we can steer the direction or leave you to create your own subjects. I'll pay you directly into your bank account within a fortnight of each article's acceptance.' Michael is all crisp business now. I can send you a contract to confirm all this. How does that sound?'

'Do you have deadlines?'

'As soon as you can write it, I'll want to look it over,' says Michael. There's flexibility around deadlines... it depends what the fashion is. We don't write Christmas articles for Easter do we?' He chuckles at his little joke.

'Okay, thanks. I'll think about it. If I decide to take you up on your offer, I'll call you back tomorrow,' says Lark, rolling her eyes. She finishes the call, intrigued but uncertain. Martin might return any day and all her energy will get caught up in their big issues. All the same, she gets online and checks the company, which seems bona fide.

'What do you both think?' She tells Jordy and Guil about it, telling how she met the man and what he has suggested.

'Hmm, it could be okay,' says Guil, jiggling Celeste on his knee. 'There is no reason not to do this. Nothing to lose.'

'But I might be gone in a fortnight, back to Australia, or

travelling again with Martin, who knows?' says Lark. 'I can't write a play based on Martin and I arguing about the baby though. It was too awful and I'm way too raw.'

'Oui, arguments can be trés terrible,' agrees Guil, swooping Celeste down between his legs. Celeste laughs and Lark soaks up the moment of exclusive adoration her parents give their little girl.

'These days skills are portable,' says Jordy. 'Guil does animation work for companies all over the world. You're welcome to use my laptop or Guil's if you want to do this.'

'True,' agrees Lark. 'I don't need the money really, but perhaps it'd be good to have a focus – other than Martin and this baby.' She grins wryly, patting her stomach. 'Thanks.'

She goes to her room and looks at the ramblings she has been jotting down on the drawing block. No, too painful and angst ridden, they bring tears to her eyes. How did this happen? For the millionth time, she agonises. Where is Martin? Is he even in London? She'd been looking forward to going to the UK. It's another disappointment. She tries again to phone Martin, sends yet another pointless text to him. To steer herself away from the unhappiness this brings her, she sends another banal text to her mum and puts a quick picture and message on Facebook for her friends. Jordy comes in with Celeste. Lark plumps up her pillow and props it against the wall. Jordy sits to lean cross legged with Celeste on her lap and flips up her shirt. Celeste latches on to her breast and begins to feed.

'Have you any ideas for writing Lark?' she asks.

'Not really. I've always done the designing, not the copy on jobs. I have been writing while I'm out sightseeing,' Lark pauses, 'but most of that is just venting about Martin. I can't write about that for an article, it's too painful.'

Jordy nods, stroking Celeste's silky curls.

'Michael wants stories about women's perspectives on love, marriage, sex. Pretty broad subject,' says Lark. 'I thought on the way home I could write about some old boyfriend type stuff.'

Jordy de-latches Celeste and swaps her to her other breast. 'Casual sexual encounters then? We had a few of those in our party days didn't we?'

Its enough to distract Lark and they both grin. Celeste pulls off Jordy's tit and gurgles at them, milk dribbling down her chin through her tiny baby teeth. Jordy wipes it away and encourages Celeste back to her leaking breast. Lark watches, filled with a grateful sense of amity. She loves the easy rapport that she shares with Jordy.

When they stop giggling, Jordy says, 'women's hopes and dreams perhaps? Our fantasies and I don't mean bigger cocks on our men,' she smirks.

'Our sexual fantasies?'

'Yeah, why not? Women all have them I'm sure. We just don't talk about them much, even to our girlfriends or husbands.'

'True,' says Lark considering. 'Without them entertaining me during sex, orgasm is far more elusive.'

'You too? Fantasies transport us from the mundane don't you think? See, that's a good place to start. There's that great quote by Isobel Allende, do you know it?"

'No I don't think so.'

'For women the best aphrodisiacs are words. The G-spot is in the ears. He who looks for it below there is wasting his time.' Jordy smiles and gives Celeste a gentle squeeze.

Lark nods. 'Wow that is just so right. But I would add that the written word is seductive too.'

Celeste nods off, Jordy's nipple slips out of her mouth. Jordy gets up and ferries Celeste to her room to put her down. Lark contemplates her advice. The more she thinks about it, the more the quote inspires her and Jordy's suggestions appeal She begins a rough outline and for minutes at a time, isn't worrying about Martin or the baby.

Next morning, Lark is up early. She phones Michael and asks that he send her the contract to look at and prepares to go out.

'I'm going to the Musée De L'Orangerie to see Monet's 'Nympheas' series.'

'The dreamy waterlily paintings, yes I love those,' says Jordy. 'Check the Cezanne, Renoir and Modigliani there too.'

'I need some inspiration,' Lark says. 'So much choice in Paris.'

Trying to sleep the evening before, ideas teemed about her, ready to expand into a story.

'Why don't you have lunch in the Jardin des Tuileries nearby? Take my laptop and do some writing there.'

'Can you make an appointment for me at your gynaecologist Jordy?' Lark asks as she washes her breakfast plates. 'She speaks English doesn't she? I'm still spotting blood. I'd better get it checked.'

'Yes, she does. She's quite busy; it's good to book ahead.'

'Okay, thanks so much.'

She has refrained from asking if Jordy or Guil knows anything more about Martin. It would just make them uncomfortable and they are being so generous already. Sometimes though, it's hard not too. She purses her lips and holds herself back as Jordy hands her a slender laptop.

'Thanks. Have fun at the mother's group with Adelyn,' Lark says, stowing the laptop in her backpack and waving at Celeste, who gives her baby waves back.

'You know there's free Wi-Fi in the centre don't you?'

'Yes thanks, see you later on. If Martin comes back, call me straight away, won't you?'

8

On the train into the city, Lark muses on Jordy's suggestions, feeling a sense of purpose that outweighs her morose ruminations about Martin. Yes there are experiences in her past she can think of that stand out as pretty sexy, the stuff of fantasy now. She jots a few memories down and decides one experience in particular could make a great story, with a few character and name changes.

What does she like to read herself? Reading about sex and fantasies can either be a real turn on or leave her cold, depending on how the author handles the imagined scene. Real put-downers are books where the sexual scenes are coarse and lack subtlety or where characters fall into typical stereotypes and as a reader she can predict all too well what will happen next.

Can she write some stories that have some intelligence, quirkiness and style? She sways with the rhythm of the train, wondering. She decides as Guil said, nothing to lose by giving it a go.

With an artist's eye she looks about at the other travellers, picking a couple bunched up close to each other, holding hands, as her protagonists. She does a surreptitious sketch of them with descriptive notes, followed by a quick outline for her first story,

45

the stuff of memory.

All the while at the Musée De L'Orangerie, her mind trips over various words and phrases, some alighting in her mind like quicksilver. She catches them and writes them down. At lunchtime, she begins to type her first erotic tale, sitting absorbed until late afternoon.

SALON MAGIC

'It's a wrap,' the Director calls, checking the gate on the film camera. The crew begin chatting as they pack up now the job is over. The product for this commercial is guaranteed to bring sheen to even the dullest hair. A new shampoo called 'Salon Magic' is to be pitched at the already saturated 15- 30 age bracket.

The choice of the trendiest salon in the city as the location delighted the client. It proved quite a challenge for the Director of Photography, with seven Victorian cathedral windows to dull down with scrims. The client insisted they be a feature in the shots, unaware of how little would be actually seen once the footage was edited down to a 30 second commercial.

The Art Director, Suchiko began work at 5.30 am. Now she picks up the product mock-ups, stowing them carefully in a box alongside her standby kit. In there are several others, to be used later in the week for the detail shots. She puts away the invisible tape, little chunks of foam for propping and the dulling spray she uses to take the shine off the products if necessary, under the intense lighting. Suchiko collects the hand-prop mock-up shampoo bottles that the actor-hairdresser has used, stowing them as well.

'Great job,' says Brian, the Director, as she passes him. 'Clients are happy. Flowers looked brilliant.'

He praises her for finding the thirty grandiflora magnolia and tortured willow stems in tall Grecian vases placed around the salon. Suchiko grins, knowing what a sweat it had been to locate and hire them at short notice on the whim of the client.

Suchiko has worked hard all day to please the client and Director. She pampered the 'talent', especially the main actress with her many washed and lacquered hair, making sure the set dressing and hand-props were trouble free. While the Director of Photography fussed about each shot, Suchiko remained cool and quietly deferential.

Suchiko runs downstairs with the Director and his Producer wife Chrissy, to help them out to their car with some of their gear. They share a quiet camaraderie, having worked on many jobs together.

'You'll be okay to finish up Suchiko?' asks Chrissy.

'Yes, I'll be fine,' replies Suchiko.

'I'll see you on Wednesday for the closeups.'

'Sure, see you then.'

The crew had noticed one of the salon staff, a young guy, checking her out as she studiously did her job. Suchiko ignored him during the shoot. She understood he'd been selected as one of several real hairdressers to feature in the background of the shots. As Brian and Chrissy belt up in their 4WD , Suchiko gives them a wave and then she darts back upstairs to continue cleaning up the salon.

Suchiko clears away the magnolias and willow into buckets, tipping out water in the staff kitchenette. She crates up the Grecian vases to be returned to a props store tomorrow. She checks all the windows and carefully removes some gaffer tape left by the lighting guys, who are also still packing up. She returns the two divans pushed out of the way, to their original, central back-to-back positions. Suchiko locates their cushions, plumping them as she replaces them. She pulls down a drop of fabric used to mask a mirror. Then she attends to the 'hero' hairdresser's caddy and table, which has had items added and removed for the shoot. When she is satisfied that the salon is back to its original state, Suchiko uses her trolley to take props down to her van. The flowers she leaves until last.

Soon there are only three of the crew left at the salon. Suchiko noticed earlier that the young hairdresser volunteered to his boss to stay behind to lock up the salon.

The lighting grip, John has almost finished coiling up cables and packing up lights and stands. A violet twilight filters through the tall windows casting a golden, indigo light on the opulent salon.

'Shoot went well,' says John.

Suchiko nods as she hands him a roll of gaffer tape 'This is yours.'Night John.'

John wanders out with the last of his cables looped over his shoulder. Suchiko picks up the two buckets of willow and magnolias with her backpack, rechecking the location with a careful look while she takes out her phone to skim for messages. The hairdresser waits at the door to lock up behind them.

'You did a great job,' he says.

Suchiko smiles. 'Thanks. How did you find working on the shoot?'

She feels fatigued and dirty, but keyed up too. Hours on shoots always does this to her. It will take a while for her to unwind. She notices the young guy's pale blue eyes, thinking of her Siamese cat 'Pharaoh', at home.

'I've never been on a film shoot before. It was fun,' he said. As an afterthought he says, 'pretty boring at moments too.'
Suchiko laughs.

My name is Micah, what's yours?'

'Suchiko.'

Suchiko,' he repeats, appraising her. 'Think you could have a coffee before I lock up?' he asks. 'Do you have time?'

She looks at the time on her phone, a nervous reflex, but knows she has no plans except to go home and crash. 'Okay, coffee would be lovely.'

Suchiko leaves the flowers by the door. She goes over to a divan and sits down, dropping her backpack on the floor beside her. Micah shuts the salon door and disappears in the direction of the staff kitchenette. She looks at the salon as she relaxes. Someone has decided that doing the place out in black and white, with gold and black salon fixtures is a sophisticated look. While she wrestles with her hair tie, she considers different colour schemes and furnishings. She realizes her hair is a mess and hasn't been done since 5am. She takes her brush from her backpack to brush her hair free of tangles.

'Let me do that,' suggests Micah who has padded back in as quiet as her cat.

Suchiko jumps. She's been so engrossed in brushing her hair she's forgotten him for a moment. He puts down a round tray of their coffee and biscuits.

'You can trust me, I'm a hairdresser.' He grins.

Suchiko looks up at him and he moves to one of the salon caddies to find a good brush and comb. Brushing her hair is one of the few moments where she abandons herself to day dreaming no matter how busy she is. Since she was a little girl in her mother's care, she has rarely let anyone brush her hair for her.

'Alright cheeky,' she returns his smile. 'I guess I AM in a salon and you ARE a hairdresser.'

She hands him her brush and turns slightly so he can sit behind her to proceed. Micah sweeps back her hair with professional confidence. He strokes the crown of her head, with his hand, rippling down her back to the finish of her hair. He pulls the brush through once, asking if it is too hard or soft.

Micah secretly loves untamed hair that is free of colourings, gels, highlights and all the endless pomp that salons create. He appreciates the sensuous slip of Suchiko's hair despite his working with hair everyday. He begins to brush, with long reverential strokes.

'Mmm,' she murmurs. It's pure pleasure to relax into the motion and pull of the brush.

Micah looks at Suchiko's shining hair running down her back like an oil slick. Where her hairline meets pale, pearlescent skin looks so edible. He runs a long, index finger over the fine hairs there.

'Would you like me to wash your hair? After today you deserve it.' Micah voices his desire with seeming innocence.

A crazy idea thinks Suchiko, so delicious. The lazy hum of distant evening traffic and the quiet of the salon is capturing them in a bubble.

'Yes, okay.' Tiny tendrils of the unknown, a frisson of desire make her shudder as she speaks.

He leads her to a gleaming salon chair in the basin area, places a black towel around her shoulders. With a light butterfly kiss on each cheek, he sets her senses tingling. They search each other's eyes and smile. He kisses her lowered eyelashes. Suchiko raises her parted lips to meet his, still wondering at this turn of events but willing to play with it. As their lips touch, she darts out her tongue tip, and sends a vivid spark running around his lips. Micah tips back her head, tracing a vein on her neck with his fingers. He licks at her thrumming pulse there.

He looks again, and drinks the desire mirrored in her eyes. Suchiko lowers her lashes and puts her head back further towards the basin, waiting for him to wash her hair.

Micah moves behind her and swathes her hair into the basin. He adjusts the temperature of the water while she gazes up at the ornate filigree on the plaster ceiling, gilded and shadowed. The fragrance of the bucket of magnolias hovers in the air.

'Temperature okay?'

'Lovely,' says Suchiko, squeezing her eyes shut in anticipation.

He rolls her head onto his hand, cushioning her. A gentle cascade of water pours over her scalp. She guesses this is their foreplay and feels vulnerable. Her sweep of hair enables her to hide in social situations. It is her crown when she dates men. Micah is stripping her of her shield. She realises she feels less nude with her clothes off.

Micah sprays waves of warm water through her hair and spoons water from her brows with his fingers. With deft movements, he shampoos, rinses, conditions and rinses again. He lifts her hair at the roots for water to filter through. It hangs like ropes of viscous, dripping molasses, an ebony waterfall. Suchiko raises her head and Micah dries her forehead and ears, leaving her hair wet. He moves around in front of her.

She sits up while he appraises her with a sensual hunger. Suchiko reaches out to brush his cheek. Micah takes her fingers and bites the tips gently as he watches her with his pale blue eyes. He bends, shaking in anticipation to kiss her parted lips.

Another deeper kiss; they both taste of coffee.

Droplets of water trickle from Suchiko's hairline. Micah licks them from her forehead, eyebrows and cheeks. She closes her eyes and he butterfly kisses droplets from her lashes. Water forms a glistening sheen on her face and nape, pooling in the scoop of her collarbone. He laps her damp neck and traces her collarbone with seeking fingers.

Her wet hair leaches water onto her shirt front. Her nipples press against her damp shirt, unmistakably aroused. Micah's fingers find them to caress through the fabric; he pinches them erect. Suchiko sighs when he slips his hands through the buttoned shirt front to hold the weight of her breasts.

With an imperceptible nod from her, he undoes the shirt and bends to lick her hard nipples, a thirsting disciple. Reality shift for moments until it slides away. Suchiko forgets where she is, who she is. Adrift, anchored only by sensory pleasure awakening the languid diva at her core.

She tugs at Mikah's spiky quiff, pulling him away so she can kiss him. She brushes his mouth with her tongue and bites his chin, noting their forgotten panting breaths. The salon is bathed in a cool moonlit polish, yet a fire builds between them.

They kick off their shoes and assist each other peeling off jeans and tops. They stand apart looking, savouring each other's bodies. They align their bodies, hip to hip, belly to belly. Their senses urge them to connect. Her hands slide down the planes of his chest, his stomach, hips and groin, to gather him in both hands, to feel the weight of his substantial shaft and balls.

Micah shudders, pulls her hands away.

'Wait a little,' he murmurs, wanting, wanting but willing restraint.

He turns her hips and propels her back to the salon chair, motioning her to be seated again. Micah arranges the long strands of her hair over her body. He follows them down while Suchiko watches him through limpid lashes. Droplets of water glisten in her creases and her pubic hair is succulent and wet. He pushes her knees apart and he kneels down between her legs. Exposure, her rosy sex open to a stranger.

Micah takes small butterfly licks of her wet mound and her diva stirs and purrs. She gasps and shudders as he bites her soft inner thighs. With his tongue he parts her labia, finding her clit to tantalize. She slides down the chair, mindless. He takes long ice cream licks from her anus to clit, feathering her opening to bite and plunge his fingers into. Suchiko is in sweet agony. Her clit bulges and tingles like sherbet and fizzing pressure builds across her belly. Her diva idles there on orgasm's threshold, like a revving motorbike, waiting for the next burst of divine power. No, she wants to climax with him and lifts his head away again to kiss his juiced up mouth. The diva urges her to draw him deep inside, into her core.

She drapes her arms around his neck and Micah carries her back to the divan. He arranges her like a Rousseau nude, once again draping and arranging her hair. Suchiko gazes at his hard muscular beauty and pushes him into a kneel next to her. She takes him into her mouth, flicking her tongue over the hot eager tip of him, plying fingers and running them down his length, followed by her mouth, something she loves to do. She nibbles down his shaft and bites the join between penis and scrotum hard while gathering his balls in her other hand. Micah groans and pushes harder into her mouth, past her gag reflex. She snorts and sucks, her teeth rasping along his shaft as pre cum lubricates her mouth. When he is writhing with want, she pulls him onto her, bunching her breasts so he can ride their soft crevice.

Minutes later, he savages her nipples with his teeth and eases down her belly. He arches his hips back and slides down through her wet pubic hair. Blur of passion kissing, they thrust and seek. thrust and find as he enters her molten centre. Breathing ragged, they probe with increasing confidence, she opening up to fit his substantial size, yet both revelling in the tight fit.

'Slow,' she orders, putting her fists under her buttocks for leverage. She wraps her legs aver over his back, She pulls her pelvic muscles rhythmically against his thrusting shaft, the curve of her cunt his ultimate pathway to her inner core.

After a time she pulls out her fists and runs a ring of fingers around his thrusting cock and into herself, feeling their sex, needing to feel him entering her with her fingers. He lunges deeper, wedging himself high inside her with each thrust, able to hit her cervix while she adjusts the angle to follow the sweetest sensations. She moves her fingers down his cock, faster than his controlled rhythm, making a contra- trembling sensation. Micah struggles to delay with this extra sensory friction and groaning, pulls out to ease his excitement.

They slow down, stop, allowing the rush to subside while he enters her in a slow, mesmerising way. Micah hooks her legs up over his shoulders. Suchiko and her diva rejoice at the ultimate surrender. They begin again, exploring each lavish sensation, staring at each other, both craving, anticipating. Sweat squelches between them, making sounds. Micah licks her face as he thrusts long, hard and deep. She contracts her pelvic muscles and holds each thrust tight and deep within herself, her cervix making love to his shaft.

Suchiko reaches down around, grasping his hips. Further then she reaches straining, following a need. She finds his scrotum, their weight of come. They are hers, she wants his hot arc to blow inside her. They transform their shape in her stroking grasp. Hard, tight. She wants to drive them inside her as well, her diva demands their contents. Mere thought and belt of rippling pressure runs across her pelvis. She closes her eyes, moaning and falling into the elusive sensation, growing it until it explodes as a rippling release. Micah slows down to feel her vagina clench and clench upon his cock as she howls. It is a cry from another dimension. He thrusts deeper, faster. He grunts as he finds her deepest places. She cries out again and he glazes over, aware only of the hot rush up his shaft. He spasms and yells out as he comes. Sweet agony creases his face and tears jump to his lashes.

Later Suchiko and Micah talk quietly on the divan for hours. They tell each other who they are, have been, want to be. The narcotic fragrance of magnolias envelopes them.

Near midnight passion takes them again in its sensuous embrace as night softens into dawn. Afterwards they raid the staff fridge for snacks. Before seven, Micah and Suchiko kiss and depart from the salon, carrying the magnolias out into the early daylight One night is enough; it's been their moment with divinity. Nothing more is needed.

Lark Connor

Lark saves and shuts the lid of the laptop. She looks about in a daze after the intensity of writing her first full story. More than that, she needs the bathroom. She stands and stretches, picks up her things and retraces her steps to the public toilets at the Musée De L'Orangerie. There is still a swirl of patrons enjoying the gallery and as a consequence, the women's toilets are busy.

She locks herself in a cubicle and relieves herself before taking her vibrator from her backpack. She blesses the makers because it is small, discreet and above all quiet. Shutting her eyes, she wills herself away from where she is and into her fantasy world. The shuffle of ladies through the toilets covers Lark's gasp and fall down shudder when her orgasm nearly gyrates her onto the floor. Writing such erotic stuff has wound her up to such a pitch. She had no idea her own writing could affect her so much and she's desperate for release.

9

He's coming back! Within, Lark shouts joyously like a town crier. She has a postcard from Scotland that arrived two days ago and she carries it with her everywhere like a talisman, like a ticket to the greatest show on earth. She can read its brief message with her eyes shut. It seems odd he hasn't just phoned or texted her but she doesn't care.

Lark,

I've been a total fool.
Time away's been necessary to show me that.
Baggage stolen at Waterloo Station- lost your papers &
passport. My phone as well.
Profoundly sorry.
Arrive Paris 9th September.

Love you, Martin.

Mixed feelings? Yes, though mostly relief and the desire to see Martin, hold him, talk and make love. She practises many imagined dialogues for when she sees him. She forgives him; she doesn't. She's angry, she's relieved. It's all mixed up and she knows it will take time to process what's happened.

She has re-edited her story several times; pondering on the kinds of women's literature she enjoys reading. Despite her reservations, Jordy insists that Guil proof read her writing as well.

'The French are not as prudish as the English or Australians,' she says, 'and Guil has a career involved in narratives.'

'Biting the scrotum? This we will 'ave to try,' he tugs his goatee and winks mischievously at Jordy, who bared her rather pointy little teeth at him. 'Ow!'

It is true; his advice from a male lover's point of view is invaluable. Lark resolves to have them both read her subsequent stories if they can, for she already has another creating itself in her mind.

She'll soon know if it passes muster because she's sent in to Michael, feeling curiously light and fulfilled. Doing something other than drifting about as a tourist has been good, even if it is just writing stories related to 'women's perspectives on love, marriage, sex.' Michael promptly gives her the flag for the first story and is keen to see more.

'He still wants the street theatre play, he calls it,' she shakes her head and grimaces at Jordy who is folding baby clothes. 'I can't do it, but I have another idea in mind.' '

'Did you really shag a hairdresser after a film shoot Lark?' Jordy asks.

Lark grins and winks, 'writer's confidentiality honey.'

'You did, didn't you,' Jordy says, grinning. Well what will this one be about?'

'Mmm, about the deconstruction of a woman's conventions?' considers Lark, raising her eyebrows

'Sounds wild,' Jordy snorts.

'Well, many women are so good at multitasking it becomes a sort of cage don't you think? Tick tock, the whirr of so much to do...' Lark taps her teeth with her fingertip.

Jordy nods, 'Yes, I guess I hadn't thought of it like that.'

'So this cage can inhibit us from letting go into pleasure, into orgasm, yeah?' says Lark, feeling her way with her idea.

'Yes, I agree with that. It is almost impossible to switch off the endless lists of things to do, plans, ideas, the past and future and worries sometimes. Even more so when there are kids.'

Nodding, Lark says, 'sometimes my mind will just let go but other times I have to transcend it with a force of will.'

'Mmm.' An impish grin spreads across Jordy's face as she pauses. 'Or a particularly luscious fantasy can arrive to help.' Lark picks some of her underwear out of the washing basket.

'Exactly. Perhaps this is my new vocation, what do you think Jordy? A writer of erotica?'

'Why not? You'll be flat out and exhausted when the baby arrives so make the most of it.'

A writer of erotic tales, a woman exploring her experiences and fantasies - pregnant in Paris – it is all so unreal, so removed from the wheel of her normal life. As a consequence Lark finds an openness and spontaneity that rarely intrudes in her late-thirties settled lifestyle in Australia. Perhaps it is travelling, or pregnancy or as scary as the idea seems, that she is without Martin.

Ten weeks pregnant and the appointment to see the gynaecologist is a couple of days away. She tugs at her miniskirt, noticing how tight the waistband is. A diary would be a smart idea, so she can remember everything about this time later. Lark makes a mental note to get herself a journal as well. Writing ideas on scraps of paper is exasperatingly disorganised.

Guil and Jordy take her to Adelyn and Remi's apartment, which is tiny, with only one bedroom compared to Jordy and Guil's two bedroom place. Like Jordy and Guil's apartment block it is well maintained but has none of the lovely style of inner Paris.

'What is the style of architecture in the inner city?' asks Lark French Classicism, it is called,' says Guil. 'Endearing is it not? But the suburbs are different.'

'Many Parisians live is very small nondescript apartment blocks like ours,' says Jordy. 'The Australian idea of a house with a backyard is unreal to most Parisians.'

Adelyn and Remi would like to move because their baby Benoit is one and a half and they want him to have his own room. Despite their conversations being mostly in French, Lark catches a few words here and there and Jordy translates off and on, so she doesn't feel too left out. They talk about many different arrondissements around Paris and some of the hideous places they have already looked at.

'One place they recently looked at, ivy was growing up the wall inside the kitchenette,' chortles Jordy. Lark smiles and tells Jordy, 'A place I looked at in Paddington, in Sydney, the floors sloped so much, the furniture was on a tilt, but the real-estate agent assured me there was nothing wrong.' Jordy translates and they all laugh.

On the way back to Guil and Jordy's on the metro, Lark finds the first couple of lines for her next story have written themselves in her mind. She mixes her memories and fantasies into a confection, working out a plausible scenario. She decides her character is a rather fussy career woman named Adriana. She is the sort who squares her tea towels and washes her clothes everyday. Very particular and hypercritical of anything that doesn't meet her particular world view.

Faulty plumbing and bad taps are like flaccid penises, Adriana grumbled to herself, pulling her car's steering wheel into a left turn. No good to any woman.

Later Lark's thoughts revert to her relationship while she drags on an old tee shirt she uses as pyjamas and crawls into bed. In two days, her life she hopes will return to its former path, at least until the time bomb growing in her womb transforms everything. Though Martin's postcard doesn't mention it, she believes he has accepted the baby. As she dozes, her character Adriana and her story takes shape so that on waking, she is able to jot down a rough outline.

'We are going to Parc des Buttes-Chaumont in the 19th ar-rondissement for lunch today, would you like to come too?' Jordy asks her at breakfast. 'I think you'll like it. It's far less formal than many of the gardens in Paris. We got married there.'

'Oh I remember you telling me you married Guil in a park,' says Lark, recalling the happy photos Jordy sent her. 'Yes, I hadn't planned anything today. That'll be nice.'

The park, when they get there, is still mildly ordered by Australian standards, but has lovely meandering paths, waterfalls, temples and cliffscapes. Jordy sets out a picnic rug and they have lunch under a tree. Celeste toddles - crawls about picking up leaves and sticks. Jordy is kept busy policing what goes into her daughter's mouth and righting her when she falls. Guil smokes several cigarettes, drinks an entire bottle of red and after chatting volubly about the animation he is working on, falls asleep in the dappled sun streaming through the branches.

Lark goes for a walk and finds a shady spot to sit and write after Jordy assures her she is fine playing with Celeste.

FIXTURES

Faulty plumbing and bad taps are like flaccid penises, Adriana grumbled to herself, pulling her Honda's steering wheel into a left turn. Absolutely no good to any woman. Resigning yourself to a landlord's cheap and nasty choices is worse than a quickie too quick, she added, raking over a personal sore point.

Adriana was still saving a deposit for her own home. It was exasperating to find the toil to save stretched into the future and as a consequence she continued to be a renter. She was at the mercy of her landlords and had recently been given notice - again. The prospect of another move meant another set of problems to get used to in an apartment that was not her own. Infuriating.

In her leisure time, Adriana found pleasure looking at home renovation magazines or surfing the Net looking at taps, faucets, lighting, shower guards and ovens. She refined her choices for many fixtures, planning their installation in her eventua lhome. A faucet sale rated with a shoe sale in giddy desire for Adriana. There, gleaming in her mental trousseau were the most unadorned, elegant chrome fittings and appliances. No wonder she felt irritated to have to move to another flat full of compromises and transience.

'This apartment has to be better than the last one,' Adriana murmured, moving with the sluggish traffic on the green light. Flung on the passenger seat with her bag, was a set of keys, exchanged for a cash deposit to view the last of several apartments that day. She shuddered, recalling hair still in the bathroom sink, overlaying rust rings and other unnameable grot she's seen today. Turning on taps with a tissue, she'd heard the rumble as water staggered up through the pipes. Disgusting!

She couldn't live with that, or the stale mix of cat-piss and cigarette smoke that underpinned the air of the previous flat, oh no. These two experiences had reduced Adriana to stopping at a suburban mall for a long black coffee and some restorative time browsing in a rather dowdy boutique. A tension headache began to build at the base of her neck by the middle of the afternoon.

Adriana turned her car into the driveway of a modern block of six flats. She flicked a look in the rear view mirror, checking her face as she switched off the engine. Grabbing her bag and the flat keys, she was away, locking the car electronically with an automatic gesture of her hand.

Opening the apartment block's security door with the keys, Adriana ran up a small flight of stairs in the foyer. Well kept she noticed, as she hauled out her self-made inspection lists from her bag.

Lists governed Adriana's life. Since the beginning of college, Adriana has regulated her life with lists as an antidote to her poor memory. Back then she became a true believer in the power of writing everything down. Collating facts, things to do Post-its, itemizing and comparative lists, events, details and thoughts were all jotted down. Like a chain smoker, Adriana would write a new list, carefully transferring the unfinished tasks from the one previous feeling feverish about throwing the old list away. She'd tried online planners and diaries and hated them. All that turning on phone or laptop, typing and saving as

*opposed to opening her trusty filofax and using a pen to
organise her life.*

*Currently single, Adriana's last partner left her because this
habit drove him nuts. He complained that she never relaxed –
even a day out of town or a holiday required another list. In a
rare moment of candour, Adriana had divulged that during sex
she often made mental lists of his virtues and vices in
comparison to previous lovers. She couldn't understand his
dismay. Not for a moment could she see that her listing fetish
inhibited her ability to relax or achieve an orgasm. Adriana
wisely resisted the urge to tell him the full extent of her
comparisons. His slightly banana shaped cock veering to the
left when erect had earned a big cross in her mental list, plus a
snort of derision in her mind despite it's efficiency at making
love to her.*

While she types up her notes later, Lark decides she'll splurge
and go to a matinee performance of Don Giovanni by Wolfgang
Amadeus Mozart at the Opéra National de Paris tomorrow. She
loves the sumptuous set design used in operas with their
extravagant storylines, going when she can in Sydney. On the
internet when she books the ticket, it appears to be a minimalist
set, but she doesn't mind; it is such a marvellous opera with the
added piquancy of a treat for herself in Paris.

On her way to Bastille the next day Lark realises it might be her
last single day for a long time, with Martin returning tomorrow.
To spend it soaking up a brilliant operatic performance in Paris
is a wonderful treat.

After the performance later, she walks out of the venue
enthralled, thinking that without elaborate sets to beguile her
eye, she could focus more intently on the plot and the singers,
who were marvellous. Blinking in the late afternoon sun, she
decides she must finish her current story tonight; writing has
already become a mental preoccupation and she doesn't want to
dwell on it when Martin arrives. How should her narrative end?
With seduction and deception, like the opera Don Giovanni?
Perhaps there could be a little - without the singing, she thinks, a

cheeky smile upon her face as she walks.

Paris is engorged with people. Many are tourists, buzzing about like the migration of Bogong moths during spring in Australia. In the crowds she catches sight of a young woman ahead with pink hair. Perhaps it is Jordy and Guil's friend Marcelle? She lengthens her stride to catch up. Walking with the pink haired woman is a tall brown haired man with a jaunty flat cap on his head. Perhaps it is Francois, both whom she met the first meal out at Soleil cafe. They weave through a cluster of people, turn a corner and disappear in the throng before Lark is able to catch them.

Adriana was chagrined to see the door of Flat 5 ajar.

'Typical,' she mumbled out aloud, recalling the real estate agent who was more interested in her cleavage than her request. 'Last lot too lazy to lock the place up when they left.'

Impatient now, she pushed open the front door and stepped into a hallway, sniffing for bad odours. The apartment enlarged into an open plan lounge room framed by the ceaseless Pacific Ocean surging past the balcony. She turned to lock the apartment door behind her, preferring to view the apartment alone with no unexpected interruptions.

Ignoring the spectacular view, she instead noticed that the paint and carpet looked in reasonable condition. Adriana took out her phone to take photos and ticked next to these items listed on her paper. Walking into the galley kitchen, the dark floor tiles earned a cross. She gave ticks for the voluminous storage and recessed lighting. Adriana pulled open the wall oven to inspect it for inadequacies. Such was her concentration and focus, she did not at first comprehend a tensing of the stale atmosphere in the kitchen. She turned as the scent of aftershave assailed her. Not an Ocker, her mental patter informed her, even as she met the stare of a casually dressed man paused at the doorway of the kitchen.

'Flat hunting too?' He asked with a faint accent, flicking a strand of shining black hair back from his face with a casual swipe of his hand. 'I arrived just before you.' He held up identical

keys to her own for Apartment 5, with the real estate's tag attached.

Adriana, arrested in her flatting list, nevertheless noticed the man's fine hands, his speckled olive eyes and the curve of his hips in his casual jeans. Her headache grasped at the top of her eyeballs, foretelling a migraine upon its way. Pigeon holing him as another flat hunter meant that she need make only the barest verbal contact to veil her annoyance. She got up from her stove inspection, piqued that his first view of her was her backside.

'Have you been looking long for an apartment?' he tried again.

'Just today, though I've looked at some real dumps since this morning.' What a bother, thought Adriana. The cleavage ogling guy at thereal estate had assured her that no one else had asked for keys since lunchtime.

Feeling cornered in the galley kitchen, Adriana sidled out into the lounge room with a tight nod at the man. She hastened her inspection, noting with a frown the dents in the carpet from bed furniture and a curtain hanging askew. More ticks and crosses plus photos to remember later. In the mirror robes Adriana could see a reversed rectangle of the balcony through the main bedroom's French doors. Out there the man was stilled in profile, caught in the ocean view.

Separate toilet, dual flush works, bowl not too disgusting - tick. Adriana could now hear the man wandering around the flat again.

In the bathroom, Adriana approached the vanity with the eye of a scientist. No rust rings or mould in the basin, but a little corrosion on the taps. Gold fittings though - could she cope with that? The tacky vase of plastic flowers with an air freshener, she ignored. She turned on the taps, glancing in the vanity mirror to see the man moving across the lounge room. Observing him, interest whispered for a moment in the deepest crease of her mind. This she quickly squelched. Adriana was a sly perver, allowing herself this sort of observation only when she was undetected.

He turned quite suddenly and saw her, caught that unguarded second before she refocused upon her list, massaging the ache at the back of her neck. He noticed her office shoes, small ankles and gauzy black hosed legs. Her maroon sheath dress was creased across the pelvis from being rucked up while seated, he imagined, on her office chair. Topped with a cropped black jacket, her appearance radiated a precise efficiency.

Flustered at being caught in that moment, Adriana resumed bustling about, intent on saying something bland and leaving. The apartment seemed reasonable, no need to stay longer. He waited at the bathroom door while Adriana turned with her mobile and took more photos. He reached to flick a strand of his hair back again.

'You have others to look at today?' he asked.

'No, last one today. It's not bad is it.'

'Love the view.'

'Yes.'

Adriana piled her mobile and list into her bag. She looked up to see a whimsical smile. Adriana stopped still, poised. She knew he had seen into her, understood something that her careful social defences usually hid. He moved towards her, hesitant. Adriana's bag dropped. She was stunned to find herself reaching for his belt buckle with a single greedy thought. Shit! She didn't even know the man and yet here she was, flicking off her stilettos in the empty lounge room as he watched with those speckled olive eyes.

Adriana's headache was forgotten. Her mind blazed through her state of fertility; last period, contraception? 'This is crazy, dangerous even,' competed with a grass-fire of serendipity. She looked up at the shine of his shaved chin, the curl of his lips caught in a surprise mirrored by her own. Their uncertainty vanished as the opportunity actaulised between them.

Once again she reached for him and his cock grew into her marauding hand. He stroked the curve of her face, following down, stroking her breasts beneath her jacket.

They pressed their bodies together and he gathered her up by *her buttocks. Turning her back into the bathroom, he pushed Adriana up against the vanity. Her greedy fingers sought out dips and curves of body though his shirt and jeans.*

He reached for her wrists then and whispered, 'Turn.' He rotated her gently. 'Look.'

Adriana stared at their reflections in the mirror, amazed. He bit her shoulders and released a thrum of breath upon her nape, igniting her inside. The whisper frisson of her zip lifted the small hairs on her back as he undid and slid off her dress, tucking his thumbs in to her pants and dragging them down too. She arched back to undo her bra, while he pulled off his own shirt. With a clunk of belt buckle his jeans tumbled to the floor.

While one hand curved around Adriana's belly, snaking into her slit, his other fanned her hair across her back. Adriana moaned tipping forward over the vanity and into his marauding fingers. In the mirror she could see the edges of his muscular form around her own and watch as he wound her hair into an anchor around his hand. With sinuous caresses his fingers commanded she spread, all the while teasing her moist lips and velvety clitoris. She reached for him behind her, taking hold of his warm shaft, using their slick to anoint herself before propelling him inward.

In the mirror she watched, mesmerized by her animal self with this unknown man. She was always so guarded about any liaisons with men. Yet nothing mattered, only this most transient union in this moment. The rhythm they created uncertainly at first, aligned with confidence.

Know herself? She thought she did. All her social appearances, her lists and consumer obsessions were nothing but convenient steeplechases that kept her from her essence. She understood this in a flash. Their passion enveloped her as he pushed deep and hard into her vulnerable molten centre.

Lark Connor

10

A text comes in on her phone as she finishes correcting the type and sends 'Fixtures' to Michael's email address. Jordy has read and checked 'Fixtures' through this morning but Guil had no time as he rushed to go to work. Jordy found it funny and the sex scene minimal but hot.

Lark, arrive about 4.30pm, Martin xx

Lark hums as she readies herself for Martin's arrival, choosing from her suitcase the sexiest clothes she can find. She washes her black hair far longer than usual. In the bathroom mirror she scrutinises her face, staring into her vivid green eyes, noticing the lines of age and concern around them. Like a first date again, she thinks, nervous thoughts galloping about in her mind.

How peculiar that these stories seem to be spilling out of her is a repeated thought. Her feelings of heightened sexuality haven't diminished; on the contrary she can't stop thinking about sex. She admires buttocks, legs, the turn of a pretty profile, the curve of a sumptuous neck in both men and women whenever she is out. Her fantasies mirror her daily voyeurism when she masturbates. It feels like she is directly connected to the essence of life, life created through sex, the life growing inside her acting as a channel for this heightened awareness.

Quite by chance, her erotic stories have become a symbiotic expression of this perception. She snorts at herself in the mirror as she cleans her teeth. Deep stuff! If I'm this supercharged, how is sex going to be with Martin, she wonders, running the tip of her tongue over her sharp canine teeth in anticipation.

By 4.30pm she is on tenterhooks and changes her underwear, the first pair soaked with juiced anticipation. Jordy and Celeste have gone to meet Guil after work and will eat out at a café – their way of giving Martin and Lark some space. A knock on the door and Lark's breath catches. She pauses, eyes shut, sending a prayer for everything to be okay. She opens the door, drinks in her lover, a hyper real observation with every bit of him dear, from his brown curly hair, down his long frame to his toes. They are in each other's arms an instant later.

Lark,' Martin gulps, softly rolling the 'r' with a rusty voice.

'Oh Martin, I've missed you so much,' Lark cries on his shoulder, sniffing his sweat and unfamiliar travelling smells on his clothes. She looks at him again and then they are both laughing, shreds of conversation jumbled while he shuffles into the flat and drops his case.

'Guil and Jordy?'

'Gone out for the evening. What happened, Martin?'

'I just... freaked out. I had to be alone to think about everything.'

They kiss and kiss, soaking each other up like sponges.

'Becoming a dad is a huge step.' Martin kicks off his shoes and lifts up her top to hold the weight of her breasts. 'Bigger,' he murmurs.

Her nipples harden, Lark takes a sharp breath, 'same with becoming a mother – but millions do it.' She bites her lip to stop other more sarcastic retorts clambering to be said. Instead she undoes his belt, staring into his blue eyes. They move towards Celeste's bedroom shedding clothes, touching, grasping, kissing, stroking, their only conversation now, a sexual one. Within minutes she has pushed him down on the futon and takes him into her, both gasping with transcendent satisfaction.

She pins his hands at his sides with her fingers and nails, wanting to inflict some pain for the anguish he has caused her. She rides him, reaching behind herself to grasp his balls for control.

He grunts, eyes glazing. 'Lark,' he gasps, about to climax.

She stops, sits impaled upon him for a few moments, gets off, placing the palms of her hands on the wall as she kneels on the bed. He gets behind her and enters her again. When he doesn't fuck deeply enough she pushes off the wall to get him into her deepest recesses. She feels insatiable, driven to the edge of need. She pulls one of his hands from the wall and drapes it about her, pushing his fingers onto her clit.

A fantasy forms, one of her regular ones. A woman wears a butter yellow satin evening dress with a split at the back and stilettos. She holds a champagne flute and is leaning over a balcony wall, looking down at a party. Martin thrusts hard and Lark drops onto her fours. The woman/ self on the terrace is grasped from behind, underwear stripped down, fingers and tongue invade her, anointing her, testing her as her pubic bone grinds into the sandstone wall. Lark and Martin find a rhythm and Lark sees the pictures, repeats them, savours the fingers fucking her yellow clad fantasy, the tongue licking her anus, dress splitting further. The woman, whose face is always shrouded or replaced by Lark's own self, holds her champagne, is content not see behind her while she is plundered. It is after all why she is here at the party.

Martin! How much she loves absolutely all of him. She reached down her front and plays with her clitoris, adding her fingers into their union, ringing his thrusting cock, gratified beyond measure to be able to enjoy their intimacy again as he slides into her slick centre.

The male asserts himself in her fantasy, she peels through a variety of cocks flicking eagerly from muscular loins, settling on the thickest to enter the golden woman, her arse now protruding, vaginal lips beckoning, her nipples hard against the golden satin while Lark watches her.

Martin picks her up and turns her over. Lark flicks her hair away as he kisses her and enters her again. She stretches her legs out wide and fastens them over his back, latching onto his left nipple, biting and sucking. Wider, higher, they arch over and into each other, her nails raking his back and buttocks. Lark feels heat and pressure building in her lower belly. She reaches down and secures his scrotum in her palm forcing him to her own commands. In her mind's eye she watches the man tease and enter the woman repeatedly until the excitement overwhelms her and Lark's orgasm showers down while she floats away. Martin bucks into her and climaxes moments later.

They stay clasped together for a long time after, Martin slowly shrivelling out of her. The daylight drains from the apartment. They lie, running fingers over each other's skin until Lark has to go to the toilet. When she returns to the bedroom, Martin is sitting up cleaning himself off himself with some tissues.

'Good to get that out of the way, now we can talk. Want some tea?' Lark asks.

'Yes. Food too, I'm so hungry.'

They dress and make themselves a salad with toasted bread and cheese while they sip their tea, an unspoken understanding that they'll talk after they have eaten.

'When I left you, I'd worked myself into a crazed state,' says Martin. 'I just had to get away. I couldn't think straight. It felt unbearably ugly that I was demanding you have a termination. I was being such an asshole.' Martin paused, rubbing the two day growth on his chin. 'I left you sleeping, hung about in Paris and caught the Eurostar to London. Fell asleep on the train, woke with my luggage gone. I had my phone, passport, tickets and wallet on me. Your passport unfortunately was still in my case. I saw your messages and texts, but I felt so bad, so confused, I just couldn't answer you.' Martin picked up her hand and squeezed it. 'I stayed at a cheap bed-sit hotel in inner London. Didn't do much – you know I've been to London before and I just wasn't interested in sightseeing, especially without you. Also I had to hang around to try to sort out my lost suitcase and buy myself some new clothes. Then I left my phone in a changing room, duh! I was a real mess.' He rolled his eyes, remembering. 'Shit! You cancelled your passport didn't you?'

'Yes, when I applied for a new one, the old one got cancelled.'

'Great.'

Martin looks relieved and kisses Lark. She feels the downwards rush of lust again but schools herself to keep focussed. He reaches for her hand across the table.

'Not only was I confused about the baby, I felt terrible about your passport. I'm sorry Lark.' He looks at her shamefaced. 'I didn't buy a phone until I arrived back from Scotland, to punish myself.'

Lark feels the urge to placate him, but she resists. He has been spectacularly selfish, she thinks, quite unaware that by not contacting her, he punished her as well. Idiot.

'How long were you in Scotland?' she asked, to allay her bitter thoughts from taking hold.

'Seven, eight days. We could go again. It's really beautiful,' he says eagerly, then falters. 'Um, if you're feeling well enough.' He looks at her belly. 'We weren't too rough making love just then were we?'

Lark smiles, 'I don't know how it works with sex and babies,' she says. 'Maybe later when I'm bigger it may be an issue. I know nothing!' she grins at him, shy now, because they haven't talked peaceably about the baby since they've known about it.

'I have something for you.'

Martin bounds away to his case in the lounge room and returns to give her a small book, '50 Pregnancy Tips for Women.'

'I bought it in London. I knew you'd have difficulty finding anything here that isn't in French.'

'Thanks!' She flips through the book. 'This is great! I'm going to see Jordy's gynaecologist tomorrow – I'm still bleeding on and off. I thought I'd better get myself checked and I can ask some questions as well as she speaks English. As to travelling, my new passport should arrive in a week's time.'

'Have you been well?' he asks with an anxious expression. 'I couldn't stop thinking about you when I was away.'

'Yes, a tiny bit sick but I've dealt with that, so I'll be well enough to keep going with our holiday.'

Lark smiles and hugs him. She can't say it yet, but she knows she has forgiven him for running away and for all the turbulence before. She just can't hang onto bitterness or regret right now.

'So we can keep our baby Martin?'

'Yes, I want to now. I think my cold feet have thawed and sense has arrived.'

Lark crushes him in a bear hug and screams with happiness.

'Yes!' she shouts, 'we're going to have our baby! Woohoo!'

Martin can't help but laugh at her happiness. They kiss and caress each other. There is a small life growing between them; a brand new feeling. They don't realise they are growing into something new too; a mother and a father.

They wash up their plates and tidy away the food.

'What have you been doing while I've been gone Lark?'

'Touristic things mostly. Galleries, museums, parks, the opera.'

He nods and smiles.

'I was just so upset,' she tosses it out lightly despite the submerged depth of emotion she has endured. 'Guil said I should do some drawing, but I couldn't, so I've been writing instead. Do you remember the man who talked to us at Notre Dame?'

Martin frowns, 'Nup.'

'I bumped into him again. He's an agent for writers.' Lark takes a big breath. 'He supplies different publications in France and the UK.'

Lark flicks on her phone and slides through screens until she finds Michael Lawson Agency to show him. While he is looking at the site, she continues. 'He asked if I'd like to write some stories, so I have. It was a way to cope with your disappearance. One has been accepted so far and I sent off another this morning.' She smiled proudly, dusting her finger across the screen and flipping to a document with SALON MAGIC typed across the top. Martin scrolls though the pages, skimming.

'Really? So this is yours – 'SALON MAGIC? Pretty sexy stuff Lark.'

'Yes, fun isn't it.'

'Does he pay, this guy?'

'Of course. Money is in my account; I checked this morning.'

Martin looks bemused, then pensive. 'Lark is a writer now, wow! These stories you're writing aren't about us are they?'

'No of course not. The subject is very wide - women's perspectives on love, marriage and sex. I'm writing erotic tales because the subject appeals to me. It was either write that or write about the trouble we've been having, which I just couldn't do.' Lark's green eyes flare. 'Jordy suggested the theme of erotica.'

Martin knows better than to question her judgement. After all, he's been away and she's made her own decisions in that time. He taps her nose with his finger.

'I love you, you know that don't you?'

'Yes me too, love you,' Lark purrs, mollified.

Keys turn in the lock and Jordy and Guil arrive with a grizzling Celeste.

'Halloo, halloo!' So good to see you Martin,' says Guil expansively, giving him bisous on each cheek. He strides into the kitchen to uncork a bottle of wine he's bought home. 'Shall we celebrate, the ah... safe return of the runaway 'usband? It is from the Bordeaux region,' he waves the bottle about. 'The best after Bougogne, but that is just my 'umble opinion.'

Jordy sits and untangles a breast for Celeste, who rummages with chubby hands in her mother's bag for her cuddly, a small brown bear she wants to hold while suckling. Jordy holds her fingers to her other tit, a wet patch visibly growing on her shirt.

'How are you Martin?' She leans to give him kisses on both cheeks, oblivious to his unfamiliarity with her semi-naked breastfeeding.

Martin looks nonplussed and she laughs at him.

'Get used to it sweetheart, its what they're made for. Lark will be breastfeeding soon too!'

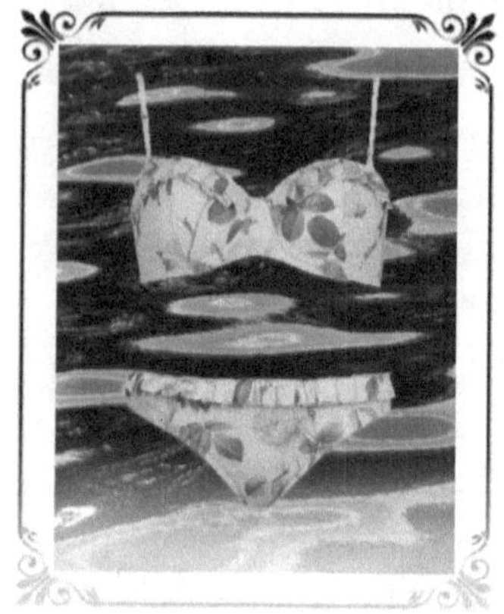

he bell on the door announces Jordy, Celeste and Lark. They sit themselves down in the waiting room of Jordy's gynaecologist, Dr Jennine Fournier, who practises not far from the Eiffel Tower on Rue de la Tour. The receptionist is on the phone, glances briefly and nods at them.

'Are there forms I need to fill out,' asks Lark.

'No, you'll talk directly to the doctor,' says Jordy.

'Okay.' Lark is perched on the edge of her chair, feeling anxious.

In the end, Martin was nervous about coming with her, so Jordy has accompanied her instead. Lark has swallowed her disappointment with his cowardice; she needs her energy for herself. Celeste writhes and is soon on the floor with her teddy bear. Minutes later she is scooped up as Dr. Fournier opens her door and beckons them into her office. She seats herself behind a large desk with chairs in front for patients.

'Bonjour, I am Dr.Fournier. She nods to Jordy who motions that Lark is her patient today. You are?'

'Lark Connor,' says Lark, sitting down again.

'We have some basic information to fill out, okay?'

'Yes, of course.' Lark provides all the details that the doctor needs including when her last pap smear was, which Lark struggles to recall.

'How can I help you today?' Dr. Fournier asks.

'I'm pregnant - about 10 weeks. I used a test from the chemist a few weeks ago. I've been bleeding, um, spotting here and there...' She fades off and bites her lip.

'Okay, so this is your first examination since you've been pregnant?' Lark nods. 'I'll have to look at you. Please go behind the screen and take off your clothes and lie down here.' Dr. Fournier waves her hand over the bed nearby.

'Just my underwear?'

'No, all of your clothes please.'

Lark disrobes, expecting to find a paper robe or something to put on. Looking at herself naked, she realises she can't see her pubes for her slightly protruding belly anymore. So, no robe, no problem, Lark is not worried about nudity. She steps out and makes herself comfortable on the gurney.

The doctor puts on latex gloves and begins pressing down on areas of the lower stomach. Lark stiffens, it is more tender than she's realised, not being in the habit of pushing deeply there herself. It feels tight and sensitive and she gasps.

'Okay, now I'll have to give you an internal examination. Legs up please. Can you come forward on the bed so your bottom is just here? Good.'

Dr. Fournier puts some gel on her fingers and puts two into Lark's vagina, probing gently. This feels fine, until she begins pressing gently on Lark's stomach again. Its all Lark can do not to writhe away. Quickly it is over though and the doctor is wiping excess gel from Lark's slit, peeling off her gloves and washing her hands.

'Please get dressed again Lark.'

When Lark has dressed and they are seated again, Dr. Fournier says, 'are you sure of those dates? You seem bigger than you would normally be at ten weeks.'

'I think that's about right, I missed a period two weeks after we arrived. She looked at Jordy, who gives an imperceptible shrug. She is feeding Celeste to keep her quiet.

'Have you been sick? Put on much weight?'

'Not much of either so far,' says Lark. Just the bleeding has been the only problem.'

Dr. Fournier scribbles on her notes. 'In France we don't advise a speculum examination when you are pregnant unless there are signs there may be something wrong. I don't think you have any serious problems but my advice is for you to make an appointment with my receptionist to have an ultrasound in two or three days time so we can see how the baby is in your womb.' She finishes writing; Lark signs a form, says thank you and is ushered out to pay and make her ultrasound appointment.

They take the metro from Trocadéro, changing at Pasteur and getting out a stop later at Voluntaries. Lark is subdued. She feels somewhat invaded despite that there was no speculum used, which always has this effect upon her.

'I know, it is a rollercoaster, pregnancy. One minute your mood is wildly optimistic, the next we are frightened by the enormity of change, like little mice,' says Jordy, pushing Celeste's pram along the narrow pavement.

'Yes it's exactly like that,' says Lark. 'Right now I feel terrified. Seeing the gynaecologist makes it more real. I'm also pissed off with Martin for not coming along too.'

'Guil wouldn't come the first time with me either. It takes them some time to find their courage I think.' Jordy answers. 'Good thing men don't get pregnant!'

'Salut Jordy!'

'Oh, it's Marcelle.' Jordy slows as Marcelle crosses the road. She has a towel over her slender shoulder and is wearing a rose and grey patterned culotte with pink platform sandals to match her hair. Bisous are given all round.

'Comment allez-vous?' asks Marcelle, her grey eyes twinkling.

'Bien merci. Well thanks,' Jordy switches to English for Lark's sake.

'Moi aussi,' says Lark shyly.

Marcelle speaks very fast in French and then tries it slowly in English. 'Guil I phone to um, découvir your plan aujourd'hui, today. 'E says to meet for swimming. So here am I.'

'Ok, lovely,' says Jordy.

Celeste has her arms out to Marcelle, with a big smile. That she knows her well is obvious. Marcelle squats near the pram and prattles on to Celeste for a moment or two, patting her aquiline nose and then Celeste's snub nose, which Celeste finds very funny. They continue on to meet Martin and Guil outside the Piscine Municipale Blomet for a swim. After purchasing tickets and separating to change into their swimming costumes, Lark feels even more insecure. Her body is changing shape so quickly. It is easy to disregard it when dressed, but in a tiny bikini, her belly is far more noticeable. She looks at Jordy, who has always been thin with narrow hips. Her boobs are big and succulent, pearlescent with many blue veins showing. She doesn't seem to notice at all how she looks, so much more focussed on getting Celeste into an Aqua Nappy and a tiny cute swimsuit, then yanking off her clothes and dragging on a one piece swimsuit with Celeste wedged between her knees.

Was that a butterfly tattoo perched at the top of Marcelle's Brazillian cut pubes? She is obviously a natural mousy blonde from their colour and doesn't shave her armpits. Lark purses her lips, thinking of her own luxuriant black bush – she prefer au natural and had scolded Martin when he decided to trim his pubes for some strange reason. It was altogether too prickly while making love.

What might Marcelle's fantasies be like, Lark wonders. Perhaps Miss Pink has studs in secret places ... perhaps her next character could be similarly coiffed below? She notices that Marcelle looks younger, her skin does anyway. Its known European women have less exposure to the elements than their Australian sisters. She still has the bloom of youthfulness, Lark thinks with a prickle of jealousy.

Marcelle catches her eye, smiles and licks her lips.

'Souviens-toi de moi?' she murmurs in a husky voice, a bloom of clove cigarette breath and sandlewood preceding her question.

Lark shakes her head; she doesn't understand. Marcelle's scent spikes her olfactory memory, She's smelt that combination before a long time ago.

'Er, you remember me?' Marcelle asks again.

'From the other day at the café?'

'Non.'

Marcelle smiles again and turns away, fishing out a flame pink swimsuit from her bag. She pulls it onto her perfectly honed body, it is high cut with crochet cutouts at the sides and very sexy. It's obvious she works out at a gym or something similar. Flinging her things into a locker and turning the dial, she heads out of the change room. Lark wraps her towel about her, bemused that less than an hour ago, naked at the gynaecologist, she had no reservations at all, but here faced with Marcelle, she feels inhibited.

Jordy notices Lark's bikini. 'Ah, that might be a problem.'

'What?' Lark looks about to see if she has pubes hanging out or something.

'In France they disapprove of bikinis in the swimming pools,' says Jordy. 'The French are very obsessive about hygiene and cleanliness in swimming pools.'

'Bikini's are not a health risk,' Lark says with incredulity. She folds her clothes and puts them in a locker, automatically folding some of Jordy and Celeste's things as well.

'Come on, we have to shower first. Did you bring a cap?'

'No, I didn't.'

'Its okay, we can buy one at the dispensing machine.'

After purchasing a cap, they head for the bank of showers running along one side of the pool. There they can hear a disturbance with raised voices. Martin, wet in new gray patterned boardies is arguing in broken French with a squat little man in shorts and a white polo skivvy. Guil is gesticulating and throwing in his comments as well.

'Vous devez quitter la piscine,' the pool attendant shouts.

'Je nage dans ces tout le temps,' Martin shouts back, looking really annoyed.

'Tell him, Guil, board shorts are totally acceptable to swim in.'

'En Australie shorts sont pour la baignade,' says Guil, smiling widely, enjoying the fuss. The attendant shakes his head, no.

'Have you men's maillot de bain on underneath?' Guil snaps

the elastic on the leg of his own togs.

'Yes, I do,' says Martin. 'Okay, je vais changer ensuite,' he says to the attendant and strips off his boardies right there, revealing new Speedos. The attendant folds his arms, smirks at Martin's togs and moves away looking for other errant attendees.

'Pompous butthead,' Martin mumbles under his breath, watching the odious man notice Lark, Jordie and Celeste standing near the showers. The attendant marches up to Lark and accosts her about her swimwear too. Martin and Guil stride over and another altercation proceeds. This time however, the attendant backs down with Guil, Jordy and Marcelle shouting at him, while Lark stands mute and embarrassed.

'He says, you can wear your bikini this time. Next time is proper swimsuit,' Guil grins after five minutes of furious French argument. 'Ees alright Lark. We French love a good fight.'

'Gee Martin, they're lairy swimmers,' blurts Lark, forgetting to say hello. Not your usual style at all, she thinks. For Martin's Speedos would blend perfectly in a Gay Pride parade. They are bright cerise with a silver shooting star decal on the front.

'All I could find when I shopped at Primark,' Martin mumbles before putting on his cap.

'I love votre maillot de bain. Il est ma couleur préférée!' Marcelle laughs, reaching out to give Martin's bottom a cheeky pat.

'What did she say?' Lark asks Jordy.

'That she likes his swimmers. They're her favourite colour,' says Jordy, with a small grin.

Martin grunts and gives Marcelle such a black look. He stalks off without greeting any of the women, dumps his boardies and plunges into the pool. Lark is surprised he's made no effort to acknowledge her or chat to her about her appointment. Knowing how much he hates officious power trippers, she understands he's furious. Later, she thinks, we can talk.

The three women and Celeste rinse themselves at the edge of the pool in the unisex shower. Around them people apply soap and lather themselves up, rinsing off before donning their bathing caps and diving in. Lark recalls as a small child, a country swimming pool where she had to wade through an ankle deep bath of water with disinfectant in it to get to the pool, but here complete washing before swimming is seriously taken concern.

'I'll do a few laps and then look after Celeste so you can have a swim,' she says to Jordy and is rewarded by a grateful smile. She steps out of the shower stretches out her cap and pokes her head and hair in and looks for a fast lane to swim in. There doesn't appear to be any slow or fast; swimmers are muddling along as best they can, so Lark dives in and goes for it.

Five laps later, she gets out and finds Jordy in the paddly pool with Celeste. Jordy hurries away for a swim. While Celeste wails for her. Lark distracts her with water squirts and by playing with some of her plastic pool toys bought by Jordy. Her belly feels tender so she 's happy not to swim anymore. While entertaining Celeste, she watches the pool goers with an impartial eye; noticing the families, the interplay between couples, the flirtations of teens and the games of children. Guil and Jordy hug at the end of a lane, a stolen moment alone. She wishes Martin would come to talk to her, surely he's calmed down by now. She notices him muscular arms heaving his lean frame out of the pool. He stands, strips off his cap and fingers water out of his ears.

'Martin!' she shouts, despite the futility of his hearing her over the cacophony of pool noise. He'll look around for me, she thinks, scooping water and pouring it with Celeste.

Another swimmer gets out beside him. It's Marcelle in her pink bathing costume. She sloughs water off her limbs and removed her cap, shaking out her pink hair. Martin and Marcelle begin talking, learning close against the noise of people thrashing up and down the lanes. They stand in a patch of sunlight from the large skylights set in the swimming pool's ceiling. Lark sucks in a breath. They glisten, slick with water droplets, looking like twin gods in their matching pink swimwear. Everyone around them seems dull by comparison.

Celeste falls over. Wet, she proves very slippery to get hold of and it takes minutes for Lark to set her right and jolly her out of her inevitable howls of fright. When Lark looks up, Martin and Marcelle are walking towards her, still chatting and laughing. And shining. Lark feels an unaccustomed stab of anxiety. Or is it jealousy she wonders, biting her lip.

'Hi Lark,' says Martin wading into the baby pool with Marcelle following.

'Hi... are you over your rage at the attendant?'

'Yeah.' Martin flicks his hand as if swatting a fly. 'Marcelle says she'll take over looking after Celeste so we can have a swim.' Already Marcelle is squatting next to Celeste who, fright forgotten, puts her chubby arms out to her; Lark has been superseded.

'Bonjour ma petit poisson,' Marcelle sing-songs, picking Celeste up for a cuddle, while pretending to be a fish.

Lark scrutinises Martin; he looks different. There is an absence of something in his face. He glows with – what is it? Cheerfulness she realises. When was the last time she saw him looking like that? Immediately she knows it was on Notre Dame before she told him she was pregnant. Inside Lark crumbles, but she manages to say, 'merci Marcelle.'

'Okay.' Marcelle is already lying down with Celeste on her back giggling.

Lark and Martin find a bench at the side of the pool. When she looks at Martin's face he looks preoccupied again and looks very mortal. That shared charisma with Marcelle has fled. Perhaps she's imagined it, she thinks, feeling rather uncertain about reality.

Martin leans over and gives her a kiss. 'How are you Lark?' What happened at the doctor?'

Lark tells him briefly, realising there is little to tell. Her anxiety about the doctor visit has passed. 'I'm alright, just a little tender.' Martin gives her a warm damp hug and she feels some of her jaggedness melt.

'More laps?' he asks.

'No, you go though.'

'Another ten, okay.'

He walks around the pool edge and dives in. The opening line for a new story evolves in Lark's mind, precipitating a loose plot line. All over the place, that's me, she smiles ruefully, watching Martin plough up and down the pool.

Wet

The chop of aquamarine water discordantly slapping around the pool, filled Linda's senses as she pushed open the door to the indoor swimming pool.

In the change room once dressed, Lark checks her phone while she waits for Jordy to dress Celeste. Marcelle chats to Jordy in French. There's a text from Michael Lawson Agency. A sign on the way into the pool instructed patrons that no phones are to be used, so she waits until everyone is assembled outside the entrance in the summer heat before phoning Michael back.

'The new story is wonderful. It needs a title change – how about 'The Listing Lady,' or 'Apartment Hunter'? Something like that. Have a think and text me your ideas.' Michael sniffed and continued. 'I'm looking for a piece with older protagonists in mind. In the thirty – forty bracket. If you are writing another, can you keep that in mind?

'Okay,' murmurs Lark, 'Are you getting any interest in my stories? At home, I'm a designer not a writer – it's a new thing for me.'

'As a matter of fact, yes. There are many LitMags that publish erotica and other mainstream magazines that enjoy articles with some spice too.' Michael chortles. 'You've a good eye for detail. It makes it all the more interesting.'

'Thanks,' Lark laps up the praise.

'Alright, I'll hear from you soon then? Perhaps we can meet again to talk more about content.'

'Yes, perhaps.' Lark thinks keeping Michael as a contact in the ether suits her better. 'I have a new idea in mind.'

'Keep them coming. Bye.'

Sliding her phone into her bag, Lark sees Martin, glasses on, looking at Marcelle's phone, a map just visible while they chat in

French. Lark feels acutely the disadvantage of knowing so little French, deciding in that moment if she spends a few weeks more in Paris, she should enrol in a crash language course.

'It's a party Marcelle's knows about in a few days if we'd all like to go,' says Martin as Lark grasps Martin's arm proprietarily. Lark slants a look through her lashes at Marcelle, to see her grey eyes assessing her with Martin unaware between them. Men are so ignorant of such subtle prevarications between women, Lark thinks, feeling her teeth getting pointier. As well as everything else, some French flirt is coming onto her man.

She looks away and rolls her eyes, turning back to say, 'shall we go away for a few days Martin, until the next appointment?'

'You feel up to it?'

'Absolutely!' Check, she thinks.

13

"Mate, so spectacular!' breathes Martin winding down the window of Guil's Peugeot to look across the tidal flats at Mont St-Michel floating like a mirage out to sea.

During the usual wine soaked evening last night, Guil, as expansive as ever, had suggested a weekend away in the north-west of France.

'My mother Leonore, she 'as a big house, we can all stay the night. She loves to see Celeste.' He says this as if it quantifies four adults descending upon his mother's hospitality at short notice. Jordy clicks her tongue, knowing she'll have to ring and arrange it. Guil is too sloshed to talk to his mum at the moment.

'Mont St-Michel is very close to where I grew up near Rennes,' he tells them. 'You'll love Mont-St Michel. 'Ow is it, you have this word 'abbaye' in English?' Martin and Lark both nod, knowing he means 'abbey.'

'It is an old abbaye out on an island. Very touristic, very crowded at this time of year, but we will go anyway.'

For the journey Lark and Martin sit in the back seat of the Citroen, separated by Celeste's baby chair. Lark has been entertaining Celeste with songs, little books and toys and her hair, which Celeste insists of grabbing every few minutes. Martin on her other side has done little to entertain the baby, he's mainly just chatted to Guil while he drives. The physical separation from Martin for a few hours in the car suits Lark. She is feeling moody and hormonal and still trying to understand her feelings about what happened this morning.

Knowing Guil's flexible idea of time now, they spent a lazy morning making love. Lark showered, collecting their swimwear from the top of the glass shower cubicle on the way back to their room. With any luck they'll get a swim somewhere on the coast, she hoped. She towel dried her hair and dressed in a pale yellow skater dress with red hibiscus pattern, thinking she'll have to shop soon for some more stretchy skirts, her miniskirts are feeling too tight now. She picked up the swimwear to pack, noticing the label for Martin's new pink togs sticking out. It's a French label. She frowns, remembering yesterday he said he'd bought new clothes at Primark, which she knows is a big department store in London to replace his stolen stuff. She picked out the pink cozzie and threw them at Martin, who was just rousing himself for the shower.

'Where'd you buy these Martin? The label is in French.'

'Primark, in London.' He looks surprised, taking the swimmers and bunching them in his hand.

'Really?' What about this then?' She peels the togs from his hand and shows him the label.

He shrugs. 'Lots of French brands there. Part of the European Union after all.'

Lark pursed her lips, uncertain. She has a feeling something isn't right, but when she thinks about it, nothing seems exactly wrong either. Ack! Maybe it's just her hormones are all over the place with the baby. Her favourite colour... is not pink. Calm, she repeats to herself. Nevertheless, her morning has been disturbed and she realises she is still unnerved by Martin's recent disappearance. Too much stuff has happened and she needs time to digest it all.

'I check the tides this morning – we can stay a few hours, the causeway will be underwater at full tide,' says Guil, in travel guide mode. All the windows are down in the Peugot because Guill can't go long without a smoke 'The river over there is the border between Normandy and Brittany. Mont St Michel is in Normandy.'

Martin leans forward to catch Lark's eye; he's been trying to befriend her for the entire journey. 'Lark?' he whispers.
She smiles a tight smile, unsure how to bridge the gap of uncertainty.

'How old is Mont St Michel? Lark leans forward to ask.

'Mille ans... a thousand years, maybe more?' Guil answers with a wave as he drives through the Bay of Mont St-Michel. 'It was created by a bishop who wanted to be closer to God and pilgrims 'ave come here since 700 AD.'

Guil eases the Peugot into a park in the mainland car park and they pile out, stretching. Celeste has a breastfeed and is quiet for the shuttle bus ride from the car park to Mont St-Michel across the causeway. Martin and Lark gaze about them in awe and Lark's gloomy uncertainty evaporates. Mont St-Michel is way too magical for unhappiness. The wide bay spreads out about them all pale golden, the sea a silver blue, topped by a cornflower sky. She misses the ocean at Bondi but has been too busy in Paris to really notice until now looking at this bay. They alight from the bus into a sea of tourists surging up the main street of the town surrounding the abbey. The usual cross pollination of languages and accents assails them. From where they stand it is obvious the main access to the abbey is through a very touristic market winding through the village all the way up to the abbey steps

'We will go another way 'round the remparts,' says Guil, lighting another cigarette and hefting Celeste onto his hip. 'Less tourists that way.'

'Ramparts he means.' Jordy has been here before with Guil. We can get to the steps that way.'

'They were built in the 15th century in defence against the cannon,' explains Guil as they all wander along the grey battlements. 'Mont St-Michel 'as never been conquered, even by the English.' He grins and spreads his arms as if he being French is unconquerable. There is definitely something unquenchable about Guil's infectious enthusiasm.

'Did you ever read 'Famous Five go to Smuggler's Top' as a kid Lark?' asks Jordy, who is enjoying daddy carrying Celeste.

'Yes, it was my favourite of them all,' says Lark.

'I've wondered if Enid Blyton based Smuggler's Top on this place.'

'Mmm, you might be right!' Lark looks around and has to agree with Jordy. There is a wondrous creepiness mixed into the awe inspiring abbey crouching over an ancient village. The place seems to draw history down from the atmosphere.

Hungry, thinks Lark, so often hungry now. She finds two apples in her bag and gives one to Martin. Biting into its succulence, she savours the juice tingling on her tongue. 'I'm here,' she murmurs, realising where she actually is; she is in her yellow dress fantasy. She looks down. She even has a golden yellow dress on. Jordy and Guil are up ahead swinging Celeste between them. She looks behind her, noting that there are people back along the ramparts, but not really close at this moment. She turns in front of Martin and kisses him with her arm around his neck. She slides the other down to rub his cock, which stiffens agreeably.

'Lark,' Martin's eyebrows rise. She undoes his fly and gets his hard-on out of his jocks, but still tucked discreetly in his jeans like an actor waiting in the wings.

'Lark. What are you thinking?'

'I'm going to lean over the battlement here. I want you to fuck me hard for as many moments as we've got before those people get too close.'

'But Lark, its risky,' Martin looks incredulous.

'Quickly,' she commands, wriggling her undies down and turning to lean out over the wall to look out at the view. She feels Martin draw close and closes her eyes, holding her apple, now transformed into a champagne flute. He places a hand beside hers; with the other flips up her dress and frees himself. She feels an immediate rush of juice as he enters her and she moans, feeling so hot she could scorch him from the inside. He thrusts hard, several times and comes, exhaling next to her ear.

Seconds later Lark follows with a cascade of energy dazzling her senses. Martin flicks down her dress and moves along the wall while he zips himself up with a discreet movement, both of them breathing hard with glassy gazes not taking in the view at all.

'Now that was so naughty,' Martin murmurs. Lark screws up her nose and grins like an imp, surreptitiously smoothing her dress and pulling her undies back in place, where they become soaked with their mutual juice. Some moments later an elderly couple stroll by talking with American accents and Guil calls them to catch up from ahead.

'Delicious though,' she says, biting into her apple again. Apple juice never tasted so good, even better than champagne.

'What brought that on?' Martin wants to know.

'Tell you later. Gotta find a tissue.' She can feel a gelatinous trickle winding down her leg.

They take the steps up to the abbey and marvel at the 11th century Romanesque Church, with Gothic additions that bring in light through arched windows. They walk around the Abbey's cloister, a gentle garden set high in the abbey. A couple with their elderly parents recognise Guil and inevitably they all stop to chat and decide to meet up the next day.

"e is an old friend from the Paris School of Art. 'e is a sculptor and has his studio over here at his parent's place,' says Guil. 'It is much cheaper than Paris and only a few hours away. We 'ave a lunch invitation tomorrow.'

On the way back down through the village they indulge in a very fluffy omelette, which both Martin and Lark love but Celeste spits out all over Guil's lap with a look of disgust.

Before the tide rushes in across the flats they all walk down onto the sandy mud from the car park and look up at Mont St-Michel.

'What is the golden statue at the top of the spire?' asks Martin.

'St Michel, the archangel,' says Jordy. 'Chief opponent of Satan. He also assists souls at the hour of death.'

'Roman Catholic?' asks Martin.

'Of course, it is the main religion in France.'

Lark wanders away on the sand, musing on an entirely different contemplation. An erotic story set somewhere like this might be fun, she thinks, taking out her writing pad to jot some ideas down. There is the sentence she thought up yesterday at the pool waiting for her on the page. Medieval romp might have to join the queue.... something beyond the cliché of the serving wench being seduced by the young master of the manor or the dungeon full of BDSM equipment. Ho hum. She wonders if Mont St-Michel had any lusty stories tucked away between the stones and then laughs quietly at her strange thoughts.

Driving back to the N176 and then along the coastal roads, they stop for a swim and an ice cream. They change in the public toilets, Lark washing out her come doused undies in the sink, noting a smear of blood again. After a swim, she sits on the beach at Saint-Cast-Le-Guildo with its quaint changing tents feeling so happy. She can even tolerate Martin's pink swimmers, inching up above his boardies as he mucks about with Guil in the water. She lays back watching Jordy holding Celeste's tiny feet in the wavelets, wondering if she'll be doing that soon. Will the baby be a girl or a boy? She's always thought she'd have a girl. She hopes she doesn't miscarry, but pushes that thought away.

Staying with Jordy has given her a much clearer idea of how it is having a baby around, though she intuitively knows she is still very self-involved - the privilege of the childless it seems. Jordy's selflessness and devotion to Celeste, she marvels at. It will be strange to not work, even if its only for a few months. Perhaps she can do a few jobs still and put the baby in day-care. It will also be hard to have so little time for herself and for Martin. She'll have to talk to him about it. If Jordy's parenting is anything to go by, it is pretty all consuming at least when babies are well, babies.

Lark sighs, feeling glutted and lazy. Fancy trekking to the other side of the world to live out one of her sexual fantasies... perhaps she needs to catch a train, ride a horse or go to a men's club to fulfil a few of her others... She rolls over and realises she it's uncomfortable to lie on her stomach now so she opts for her side to think some more about her swimming pool story. A seduction, yes... with older characters. She is enjoying writing - it is something she'd never thought about doing seriously before.

*She met him at the pool that summer. The water sparkled like
a constellation.*

She jots the sentence down on a notepad from her bag. Later as
they continue driving along the coast, she sits in the front with
Guil. Jordy breastfeeds Celeste again and when she falls asleep,
eases her into the baby chair, buckling her in with her teddy.

Lark opens her notebook again, intent on writing as they drive.

'Another story?' asks Guil, a glint in his eye as he glances her
way.

'Yes. This time about a quick liaison at a swimming pool.'

'Ah, so you 'ave been researching at the piscine?'

'Could say that Guil.' She looks at her sentence. No, it's not how
she wants to start.

~~*She met him at the pool that summer. The water sparkled like
a constellation.*~~

14

*S*he begins again, gazing out the side window at the French countryside every few lines, with half an ear on the banter between Guil, Jordy and Martin. Their chatting in another language frees her to concentrate in English.

WET

The chop of aquamarine water slapped the pool sides as Linda pushed open door to the indoor swimming pool. She used her foot to hold it open for her toddler to walk through holding his toy truck, while she held their towels, bags and food. With her last free fingers Linda nudged her bikini top over a piece of her breast that felt like it had slipped out. Unreliable and slippery these breastfeeding breasts she mused, keeping an eye on her son.

'Don't run, only walk,' she called out to Joshie, who stopped transfixed at the shallow end of the children's pool, in no hurry. Linda dumped their stuff, picked Josh up and deposited him on the wooden bench.

'We'll just get you changed Joshie.'

She stripped off his day clothes and nappy, changed him into an aqua nappy then helped him step into his togs and rash shirt. She rummaged deeper in the bag to find him a snack and drink. While he sat nibbling, she kicked off her own shoes and unzipped her skirt. Picking up their clothes, she stowed them while unearthing some little buckets for Josh. She sat waiting for Josh to finish his snack with a sense of relief to be here. Paddling with Josh has become a happy weekly event.

Ten minutes later, Linda sensed she was being watched from the other side of the pool. Following the beam of energy across the glittering pool, Linda discovered an older man playing with two children. Even from a distance she could see they all shared similar facial characteristics including extraordinary blue eyes. As he rough-housed with his kids, he perved on the few women doing laps, flashing a look a few times at Linda. She arched an eyebrow and stared back. Joshie finished his snack and made a beeline for the shallow end of the kid's pool.

'Mummy come now.' Linda's attention snapped back to him.

'Hold on Josh.'

'Bringing Teddy too.'

She quickly rounded up the snack box and drink bottle, grabbed the buckets, shut the bag and joined Joshie. They both waded into the infant's pool to play. Teddy waded too, becoming a sodden mass of fake brown fur.

All the while Linda was aware of the man's observation; for early forty's, post childbirth she was in good shape. In fact she mused, just getting back some libido after a late child. Was it nature's bonus to increase her erotic appetite in her years before the turbulent times of menopause overtook her?

Linda glanced a few times at the man. Older, yes – perhaps late forties or early fifties, but it was hard to tell, him being wet and at a distance. Pretty fit, he was throwing his two boys over into back-flips in the pool under the glare of the pool attendant. The big boy of thirteen or fourteen and the younger, around eight years old were having a lot of fun. So, greying but not balding. Strong shoulders and chest with no flab at his waist. Perhaps it was the water gleaming on his lashes that gave them such a cute blue anemone look. Lovely.

Somewhere between six and seven, Guil turns the Peugot into the driveway of a rambling stone farmhouse with dormer windows in Saint Mayeux.

'My home,' he says, 'or at least my Maman's now. 'I grew up 'ere.'

The front door opens and Mrs. Fontaine greets them all with double kisses.

'Bonjour, bonjour et voici ma petite-fille.' She takes Celeste from Jordy's arms. 'She gets so big now.' Mrs. Fontaine smiles and jiggles Celeste who freshly awake, gurgles with pleasure at seeing her grandma, who in turn pulls a face. 'Elle a besoin d'un changement de couche.'

'Yes, pretty smelly,' says Jordy, 'I'll go and change her nappy now.' She takes her bag from Guil, recovers Celeste and heads inside.

Mrs. Fontaine looks to be in her fifties, dressed in slacks and a crème shirt, epitomising typical French style.

'Bienvenue, welcome,' she nods at Lark and Martin.

'Bonjour.' Lark smiles and Martin shakes her hand.

'Maintenant que vous êtes arrivé, nous pouvons faire le diner,' she says to Guil. 'Entrez.'

Lark looks askance and Martin translates as they enter the house. 'We can make dinner, now we've arrived.'

'You don't speak much French?' Mrs. Fontaine asks Lark.

'Not much.' Lark is a little embarrassed by her lack. 'I will take some lessons in Paris I think.'

'Ah, wonderful. Do you enjoy your time in France?' she asks them both.

'Yes, I have been here before, but its Lark's first time,' Martin answers.

'Take them upstairs Guiliame. Your bedroom is the third along. I have seven bedrooms here. Put your bag in there and have a shower if you wish.'

They pass through a large open plan room with three different lounge settings – one surrounding a pot belly stove, another in a glassed in deck, windows open and another near a long wooden dining table next to a wide galley kitchen.

'Your house is so lovely Mrs Fontaine,' compliments Lark.

'Call me Leonore.' Guil's mother smiles.

Upstairs there is an internal corridor with several doorways leading from it. A double bed under a slanted roof with a dormer window is their bedroom for the night. Lark drops her handbag on the bed and looks out the window; the sea is visible just like at Bondi.

'Look,' she says to Martin. 'I love it.'

Guil returns from one of the further bedrooms where they can hear Celeste talking to Jordy. he stops at their doorway.

'You were so lucky to grow up here,' says Lark.

'Oui, my brothers and sisters, we play a lot, its true. There is a hectare of our land to the beach and five of us so it was very busy.'

'How could you leave this lovely place Guil?'

'Art school in Paris, mmm. That is what I wanted. Then I met Jordy when she was, how you say... un étudiant d'échange.'

'Exchange student,' says Martin.

'Then the jobs in animation... and we can always visit.'

They take quick showers and make a meal with cold meats, salad and herbs from the garden, sautéed vegetables, white wine and convivial conversation.

What Lark remembers later when she thinks of this gentle evening is the marvellous taste of julienned vegetables sautéed in balsamic vinegar which she wanted to eat and eat.

'Italian cuisine, not French,' according to Leonore.

How, as the wine flowed, the conversation reverted mostly to quick-fire French with Martin and Jordy translating bits when they remembered her. She could catch words here and there, occasionally understand the nuance of a phrase and heard the regional dialect as different to Parisian French.

'They are talking about light, atmosphere and how a couple of times here the family even saw the Aurora Borealis above the la Manche - the English Channel. Saying also that when Guil was a small boy he loved to try to draw light coming through the clouds,' translated Martin.

'Hundreds and hundreds of pictures,' laughed Leonore, waving her hands to show fluffy clouds.

And now, it is what I do for work. I use lighting to create beautiful backgrounds for animations,' said Guil.

Celeste crawled up on everyone after the meal, finally falling asleep on Lark's lap. Thumb in her mouth, her soft breaths puffing in and out, oblivious to the adults' chatter. Lark could not help but admire the perfection of her – her chubby brand newness and wondered again about the child growing inside her. We are all made from sex, a truism of course, she thought, yet often forgotten. She looked around the table anew, thinking how most often we are made not just of sex, that irrepressible biological urge to replicate ourselves, but of love too.

Worn out from the day, Lark retires first and drowses, the shush of the waves lulling her. Martin comes to bed not long after and they curl around each other like two cats, listening, content. The word 'romantic' comes into Lark's mind; old and clichéd - yet the lovely farmhouse they are in with each other and the sea lapping the shore nearby, feels infinitely tender.

'I love you Lark, no matter what happens,' whispers Martin.

'I love you too,' Lark purrs back. 'What do you mean, whatever happens?'

'The baby,' he says.

'Together we can make it work.' She kisses him, feeling her passion uncurling itself.

'Yes, I think we can,' answers Martin. 'Worry free sex until then, how's that... I like it!'

'Mmm,' murmurs Lark, rubbing her chin against his stubble.

She's already aware what a relief it is to be free of the constant concern over different sorts of contraception, the relentless cycle of monthly blood, fertility and the fear of late periods.

They disentangle, stroking and kissing. She sniffs his skin deeply, wishing to never forget his scent, even overlaid as it is with the wine he's been drinking.

'That was pretty wild at Mont Saint-Michel. What inspired you?' Martin asks, twirling a coil of her hair around his hand.

'Ah,' says Lark, debating whether to tell him her yellow fantasy. In words it might sound trite so she dissembles. 'Got terribly horny. This baby is really winding me up sexually.'

'I noticed,' says Martin and she can feel his smile as she runs her fingertip over his bottom lip. 'Can't say I mind.' He plays with her nipples, his interest prodding her in the leg and leaving a silver slick there.

'Do you fantasise when we make love Martin?

'Sometimes.'

Lark can hear the slight caution in his answer. Like herself, she senses that fantasies can be a private thing, but she asks him anyway. 'You do? What about?'

'This and that,' he replies and begins a journey lower, taking her sensitive nipples into his mouth and biting hard enough to make her catch her breath.

'One day let's compare some fantasies,' whispers Lark to his curly head. She rolls slightly and spreads her legs, demand implicit. Martin murmurs and then Lark no longer cares. Her clitoris hardens under his tongue's laving. Her thoughts unravel, words from her story hurry by her mind's eye and flow away. She shuts her eyes as he laps and nibbles her. When she begins to peak, she reaches for him. Martin wipes his mouth and kisses her while she manoeuvres his hips to plunge into her. They both groan with pleasure. Lark claws his buttocks and returns to grasp his hips, wanting to exert some control over his thrusting. She interrupts his rhythmic determination, forcing him away, then into her, against his own tempo. She adjusts his frame to allow for the small lump of her womb and they settle into a slow timeless pace, feeling every minute sensation.

Lark imagines she has a penis and she is the one screwing Martin with it. She embellishes and repeatedly admires the slickness of her imaginary cock and what it is doing, flicking and eager to plant its seed deep in nameless maws, full of ripeness and readiness to conceive.

A gay client told her months ago about glory holes in wine bars and public lavatories on Oxford Street in Sydney. Fascinated, she'd googled it - the utter bizarreness of a wall between you and another person, engaging in anonymous sex. This comes to mind and she inverts it, conjuring a wall of undulating protuberances suitable for women to use, then imagines herself balanced on an enormous phallus that splits her as it cleaves her, again, again.

She is dimly aware of the heat in her belly as she arches to meet Martin; it flickers and firms while she bites across his fine haired chest to each nipple. Moments later she is rushing down a rising slope of orgasm with Martin still beating a rhythm into her. He smiles and kisses her and builds himself his own crescendo, coming hard into her minutes later.

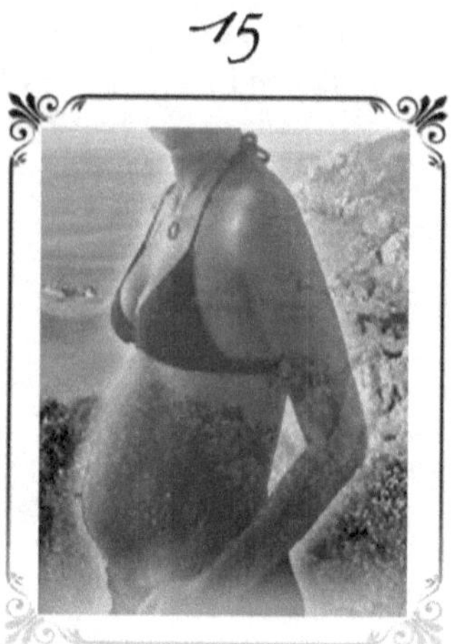

15

*L*ark wakes in the grey light of dawn, the unfamiliar feather pillow has flattened out and no amount of pummelling gives it substance. She lies for a while listening to the first birds peeping over the ceaseless tide. She plans some more of the story 'WET.' Soon there is enough light coming in through the dormer window to get up.

She visits the bathroom, and takes the laptop downstairs, writing until she hears Jordy and Celeste stir around 8 am.

WET

Josh wanted to walk to the deeper end of the pool, so Linda guided him, making sure he didn't slip over. She picked him up under the chest and tummy to help him 'swim', a couple of times. The next time she looked up, the magnetic sensation was gone. The man and his children had left. The pool seemed empty, just an impersonal reflective beast without that beam of energy cast across it.

After twenty minutes, Joshie tired of the infant's pool. Linda took him down the ladder into the 25mm pool with an inflated ring and his arm floaties on. Ten minutes in the cooler water and he became whingy and cold, so they got out and grabbed their things, heading for the family rooms to have a hot shower.

'Fishy curtain, fishie curtain,' shouted Josh.

He knew the family room shower curtains sported either ducks or fish. The 'duck' family room was engaged but the fishie one free. Linda put her bag on the change-room chair and immediately turned on the taps, adjusting the shower heat to suit Josh. He climbed onto the little shower seat installed on the tiled wall.

'Truck now Mummy,'

She took the sodden teddy, stripped off her togs, rinsed them and bundled them into a plastic bag. She gave him his truck and bent to strip off Joshie's swimwear and nappy. The door handle rattled and opened - Linda had forgotten to lock it.

'Excuse me.' A head poked in before the door closed.

I'm naked, Linda thought with an inner shrug as she squatted in front of Joshie. She was ambivalent to nudity in general, yet even more so at the pool. The change-rooms filled with women in their collective nakedness posed an eternal delight for Linda. Divested of clothes, gleaming with anticipation for a swim, or satiated by one, the parade of bodies gave Linda a pleasure she'd enjoyed since a small child. Consequently she couldn't have cared less to be seen attending her child in the buff.

Joshie demanded soap, wobbling off the little seat. She caught him and set him on his feet, forgetting again to lock the door. She reached into her bag for three little containers to fill from the liquid soap dispenser. The door swung open again with a hiss.

Standing there freckled with shimmering water, stood the man with sparkling blue eyes. With his hand on the locking device, he observed Linda again.

'S'cuse me for barging in again. My kids are in the shower next door and I, er wondered if you had some shampoo I could borrow. '

Linda's initial surprise fell away as she looked at the man poised by the door. She'd heard children next door shouting over the pelting water.

Bemused by this neighbourly explanation of his appearance in her change-room, she continued to squeeze pink liquid soap into Joshie's containers, wondering what to say. Josh reached for them with stubby fingers and sat on the floor to wash his truck, ignoring the adults with childish absorption.

Still impervious to her own nudity, she accepted that a small strip of lycra across his taut loins hardly rendered him clothed either. They both looked like old drowned rats so it didn't matter much. Nevertheless, she reached for a towel to drape about her as she rose, purely for social decorum.

She rummaged in her bag and passed him their shampoo, a smile twitching her mouth. It was hard to keep a straight face, especially when they both knew that attraction zinged between them irrespective of the unusual circumstances.

'Ahh, mmm, well, thanks, I'll bring it back,' he faltered, bouncing on his toes, as he backed out.

Linda knew there were more than a need for shampoo going on; this man had a different agenda in mind. She took a nervous breath as possibilities flitted through her thoughts. She heard the other door opening and imagined the man administering shampoo to his kids. Moments later he returned with the bottle, which she received with a gracious nod. Linda retucked the towel a little tighter. Trying to be stern in the circumstances didn't have much impact.

'Thanks. You're pretty outrageous y'know'

'Yes, been told that before.' The man grinned.

'Inviting yourself in here. You could be anybody. WE could be anybody. The shampoo's just an excuse isn't it?' said Linda.

He looked so much like a wolfhound puppy she'd owned as a child. Solemn and contrite while he idled at the door. Even though his tongue wasn't hanging out like her dog, his grizzled grey body hair, lean form and blue eyes had an anticipatory air. His eagerness disarmed her as she stood next to Josh and his truck, the shower running behind her.

'Alright, a daft impulse, pardon me,' he muttered.

She watched the effervescence drain from his face as he stepped back to pull the door shut with him.

'On the other hand,' Linda said, cocking her head, 'we could acknowledge this energy between us and consider a little fun.'

She reached up for the handheld shower faucet and sprayed him as he hesitated, resettling its cascade back on Josh. Spontaneous, yet it was enough time for her to think through her options and to weigh the situation. She'd been on her own for months, what was there to lose? He didn't strike her as trouble, just an opportunistic family man.

He laughed, taking in Linda's imperceptible nod. Her wolfhound-man all but wagged his tail with joy as he re-entered her family room.

Joshie looked up and asked, 'What's my name, Joss, your name?'

'Robert.' He grinned down at the little boy.

'More soap Mummy.'

Josh held up his truck and settled back into his soapy games. Linda let her towel drop as she reached deep into her bag where she found a battered condom packet which she handed to Robert.

'No questions asked,' she said, 'if we get that far. We stop if Josh is disturbed or if I say so.'

'Yes,' he agreed. 'If my kids get crazy next door, we stop too.'

Robert reached for Linda's hand, and pulled her to him, all the while scrutinising her face, the angles of her body, her nipples dimpled with damp. They touched noses and kissed. Linda felt his erection stretching like a spear in his Speedo's while it nudged her pubic bone.

She pulled away to squat beside Josh and make sure he was okay. Turning, Linda found his erect penis nuzzling her cheek. She guided it into her mouth, licking and sucking, the shower streaming over their bodies. He pulled her up from the floor and ran his hands over each succulent plane of her wet skin. They kissed again. Linda pushed Robert down onto the small shower seat. She turned and sat on his lap, noticing his togs already looped around his ankle.

'Perfect,' whispered Robert, stroking the taper of her wet back and rubbing his stubble over her shoulders.

He bit the edge off the packet, pulled the condom out and eased it onto himself. She twisted around and they kissed again across her shoulder while she lifted her torso up just enough for Robert to plunge into her. The cascades of water were loud enough to mask their gasps at each discreet thrust. Robert's held her hips and lifted her while she pushed off from her hands gripping his knees. Inside, their sex danced like two darting fish.

Joshie glanced up briefly and then returned to his game, making small truck talk. 'Brrm, brmmm.'

Linda leaned forward to touch Joshie's bowed wet head.

'Brrm, brmmm,' whispered Robert as he pushed a finger into Linda's anus. With unexpected vigour, the flick of his cock reached in deeper. Over the sound of the water rushing, Linda could hear the kids next door shouting with glee and see the lovely wet crown of Joshie's head, yet enjoy the molten sensation with this stranger. All of it fused into a wild ephemeral moment and she felt her climax darting and threshing across her belly. Up, up glinting, scintillating, boiling over like lava. Rushing, crushing, and ringing down his cock as he bucked into her, his own surge exploding.

Into this moment, Josh thrust his empty soap pots.

'More soap. More soap, more, Mummy.'

Linda gasped and shimmied forward from Robert's lap, flushed and exultant. Murmuring to Josh, Linda stood and squatted to top up his soap and resume her own ablutions, with an otherworldly aura still haunting her. Robert looked glutted, transcendent. He hauled up his Speedo's as he got up and raked her with his sparkling blue eyes.

'Thank you,' he whispered, touching forehead and heart in a sign of devotion. He kissed her wet forehead, nose and mouth before leaving for the next change-room.

Linda locked the door. Now she showered, feeling like an errant teen-queen. It had been years since she'd done anything quite so spontaneous.

Or quite so naughty.

For months after, she looked for Robert's sparkling gaze at the pool patrons but did not see him again.

Well, still needs some polish, Lark thinks as she signs, 'Lark Connor,' but it will do. I think I am saying what I meant to say. Perhaps it'll be seen as risqué with a child involved. Or he, Robert could be a mad axe wielding rapist. She bites her fingernail. It's enough for now and anyway – in any story there are dark possibilities, just as in life. She saves and shuts the laptop, returning upstairs to where Martin still sleeps. There's a faint reek of wine in the air as he snores. Dear man, I love him so much. He must have really freaked out to leave me like that, but he really was being a horror. But that's finished now and he's accepted the pregnancy. I'm so glad he wants to come to the ultrasound with me tomorrow.

There's a light tap on the door and Lark pecks around the door.

'Wanna come out for a walk before brekky Lark?' says Jordy.

'Sure, I'll just get dressed,' Lark whispers.

A few minutes later they take Celeste for an early morning toddle past the slight hill behind the house, through an old wooden gate to a similarly old bench where the sea is visible.

'Oh,' says Lark. 'I'd love to own a little piece of this part of the world.'

'It is lovely isn't it,' replies Jordy. 'The English Channel is full of greys and pale blues... nothing like the steely aquamarines and bright blues of the sea in Sydney though. I miss that.'

'I'd love to paint this soft view.'

They sit companionably for a while. Jordy breastfeeds Celeste, while the pale early sky segues into a cobalt canopy with small clouds on the horizon.

'So, how is Martin? Has he sorted himself out?' asks Jordy.

Yes, he has,' says Lark. 'He's still reserved about the baby but is happy too.'

Jordy sighs. 'Well that's a relief for you both. Having a baby is such a life changing experience.'

Lark turns to her friend. 'Are you happy being a mum Jordy?'

'Its exhausting and exhilarating and I love Celeste so much.'

Jordy squeezes Celeste, who squawks and wants to get down from Jordy's lap. They get up and wander back towards the house. 'Yes I am happy. I don't know how long I can avoid going back to work and putting her into day-care, but it will be as long as I can.'

Lark is thrilled to find that Leonore has oats so she can have porridge for breakfast. She is so hungry she eats a second bowl, feeling like she is one of the children from the Famous Five.

'Rolled oats are called, 'flocons d'avoine,' in France and you can buy them in bio shops', says Leonore to Lark's enthusiastic question. 'It is not at all traditional to eat for breakfast in France, but I like it in winter. Not summer like you! But I hear you are eating for two, yes?'

Leonore is the first person to know outside of Martin, Jordy and Guil. Lark finds tears pricking behind her eyes and nods, wishing she could tell her own mother.

Leonore gives her a gentle hug and kisses each of her cheeks. 'Félicitations à vous. I hope everything goes well.'

16

After a swim in the sea, they leave Leonore's house and Guil drives them over to have lunch with the friends they met at Mont Saint-Michel, who live in Saint Brieuc nearby. It is a very rural district with two rivers running through the township, aged stone and wooden buildings with latticework upon them, squatting on cobbled streets. All very picturesque.

Gisella and Phillipe live in a quaint stone house set on a corner. Their property has four sheds, a plump black faced sheep with a lamb, a rooster and several chickens busily rushing about a trail of sculptural forms that spread from the front door all over the yard. Mostly these are large amoebic ceramic forms but there are also corroded metal conglomerates and wire kinetic shapes as well. When they both discover Lark is an also an artiste they all chat in a mix of enthusiastic French and English, everyone using gestures when words fail.

Once again the wine flows under a trellis of wisteria set on old flagstones out the back of the house. By the end of lunch, it is decided that Gisella and Phillipe will follow Guil back to Paris for the party tonight. They have friends in Paris they can crash the night with.

Actually Guil is rather too drunk to drive, so Jordy drives instead. Talking in the car, Lark mentions that she still can't drive on the right-hand side of the road, so Jordy gives her some time behind the wheel to get used to it. 'Better learning in the country than in Paris,' she says.

While she has a driving lesson, Lark gives the laptop to Martin to read 'Wet.' Guil dozes next to Celeste, who strains to look at her dad around her baby chair, while chattering baby talk to Jordy, who reassures her from the passenger seat.

'Did this happen to you?' is the first question Martin asks when she settles in the back seat again as Guil moves to the front.

'No, I've just made it up.'

'Really? It seems so... possible. Considering you've never written much before your stories have surprising verisimilitude Lark.'

'Well, I do have a highly detailed imagination, you know that Martin. And I have been an avid diary writer for years and years.' Lark runs her tongue over her pointy dingo teeth as she grins.

'Yes, I know.' Martin frowns. 'Are you sure you want to be writing this kind of material?'

'Why not?'

'It's pretty risque. Is this really the sort of stuff women like to read?'

Lark curls her hand into Celeste's sitting next to her in the safety chair.

'I love some erotic fantasy in my reading material especially when it is unexpected. I've just written what I might like to read myself.' Cheeky, she says, 'Don't you?' She knows most of what Martin reads is related to dry history, doctoral theses and news online.

Martin splutters, 'It doesn't usually figure in my reading criteria.'

The rest of the trip Lark entertains Celeste as before and muses upon the ending of 'Wet'. Perhaps there is more to this story than a one off seduction. Could Linda and Robert meet again in an unlikely situation? She scribbles in her journal when Celeste falls asleep, wondering if her alternate ending works.

WET (alternative ending)

Some months later, Linda decided to rearrange some of her bank savings. Approached in the shopping mall by a bank's promotional team, she discovered that there were new products available with better interest rates than her old accounts. With Josh in day-care, she walked into a banking branch near her work one day.

She enquired at the customer service desk and was soon directed to a man just emerging from his office. He shook hands and said goodbye to the client he'd just seen. The man turned, and there stood Robert poised like a wolfhound in a charcoal grey suit. An instant of recognition passed between them. Surrounded by a multitude of people doing banking business, the sounds morphed momentarily into a blur of rushing water.

'Good morning, you'd like to arrange a Term Deposit?' Robert said, his smile lingering on the harried worker on the Customer Service desk, then onto Linda.

'Yes I'd like to discuss options for a Term Deposit or any other suitable products your bank has,' Linda answered, her eyes betraying her amusement.

'Please.' Robert guided her into an office. Linda sat down while he folded himself into a chair behind the desk.

'I work here part time,' he said. 'Stay at home single dad three days a week the rest of the time.'

Linda thought his choice of explanation unusual. She wondered what she could say. Should she mention her widowed status? Did it matter to her whether it should matter to him? She wasn't sure and besides, she'd developed an aversion over time to new acquaintances that told her all, right down to their astrological sign in the first ten minutes of meeting.

'Well at least you're in the right room this time,' she answered, deciding to delay any personal repertoire for now.

They faced each other across the desk, both acutely aware of each other's cumulative appraisal. She knew their previous encounter had just been a one off with no further intentions for either of them. Yet here they were.

'Your name is?'

Robert tried to wrest the situation back into the banking request posed by Linda. He moved his fingers to the computer keyboard and opened up a menu.

'Linda Greythwaite.'

'Ah I didn't know your name.'

He paused looking at her again, remembering. They were behaving like two cautious old dogs discovering each other in unknown territory. Stiff and sniffing, she'd describe it to herself later. This won't do she thought; we know nothing about each other yet paradoxically have such intimate knowledge.

'Robert?' Linda leapt in. 'I have accounts here and I am sure you can tell me what I want to know – later. Right now, do you think we could go with our instincts a little?'

She saw no point in being insipid and could see she had his full wide eyed attention.

'Do you get disturbed in here once the door is closed?' She asked, gazing at the door semi ajar.

'No,' Robert murmured, 'though it isn't protocol to shut it.'

'If I'm not mistaken you'll need my details to process and approve my application?' Robert quirked an eyebrow, not sure where she was leading him.'How about you pull the door shut as far as codes of behaviour allow?'

Robert nodded, the anticipatory grey puppy again, and came around the desk to comply.

Linda stood. Tucked in a corner out of the line of sight of any casual observer in the main banking foyer, they looked at each other for a long moment There was no doubt about the electricity between them, fusing on altogether different circuits to the office reality. She began to kiss him but retracted at the last moment, teasing.

His iron strong swimmer's arms encircled her waist, moving up to catch her nape with his hand. He tipped her head back to burn a kiss on her neck. It lit her senses and she felt the familiar rush burn downwards inside. Another brush of lips shimmering and teasing led them to pull apart wide eyed.

'Will this sort of detail be beneficial?' she mocked.

'Is it a nine month sperm deposit you are interested in Linda?'
Robert grinned.

'Definitely. I'm sure you can arrange it for me,' snorted Linda,
rolling her eyes at his overwhelmingly tacky joke.

Robert answered by pulling her close. They opened their kiss
to explore, their tongues flicking and twining. As before the
undertone to their spontaneous passion was a limit on time, in
a risky place. Lust grew into a pervasive presence wrapping
them in a body tingling cloak.

With a quick careless glance at the door, Linda slipped down
to kneel on the Bank's floor. She undid his fly and filled her
mouth with his engorging penis.

'Mmm yes, the necessary details,' Robert gasped.

Lark Connor

17

They arrive back home around seven and raid the fridge for a meal. After showers to freshen up after all the travel, they catch the metro to the party near Pére Lachaise. It's been a scorcher in Paris and it is still fuggy and hot outside. Lark wears a white top and shorts with a pair of Jordy's tangerine platform shoes, while Martin has dressed in unfamiliar shorts and a shirt he bought at Primark in London.

Parties are the same the world over, thinks Lark, listening to the loud familiar dance music and burble of excited voices coming from the apartment they climb stairs to. When they come through the door, several people approach to greet them, including Gisella and Phillipe who introduce them to other friends. Adelyn and Remi say hello. Baby Benoit is with them, just as Jordy has brought Celeste. Bisous all round with lots of broken English greetings and questions about Australie and Martin and Lark's European travels so far. Hand gestures and laughter diminish the gaps in understanding for Lark but Martin chats easily in French. Lark is soon sidelined by the language barrier and her teetotalling so she dances instead.

She notices Marcelle arrive, dressed again in pink, this time in lycra hipster jeggings and a crop top that accentuate her supple figure. She lights a cigarette at the door and a cloud of clove scented smoke has the desired effect. People catching the fragrance turn her way. She grins and begins to dance as well. Marcelle arrives in front of Lark, nods a greeting in time with the pounding beat and gyrates provocatively in front of her. Lark moves away but Marcelle reaches for her hand, sliding her own up and over Lark's breast, looking at Lark intently.

'Souviens-toi de moi?' she shouts in her husky voice.

Lark twitches away from Marcelle's gesture and frowns as she dances. What is Marcelle doing touching her like that? It wasn't an accident. Why is she asking if I remember her? She rubs an arm over her breasts, feeling invaded.

'No, I don't know what your'e on about,' she yells over the music and moves away.

Martin joins in, dancing with his unique jerky movements. Remember me – Marcelle has said that before but Lark can't think what she means. Maybe she has mistaken Lark for someone else. Maybe she's crazy.

The rooms are fuggy with wafts of cigarette and marijuana smoke. Lark begins to cough. After three or four dances she is covered in sweat and brushes through groups of people to the kitchen for water. An athletic looking negro guy starts up a conversation in English with her. He's from London, a friend of the hosts, here for a weekend. They chat loudly to each other with the intimacy of strangers, leaning close to hear each other over the noise. People drift in and out to get drinks.

Eventually he propositions Lark - perhaps he was planning it all along. She lets him down lightly and returns to the lounge room with an extra glass of water. She looks for Martin and she sees him leaning against a wall, deep in conversation with Marcelle, who is insinuating her lithe body against his.

As she approaches she hears him say, 'Non Marcelle, je suis avec Lark maintenant.'

More nonplussed than angry, Lark clasps Martin's hand and he jumps. The look he gives her is preoccupied as if he's in a different world but Marcelle just smiles her vixenish smile and drifts away. Lark drops Martin's hand and evades him when he lunges for her, a proud dingo on the run.

'Lark!'

She finds Jordy on the small veranda and says she's not feeling good, could we perhaps go? Jordy, who also doesn't drink and is tired from driving, acquiesces. She collects Celeste from where she is asleep in one of the bedrooms and the two friends catch the metro home. Lark travels with Martin's words reverberating in her mind: 'non Marcelle, je suis avec Lark maintenant,' which even she understands.

'No Marcelle, I am with Lark now.'

On auto pilot, she finds her way to bed and lies in the milky warm darkness. Her mind churns the words across a crest of emotional waves, while in the troughs, murky ideas and uncertainties manifest. How long she lies there blinking in an altered state of reality, she doesn't know. She hears Guil and Martin arrive home, hears bathroom sounds and then Martin's darkened shape is in the room, breaking the congealed atmosphere. He undresses and slides into bed. She waits for an explanation, but if he has one, he's not going to divulge it willingly.

'What was all that about Martin?' asks Lark. Her hands tense into fists.

He sighs and rolls over, a world away.

'You know what I mean. 'Non Marcelle, je suis avec Lark maintenant,' she repeats the phrase badly. 'I am with Lark now.'

'Yes.' There is another pause, the sense of a giant bird tensing itself for flight.

'Martin?'

'Okay, okay.' He clears his throat. 'I used to be with Marcelle. We were together a long time, bought a house together in Manly.'

'Oh shit.' Lark feels like she's been sucker punched. 'She's the one.'

A long pause from Martin. 'Yes she was the one.'

The wave has crested and plunges, with both of them scrambling in its depths.

'When were you going to tell me Martin,' says Lark.

He snorts. 'Preferably never. Remember I've been with you the last three years and she's been on the other side of the world. You didn't need to know.'

Shaky, Lark feels confused, relieved and angry all at once. Can't decide which to be and feels tears springing to her eyes. She dashes them away, furious with herself.

'I've never pried into your past Lark, though I know you'd tell me without reserve. I'm different. I find it hard to express stuff like that. Especially... especially when it was so murky.'

Lark bites her lip, her compulsion is to soothe him and forget her own anxiety, even when it appears valid. 'Maybe so, but what is she doing coming onto you like she was at the party?'

'Drunk and stoned or tripping on something I think. '

'And?'

'Marcelle is a strange woman. She has these appetites... compulsions. She'll act upon them without thinking of the consequences or anyone she hurts.' Martin says. 'That's why we parted ways. I loved her but couldn't stand that carelessness of hers after a while. With me. With others.'

'Appetites? What do you mean – what sort of appetites?' Lark can't help asking.

Martin hesitates. 'She was into all sorts of kinky stuff. Whips, leathers, S &M, three ways. Lovers. She's bisexual, probably still is.' Reticent about his time with Marcelle before, now he's begun he doesn't hold back.

Lark feels her nipple tingle, the one Marcelle touched. 'And you?'

Martin sighs. 'Yes, I was involved too.' His words flutter like stabbing crows in the milky darkness. Involved. A pathetic word to cover a chunk of his life. 'But that's not what we're talking about.' He tries to shut the Pandora's box.

Lark lies there saying nothing, just listening to their breathing. Inhale and exhale. Heck, he kept all that well hidden.

'Lark?' Martin turns over.

'Are you happy with my simple tastes Martin?' she can't help but ask, aware how selfish her insecurity is, her need for reassurance greater than asking him about his own emotional fallout.

He curls around her, threading his arm under hers to hold her close. 'Yes, more than happy these last three years Lark.' She can feel his words upon her shoulder. 'I see it now as part of my crazy experimental youth.'

'You mention your hurt in such a general way Martin. I'd like to know how you felt,' she says.

Martin sighs as if dredging through the mud of his past. 'I was a young guy and felt sorry for Marcelle. She'd recently arrived from Paris. I thought we could lead a simple life, look out for each other. We bought the house in Manly. I caught the ferry and bus to Uni to work.' Another pause. 'Left at home with too much free time and imagination, Marcelle began experimenting beyond Manly's confines let's say. When I found out, I was angry. I didn't want her to run back to Paris, so I joined her games. Until they became too extreme and hurtful and she left anyway.'

'What does she want? Why did you tell her that at the party?'

'Parting ways was very difficult for both of us, but we'd really gone off the rails with each other,' he said. 'See, Marcelle is always on the make. If it wasn't me tonight, she'll have found a lover by the party's end. She consumes people and discards them like lolly wrappers. I was just a sucker to stay with her so long.' There's his bitterness hiding pain. 'Having been with you, I can see what a deviant she became back then.'

Lark thinks back to a time in her past when one night stands proliferated. By her early twenties the novelty of waking up with some guy you'd only met the night before and didn't want to see again wore off. Had Marcelle made this a lifestyle? With her own variations?

'I hope all this is true Martin and there's nothing between you and Marcelle.' She turns over to face him.

'Scout's honour.' Martin holds his first three fingers up and gives a sad grin in the semi- darkness.

'Why did we go to the party then?'

'Marcelle is an old raging friend of Guil's from way back. You'll have noticed Guil is always ready to celebrate.'

'An old friend?'

'Yes, they met in their early twenties when Guil's family

holidayed in England one summer I think.' He seems about to say more but stalls.

Lark frowns. 'But she's not English.' She doesn't get the connection.

'Actually she is. She speaks perfect French and she affects to be so.'

Her instincts tell her there's much more to this story, but it will take some inner reflection to find some sense in what Martin is saying. Perhaps she'll ask him some more exacting questions another time.

'She keeps asking me if I remember her. I don't know what she's on about. Do you know?'

'No.' Martin pauses. 'Don't worry about it. Marcelle is very strange and she wants to unsettle you, I'd say. Even though we finished and went our own ways a long time ago, creating doubt and chaos would give her pleasure.' Martin kisses Lark gently and hugs her. 'I'm here now and we're going to get married and have our baby, that's what matters.'

'Yes we are,' whispers Lark, a tear of relief sliding from the corners of her eyes into her hair just to hear him say it. She feels her mental claws retracting, the wave of anxiety slowly subsiding. She reaches for his hand in the dark and the gentle nebula of sleep whirls them into its embrace.

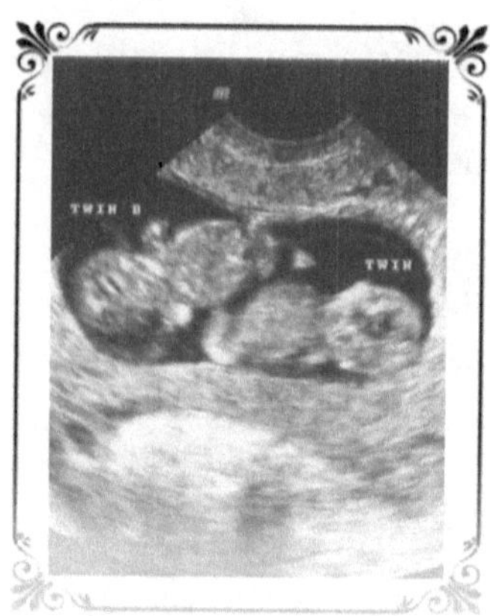

18

*L*ark looks up from typing when Martin tentatively runs a fingertip across her nape. In that glance, it's obvious they both feel fragile with each other. Martin's revelations and the sight of Marcelle virtually giving herself to him will take getting used to, as will the awareness that he has a past which is unknowable and lascivious. Even in the relative present he's resolved into a stranger by walking out the door and leaving her and by being propositioned by his ex- wife. Lark has been turning these conundrums in her mind since waking. After all, she has the same capacity to be unknown, as does any person and is honest enough with herself to acknowledge it. She's thought about that man coming onto her in the kitchen last night. What if she'd just followed that offer? Look at these fantasies she is writing: some parts her own experiences and some parts imaginary and who really knows which are which, except herself? For the first time too, she doubts if her writing about straight heterosexual experiences is adequate.

She gives him a wistful smile, wondering about his two business trips to Paris and London during the last three years. Has he had anything to do with Marcelle while he's been away? She hates this corrosive doubt guillotining their togetherness.

'Guil's gone to work and Jordy's taken Celeste to the park.' Martin reads her typing over her shoulder but doesn't comment. He gets baguette slices, fruit and coffee, sitting with her as she taps away at the keyboard.

'You okay about last night Lark?' he asks. 'Sorry you found out that way. I just didn't think it was important.'

'Hey, understatement of the year, but yes, I'm good with it. It was a shock but I'll get over it. We've got more important stuff to worry about today,' she says, still brittle, but better.

Martin nods, a look of relief creeping over his face. 'I was thinking... we should get Guil and Jordy some presents for having us stay. Have you been to any of the big department stores in town - Galerie Lafayette, Printemps or GHV?'

'No I haven't. What were you thinking we should get them?' Lark grabs at the project, it's a perfect distraction. 'Jordy is notoriously hard to buy anything for.'

'I've got a couple of ideas. We could go into the centre, see what we can find, and have some lunch before your appointment,' suggests Martin.

'I'll just finish this and send it.' Lark nods and smiles.

'Okay, I'll take a shower.'

Lark and Martin take the metro in and prowl through the stores, buying Jordy an overdyed violet halter dress and Guill a psychedelic shirt. They buy some little skirts for Celeste hoping they'll be the right size and a slow cooker which comes in a rather awkward rectangular box. At La Verrière café on Avenue de Tourville near the Eiffel tower and Dr. Fournier's rooms, they find a delicious array of vegetarian and vegan foods to choose from.

'I have to drink an ocean of water before I have the ultrasound,' says Lark and proceeds to drink several glasses before leaving. Outside Dr. Fournier's rooms they stop for a moment to hug, searching each other's eyes.

'Ready?' asks Lark, who hopes the ultrasound will be done soon. All that water feels pretty uncomfortable; she wants to piss.

'Yes.' Martin takes a deep breath. 'Lead on fair damsel.'

'Shall we find out what sex the baby is Sir Knight?
'May as well.'
'Some people don't want to, but I'm too curious. I'd like to know. I want some pictures too.'
'Okay. You realise are only two choices anyway,' Martin says.

As directed Lark and Martin takes the elevator to the floor above Dr. Fournier's rooms. Lark presents the confirmation of appointment form to the receptionist there. They wait ten minutes and are ushered into a dimly lit room with a gurney, two monitors and a large keyboard nearby. Off to the side there is a sideboard, sink and cupboards.

'Bonjour, je suis votre technicien ultrasons. Je m'appelle Suzy.'
'Can you speak in English for my wife?' asks Martin.
'Of course I can,' smiles Suzy, who has a broad Scottish accent.
'Where are ye from?'
'Australia.'
'I've heard its lovely over there. Have ye had an ultrasound before Lark?'
'No,' says Lark.
'Unzip your skirt and lie on the bed. Tuck your top up into your bra. And push your skirt and undies down to your pubic hair. That's right, like that.' Suzy tucks Lark's skirt down further with cool fingers.

Lark holds Martin's hand as Suzy explains. 'I'm going to apply a special gel to your abdomen and pelvic area. This gel is water-based, so it won't leave marks on your clothes or skin. It helps the sound waves to travel properly.' She squirts a thick transparent gel onto Lark's tummy. 'This is called a transducer or a wand,' she continues, holding up a stubby plastic rod attached to the monitors. 'I think of it as my fairy wand,' Suzy smiles, smearing the gel on Lark with it, while typing a few characters on the keyboard with her other hand.

She moves the wand around firmly while Lark clenches her jaw against the pressure; her bladder feels overly full. For a moment or two, Suzy moves the wand over Lark's belly typing, capturing and measuring the black and white images on her computer screen.

'What is that?' asks Martin, unable to stand the suspense.

'Just hold your breath a moment Lark,' Suzy says, ignoring Martin as she clicks to take another image. 'Ye can let it go now. So you think you're about 10 weeks pregnant Lark?'

'Yes I think so,' Lark murmurs through gritted teeth.

'Alright, now I'll do a transvaginal ultrasound. I'll insert a smaller probe into your vagina to get clearer image.' Suzy wipes the gel from Lark's stomach area. 'Can ye bring your legs up Lark? The gel will be a bit cold, but here is a clearer image.' Suzy turns the top monitor around so Lark and Martin can see. 'Here is a head, backbone, legs and arms – can you see it now?'

'Yes,' both murmur in awe, getting a grasp of what the image is showing them. The little being moves around and appears to sense the probe. It is a shock to see how well developed the baby is and it's only ten weeks old.

Suzy moves the probe a little. 'And here, is your second baby, see? Head, trunk, arms, legs.'

'Second?' gasps Martin.

'We've got two?' whispers Lark, shocked to pieces. Her world shakes. She doesn't know whether to laugh or cry. Tears come anyway and she lets go of Martin's hand to run her own over her face. 'No!'

'Yes, ye have twins, congratulations!'

Martin just looks at the screen, too stunned to say anything.

Suzy busies herself taking more images and measurements as the couple try to compose themselves.

'We're going to have twins,' Lark mutters stupidly. 'Martin?' She reaches for his hand again.

'Would ye like me to tell you what sex they are?'

'Yes,' Martin rasps.

'A boy and a girl.'

'Uh! This is just too much to take in.' Martin stares at the screen, watching the tiny forms move about.

'Do ye have twins in either of your families?' Martin and Lark look at each other with shock haloing their features.

'No, don't think so,' says Lark. 'Are they identical?'

'No, if you look ye can see that they are in separate amniotic sacs.' Suzy points at the screen, trying to put it simply. 'It means they are non-identical or fraternal. Older mothers have non-identical twin pregnancies, whereas younger mothers are more likely to have identical twins. Identical twins share the one amniotic sac in the womb. Dr. Fournier will tell you more.'

Suzy continues typing and the seconds drip like honey from a spoon, soft, viscous and rich with awe.

'Can we have some pictures Suzy?' asks Lark. 'I'd like to show my mum.'

'Of course.' Suzy moves the probe here and there, tapping on her keyboard a few times. 'There. I'll just take out the probe and here are some tissues for ye to clean yourself up. Go and empty your bladder: There's a toilet just outside the door. You'll have been even more uncomfortable with two babies and all that water,' she chuckles.

'Agh, too true. Thanks.'

Suzy busies herself with the computer and leaves the room while Lark bolts for the toilet, returning to the ultrasound room utterly relieved.

Martin has a packet of photos in his hand and still looks like he's been hit by a cement mixer. 'We go down to see Dr. Fournier now,' he says, picking up their bags and the slow cooker box.
They wait in Dr. Fournier's small reception area until she calls them in. As before, Dr. Fournier seats herself behind a large desk and beckons them to seat themselves on the chairs provided.

'Hello Lark, this is your husband?' She reaches over her desk and shakes Martin's hand over the top of the box in his lap.

'Martin.'

'So Lark and Martin. You have dizygotic or fraternal twins and it is confirmed; you are ten to eleven weeks pregnant Lark. Such good news!' smiles Dr. Fournier. 'It is why you have been bleeding; the uterus expands very quickly to accommodate twins and it bleeds as a result. Do you already feel bloated Lark?'

'Yes I do actually.'

'It is not your first pregnancy,' Dr. Fournier checks her notes. 'But the first you have carried this far. Have you been feeling well?'

'Yes, very well, just a little sick, but I got some clay tablets and that solved it. I am mainly just hungry a lot.' Lark grins, her shocked torpor lifting.

'I advise you not to fly or travel extensively for another three weeks until you are past your first trimester. There is a greater chance of miscarrying in the first trimester than at any other time.'

'So, does that mean short trips are alright, but not long road trips and not flying home to Australia yet?' asks Martin.

'Yes exactly,' agrees Dr. Fournier.

'Will sex still be alright?' asks Lark.

'Of course, until much later in the pregnancy. Just be guided by what feels comfortable,' smiles Dr. Fournier. She writes in Lark's notes. 'Do you have any other questions?' Martin and Lark are just too stunned to think of what to ask. 'No? Then I would like to see you again in three weeks to check your progress.' She smiles and goes through the formalities briskly. 'Next time I'm sure you'll have many questions.'

wins!' screams Jordy when they let themselves into the flat and tell her. She throws her hands in the air and hugs them both repeatedly. Celeste joins in, hugging adult legs and chirruping with joy. 'What wonderful news!' says Jordy. 'Did you find out what sex they are?'

'A boy and a girl,' answers Martin, a small smile tugging at the corners of his mouth. Jordy's reaction is infectious.

'We'll have to get balloons – pink ones, blue ones and purple in between!' Jordy sings to Celeste, picking her up and whirling her just a little in the small entranceway while she giggles. 'Two babies! Two! You are so blessed.'

Lark feels heartened by Jordy's happy response and the catatonic state she and Martin have been in, diminishes.

'Ah, it's a shock I can see,' says Jordy. She puts Celeste down and takes their hands, leading them to the couch. 'Sit, I'll make you some calming tea.' She busies herself in the kitchen. 'How was the ultrasound Lark?'

'Everything went well and Dr. Fournier was kind. She wants to see me in three weeks. Said I shouldn't fly or do any rugged travel until the first three months are up.'

'Yes it was the same for me too.' The kettle clicks off and

a lovely herbal aroma pervades the air as Jordy pours hot water on the tea. 'I had two miscarriages before, so Dr. Fournier was very cautious.'

She brings in the tea and they sip with relief.

'Another as well as the one after Celeste? You never told me that.' Lark is a little indignant. 'That's sad.'

'Yes, that's why. I didn't want to tell anyone at the time and then when I'd gotten over the sadness, I didn't want to divulge and upset myself again.' Jordy gives a wistful smile. 'But now we have the wonderful miracle that is Celeste.'

The little girl sidles along the furniture hoping for a taste of Maman's tea. She has a new bib on covered in un-nameable splats; she's been eating solids again. Jordy kisses Celeste on the top of her head.

Martin has been quiet, sitting there next to the slow cooker. 'I really don't know how you women cope with all this. I nearly fell through the floor when I saw that ultrasound. Blood and babies and probes put inside you. Loss and birth and pain... I'm in awe. And now we have twins – it will be such a shocking change!'

Jordy turns to Martin. 'Lark and I are thirty eight and you are what?

'Yep, thirty eight too.'

'We have had many years just to do what we want Martin. Much more than our parents or any parents before them. Is the loss of your individual feedom frightening you?' Jordy can be very direct; it's one of the things Lark likes about her.

'Frankly, the whole thing is overwhelming. I don't know if I'm ready to be a parent.' Martin looked apologetically at Lark.

'He's worried about bills and loss of freedom as well,' says Lark, frowning. Not again, she thinks.

Jordy nods her head. 'I can understand it, because I went through the same kinds of worries and doubts; believe me, we all do. You might not realise it, but it's hard for the modern woman as well.'

'How so?' Martin frowns.

Jordy blew on her tea, letting Celeste puff on it as well. 'Well, there are women who opt to use day-care for their babies from a very early age so they can return to work or there are wealthy couples who have nannies to help raise their kids and there are many mothers swinging between these two options or the third, being a stay-at-home mother. For most women it's a juggling act; motherhood is a career in itself!' Jordy sniffs and grins. 'Women are most often the primary carer for their kids whether they are, a full time mum like me or otherwise. It's an enormous responsibility, especially with the pressure to work, pay taxes and be a productive unit in the world, not to mention the profound loss of independence.'

Jordy lets her child take a tiny sip of the cooled tea. Satisfied, Celeste plumps down to play with toys at Jordy's feet. Jordy takes off her bib, scrunching it in her hand. 'On the other hand there are men who involve themselves in child rearing and its responsibilities in a big way. But again, it is subject to many variables – conditioning, work and career commitments, personality – stuff like that.' She could see that Lark and Martin were hanging on her every word. 'And if your man is out there earning the majority of income, then mothers inevitably take on more of the burden of child rearing, even if they are earning too.'

'I just feel so overwhelmed and ignorant,' blurts Lark, looking at Martin, who agrees with a nod and a widening of his eyes.

Celeste has decided to hang onto her knee. 'Uh,' she says. Lark knows some of her partial words well enough and pulls her on her lap where she plays with lark's necklace.

'It'll pass Lark,' says Jordy to both of them. 'It's not rocket science looking after a baby, but it is exhausting, exhilarating and probably the best thing you'll ever do. Both of you.'

Guil's key turned in the lock. Celeste squawks and writhes down from Lark's lap on a mission to see her papa, who puts down his bag and kneels with open arms.

'Comment va ma petite fille?' Guil hugs Celeste, giving her two smacking big kisses, followed by two for Jordy, who has come to greet him, whispering in his ear while she embraces him.

'Hallo!' Guil says to Lark and Martin as he comes to the lounge room, looking rather sweaty from the heat. 'Ah so, you 'ave some incredible news? The baby has ten fingers and ten toes?'

'We have twins,' says Lark, enjoying the look of shock the words create.

'A girl and a boy,' adds Martin.

'Twenty toes and twenty fingers, vingt et vingt. This is amazing good news!' Guil squeezes Celeste too hard and she wriggles to get down. 'Are there twins in your families?'

Lark and Martin look at each other. 'Not that we know of,' says Lark, cocking an eyebrow at Martin, who takes a breath and hold it.

'What?' She asks.

'No, no twins,' he murmurs. 'Its just - wow!'

Guil kisses them both and shakes Martin's hand. He peers at both of them saying, 'Ah, it is a big surprise for you both, this idea?' He smiles and waves his hand. 'Yes it will be a géant change in your lives its true. If your babies can be healthy it is the most important thing...' He looked serious for a moment, a rare enough expression on his constantly animated face.

Gone the next moment, he smacked his palms together. 'Wine! A toast to the new maman et papa! We must celebrate of course!' He is already in the kitchen unearthing a dust covered bottle from under the sink. 'A special old Pinot Noir from Bourgogne district. Martin you must uncork it, after all, you 'ave with half the action, both created twice the result!'

It is impossible not to laugh at Guil's innuendo. Martin tugs out the old cork and pours, feeling infinitely lighter. It's a novel idea – they'll be parents soon of two!

'Music of course we must have.' Guil plugs his Ipod into the speakers and selects up tempo top forty French songs on a loop.

'Will you 'ave the bébés here in Paris?' he asks, handing Lark a glass of wine. 'No I shouldn't have wine,' she murmurs.

'Ah, a mouthful or two won't hurt,' says Guil, holding up his glass. 'Here! Congratulations! It is amazing. A miracle and you should both be very proud.'

They clink glasses, even clinking Celeste's little mug with a spout which she holds up. They do feel proud, nervous and excited, smiling at each other.

'As to where we'll have the babies... we haven't thought that far. Probably we'll return to Sydney?' Lark answers Guil's question, shrugging her shoulders at Martin.

'You know there are reciprocal healthcare agreements between Australia and the UK, Italy, Sweden and quite a few other European countries, says Jordy. You can look it up. It's worth knowing if you are in Europe for another few months.'

Lark makes a mental note to add it to her list of research and perhaps she can ask Dr. Fournier as well. The wine is delicious, tart on her tongue, then opening out into a full fruity taste with a tang of autumn. Lark savours it, knowing it might be her last for quite a while.

'And what is this?' Guil asks, moving the slow cooker box off the lounge so he can sit down.

Celeste immediately begins to tip the box upside down to sit on. Martin swoops before she can. 'We forgot. Here's a present for you both. We thought it might be good for, well, slow cooking.' Martin grins, passing the box to them. Lark meanwhile is pulling other presents from her forgotten bag on the floor.

'And these are for you as well. You have been so kind to us, so generous letting us stay with you,' she presses her arms to her chest and shrugs her shoulders up. 'I hope the clothes for Celeste fit. I've never bought clothes for a little girl before.'

'Thank you.' Jordy takes the gifts, opening the box and taking out the clothes. 'I love this dress Lark, you know my taste.' She kisses her friends. 'I'm enjoying having you both here and so is Guil.'

'This is for you Guil. I hope you like your shirts wild sometimes.' Guil takes a peak, pulls out the psychedelic shirt and immediately puts it on over his work shirt. 'Oh, this is truly wild. Merveilleux,' he murmurs, inspecting himself. 'A true artiste's shirt I think.'

A moment later Jordy returns from her bedroom where she's changed into the new halter dress and violet really does look great on her. 'I love this!'

She does a twirl and the dress swirls around beautifully.

'Little princess, come here and we'll try your presents on.' Jordy holds up the little skirts against Celeste. 'They seem a good size too, thank you.'

'The shop attendant showed me the adjustable waist elastic button things,' Lark pointed. 'They're a good idea aren't they.'

'Yes,' smiled Jordy, thinking that Lark would learn. 'I'll just take this dress off and we can prepare something to eat. I bet you're hungry.'

Lark notices her stomach is clambering for food. She's been so preoccupied she hasn't noticed. 'Hell yes, I could eat double helpings. I could eat...'

She lunges at Martin and bites his arm, his glass of wine sloshing. Martin gives her a funny look. A ravenous Lark is a new thing.

'Steady on!'

They all laugh.

An hour later, they've made couscous, pancakes made by Guil and a green salad with rounds of French bread. There's a knock on the door. Marcelle and her friend Francois, who Lark and Martin met when they first came to Paris, are standing behind armfuls of pink, purple and blue balloons. Lark bites her lip and gives Martin a look. He shrugs, only too aware of her sensitivity about Marcelle.

'Bonjour! Nous avons apporté les ballons,' says Francois, handing out the balloons.

'Merci Francois, Marcelle.' Jordy gives two balloons to Celeste to play with. 'I hope you don't mind, I texted them to buy balloons and come for dinner too.'

'Hallo Lark,' Marcelle gives her brief air kisses near her cheeks. Lark can smell her fragrance, a combination of clove and sandalwood. She is once again struck by a scent memory.

'Martin.'

She also gives him kisses, letting go of her balloons. Francois follows suit. Lark, her day already so overwhelming, forgot last night revelations, until now. Automatically her radar is up, alert to any undercurrents floating between Marcelle and Martin, noting only a stiffness emanating from Martin. Marcelle smiles at her through her lashes. Her look is not hostile as Lark imagines it might be, but provocative or perhaps challenging, she isn't sure.

'Bonjour mes amies,' says Guil, well into the second bottle with Martin and mildly drunk. Kissing their cheeks, he blurts, 'Martin et Lark ont des jumeaux à venir!'

Lark looks at Martin for a translation. 'He's told them we are having twins.'

Nobody notices Lark's brief frown at Guil's lack of guile; she really wants it to remain a secret until she is over the first trimester.

'Twins…' says Marcelle with a heavy accent. ''ow wonderful,' she quirks her eyebrow, staring at Martin. 'I have similar news.' Marcelle has no trouble speaking English when it suits her, thinks Lark, noticing that even her English is embellished with a French texture. 'I am pregnant too. I did a test today. I'm only perhaps two weeks overdue.'

'Amazing! Congratulations. What a special day!' Guil passes glasses of wine to Marcelle and Francois. 'Another toast!' he picks up balloons and throws them towards Celeste on his way to the kitchen for more wine.

Martin pushes out his chair and stumbles away from the table towards the bathroom, which only Lark seems to notice. There is a brief lull while everyone serves themselves food, but when he returns, Lark notices how drained and waxy pale Martin looks.

'Drinking on an empty stomach,' he murmurs to Lark, shouldering on a fleece jacket despite the warm evening and wiping his hand across his mouth. He stares in a drunk way at Marcelle and Francois, still smelling faintly of vomit.

'Do we get to know who the papa is?' asks Jordy. She smiles at Francois while she bats Celeste's hand away from her fork. 'Of course not you, unless you have donated sperm to this worthy woman Francois.'

Marcelle translates for Francois. His elegant eyebrows shoot up. 'Non, pas moi, je suis gay!'

They all laugh at his reaction.

'The father, he's been on holiday in Paris. I've only just told 'im,' Marcelle smirks. 'We'll 'ave to work out what to do. Another termination perhaps.' She flaps an indifferent hand, unaware of the momentary silence at the table.

Lark knows that while not anti- abortion, Guil and Jordy are still sensitive new parents, too aware of the wonder of new life to accept Marcelle's cavalier attitude with ease.

'Come sit with Tante Marcelle while Jordy feeds you your petit dîner,' says Marcelle, wriggling her pink sheath dress down and picking up Celeste.

Martin continues to look blanched, only picking at his food. The shock of today has been too much for him, thinks Lark and rubs his back with a sympathetic hand.

Jordy feeds Celeste with no spills on Marcelle's pink lap. She cleans Celeste's face and takes her to their room to put her down. Guil, as is his custom after a vegetarian meal, gets up and cooks himself a big rare steak - every evening it is either steak or pancakes. Martin looks bilious again when the area fills with the smell of frying meat. He murmurs his goodnights and takes off to their bedroom.

Lark follows not long after him. They curl around each other under the sheets, talking a little and resting together. Lark deliberates whether to ask Martin about his previous business trips in Europe but by the time she decides to ask, he has fallen asleep.

20

*A*wake, and the time is 5.10 am when she turns on her phone. Sleep has fled and Lark's mind is already going full pelt trying to catch up with the astonishing fact of her twin pregnancy. Martin is restless too, but doesn't break through the surface of sleep.

Lark rolls off the futon into a squat and dressing quietly, picks up her phone, bag and the flat key. She lets herself out, catching the lift downstairs for a walk in the new day. The air is muggy – not the humidity of the Sydney summer, more the stuffiness of 2.25 million Parisians slumbering together under the arc of the city. She finds solace in movement, power walking careful blocks that return her to Guil and Jordy's street. Time alone to think without the overlays of Martin's presence, feels like a necessity. She puts her hand on her belly and hums quietly to herself, murmuring 'bonjour,' to the occasional person out for a walk or to relieve their dog.

Such an intense time, so much is happening, she thinks. How blessed am I! So many certainties she left Australia with have been transformed; their holiday for starters, their childless status, Martin's dependability – huge. Even her identity as an artist-designer has shifted into something else. She stops to lean against one of many trees bisecting a street, a Linden or Horse Chestnut she remembers someone telling her. Her fingers drift over the bark and she plucks a leaf.

What more will change, apart from her belly? She thinks wistfully of her family and friends experiencing winter at home and misses them. She misses Purzia and his feline comfort. She checks her phone; there's been a text from Michael and one from Mum. She remembers she turned her phone off before the ultrasound yesterday and had clean forgotten to turn it back on. Mum asks how she is and says all is okay at home. She scrolls to Michael's text:

Lark, 'Wet' well received. See a couple of the many here:

http//www. Eloiseérotique.com
curvelurve.com

You're a natural maven for this genre
Next article subs: Losing Virginity
Same word count arrangement
Deadline: Monday 9/23/16
Contact me any problems
Michael Lawson

Lark flicks over to the sites and skims for a moment or two, amusement twisting her mouth. So her stories are being sold to sex blogs and story sites... she guffaws to herself. The quiet designer living in Bondi seems a far distant self. She's always had a healthy sexual appetite, but writing about it while pregnant with twins on holiday? Never in her most bizarre imaginings could she have come up with such a thing. Life can definitely be stranger than fiction.

For the moment though, Lark has weightier matters to consider; on centre stage her twin pregnancy.

When thinking about babies, she never imagined more than a baby girl, yet growing inside her are two babies – a girl and a boy, star-fishing in their amniotic fluid. Though brimming with

with uncertainty, Lark is filled with a rush, much like the beginning of a thrill ride at Luna Park. She hurls a scream of pure joy into the air. Oops! She smothers it with her hand. Its still only 6am on a Tuesday morning and despite that there are some citizens emerging in their office-wear, most Parisians are still asleep. Lark sends a prayer into the early morning light instead, to Nature, thanking and requesting an uncomplicated pregnancy.

Which leads to her fiancé, Martin. He's become increasingly unknowable since I told him I was pregnant, she thinks. We've been together three years, highly compatible, easy and happy. Loving and intimate. Secure together. Perhaps I am overstating it and being melodramatic but I feel I'm with a secretive stranger on this side of the world.

Truly the advent of a baby, two babies is a ginormous issue, even for her. Martin isn't carrying them, so she empathises, considering that he just doesn't have that inner connection to the babies she has.

The revelation about Marcelle is also shocking. Really I haven't got my head around that at all, Lark thinks with a slight twist in her guts, shredding the leaf she picked. That he was once married to her is just so weird, and here we are having a holiday in the same vicinity as this ex, who is a strangely slippery customer – still with possible intentions towards Martin.

Gotta wonder why he didn't tell me ages ago. Lack of trust is a non issue; I trust him entirely, she thinks. I really hope Martin will settle down and accept me and the babies now. Lark sighs, pushing off from the tree to return to the flat.

I'll wake him to make love, she plans. Lark lengthens her stride; knowing the transformative energy of sex and even better, a good orgasm to render problems less significant.

Back at the flat, no one has stirred; it is only 7.15am. Lark quietly makes tea and taking it to their room, strips and slides under the sheet covering Martin. She runs a hand down Martin's side and reaches over, to find him morning-stiff. As he wakes, he begins to move in the clasp of her hand, seeking pleasure. She feels a responding shimmer of heat trickling down inside her and lifts a leg to balance upon his hip so she can stoke her own heat with her fingers. Martin rolls into the apex of her legs. Kissing him, she guides his cock to her clitoris, rubbing their slick back and forth from her clit to her opening, drifting with hypnotic pleasure. She takes hold of his hips, he is awake now and wants in, but she restrains him, biting her bottom lip, a smile playing there.

Determining 'when' is an illusion they play with, because she knows his greed to be inside her will override her restraining grasp soon, but she likes to play with this moment of control – until – she shoves him hard into herself, gasping at the tight pressure of him pushing the top of her vagina. He nudges her unpinned leg up and out to manoeuvre more depth and she can feel the nub of him thumping her cervix. Both breathing heavily, they fall into a mindless pattern, a place between thought. Friction and rhythm simplify existence. Revelling in each other's bodies, in their union, nothing else matters.

Lark's fantasies trawl past the eye of her mind like an erotic zoetrope: she selects and discards, while she bites his shoulder and finds his closest nipple to suck. She chases and simultaneously is, a nubile girl in a forest, she is the horny guy that chases her. She moves onto flickers of a three way encounter, where she has a man on either side of her. While Martin thrusts, she explores, watching the woman being entered front and back.

Reality intrudes, she hears Celeste crying and inexplicably, Marcelle's vixen face follows. Lark pushes away from Martin and they disentangle. She stands, pressing her palms against the wall and tilts her pelvis out for Martin to enter her. He groans again as he plunges into her, while she pushes away from the wall to get maximum pleasure. Martin reaches around her body and finger fucks her clit, driving her past reality, into a stupor of imaginings.

Her mind hovers while their combined energy rushes and tingles. She is the Parisian girl she saw on to way home in helmet and bike leathers, riding her Honda, hair matted and carelessly flying into the face of her pillion passenger. Look, her leather pants are like black cowboy chaps, covering her legs with her ass nude. The rider rides into the wind as she handles her powerful bike, leaning into the turns. Her pillion passenger mimics her moves. She lifts her ass and he takes her from behind. He's delectably big and she is impaled while gripping the handlebars, concentrating on the torque of her motorbike while being screwed lavishly. He's slipped one hand into her chaps at the front to work her clit. He reaches past her with the other hand to hold the bike upright as she orgasms. Lark rides the crest, her come showering down inside her as her alter-ego on the bike glitters and fades. Marin climaxes into her, pumping her full of spunk.

Minutes pass and the wave of euphoria passes slowly. They remain bonded, united. Lark realises Martin is crying into her hair while he holds onto her. She turns in his grip, spent penis falling from her as she traces his wet lashes with her finger. This isn't the reaction she expected.

'Martin?'

A guttural noise from deep within him expresses Martin's angst. He dashes a wrist across his eyes.

'All too much, Lark,' he mumbles brokenly. His shoulders shake with more tears, Adam's apple jerking while he tries to swallow the eruption of emotion.

Lark doesn't know what to say, believing she and the babies literally embody his problem. She holds him as he weeps, feeling the agony of going against him if he wants her to terminate again. She can't have an abortion, she won't – even if it means losing him. She pulls herself away from her internal wrangling to be a support as he cries such rare cathartic tears. All the platitudes in the world are pointless.

'I've really fucked everything up,' he gasps. 'We were supposed to have a fabulous holiday. A pre-marriage holiday...' He groans and turns away, collapsing onto their bed and with a shuddering breath.

Lark reaches for a couple of tissues to wipe the come trickling down her inner thighs, wadding another couple into her pubes as she squats down in front of Martin.

'We can make this work together,' she says, injecting as much positive determination into her voice as she can while Martin shudders with involuntary sobs. They fill her with foreboding now.

'Are you going to bolt again Martin?'

'You don't understand Lark.'

'Tell me what I don't understand.' Lark bites back the desire to harp, to shape their dilemma in the frame of survival she worked out on her walk back to the flat, one that accommodates the enormity of twins in her own mind and has a victorious outcome.

'You don't understand,' repeats Martin, palming away more tears.

'Tell me!' She gets irritated by the obtuseness and lack of articulation most males have with emotional expression. Her women friends get it out, say it, express it!

He just shakes his head, mumbling, 'Can't yet.' He topples and rolls himself into bed, drawing up the sheet. 'Exhausted, just want to sleep.'

Lark feels like screaming. She looks at his huddled form and knows the mere act of tears and whatever has caused them, has wiped him out.

Try being a woman for a day, the caustic thought shreds the last whispers of her orgasm. She picks up the slender '50 Pregnancy Tips for Women' book to finish reading and stalks out.

Lark looks pale and distracted when she emerges from Celeste's bedroom. She's been up earlier; I heard her go out. She puts a mug of tea on the kitchen table, looking at it from some faraway place.

'Morning,' I say over Celeste's crown.

She sees me feeding Celeste, watches her rhythmic sucking. A tear threatens to spill from her eye.

'He's freaking out again Jordy. If he runs again, I think I'll go home. Get on with it at Mum's. She'll help.'

I can see her agonising. I know Lark really doesn't want this but also know how naïve she is about the effect and effort that babies are. Two tiny babies, I can barely imagine. I sigh, de-latch Celeste and swap her to my other breast.

'Wish I knew how to help Lark. Crazy guy. So many people would be thrilled to be having twins. But yeah, I agree it'd be wise to have a plan B in case Martin doesn't accept the idea.'

Lark lets out a choking noise and takes a gulp of her tea.

I pick up the book Martin has bought for her: '50 Pregnancy Tips for Women.' It's woefully inadequate.

'Guil's cousins are coming to stay for a week in a couple of days,' I say, changing the subject. I feel uncomfortable telling her.

'They'll be staying a week - it was arranged ages ago. You're both welcome to stay again after that.'

'Ah, okay.'

'I know it's a difficult time for you and Martin, but...'

'Oh, you and Guil have been so wonderful,' Lark rushes in. 'My thoughts are all over the place, but we had planned to visit Leisje in Amsterdam. Do you remember her?'

I have a vague recollection of a tall girl with brown dreadlocks dancing crazily at the Chinese Laundry nightclub and the World Bar, both venues that were our late night rage haunts in younger days. 'Yes I do.'

'I just hope my passport comes. It's due today or tomorrow.'

Celeste looks up at me and pulls off my nipple; she's full now. She gives me a milky smile, sits up and is ready to get down. I put her in her walker and start making breakfast. Lark picks up a knife and helps to cut up a fruit salad. Celeste muscles her walker into the galley kitchen and bangs up against Lark's legs.

'Ah,' Celeste says. 'uk.'

'She's trying to say Lark. You're part of the family,' I laugh.

Lark squats and kisses the top of Celeste's head. 'I'll have another talk to Martin and see what we'll do. Or what I'll do,' she adds, lips compressed in a tight line.

Fruit salad is ready and I'm ravenous after feeding Celeste so I take a heaped bowl and begin eating. Lark has none. 'Come on Lark, eat up. You can't starve yourself,' I say, mock stern. 'You have two others to think of now girl, no matter how you feel.'

'Okay mum.' Lark serves herself and between mouthfuls, switches on her phone. She checks for messages, sending a message to Leisje she says. She chats about her stories and what the next one is going to be about – virginity and its loss – while sending a text to her new story 'boss'.

I can see her mind is still in a whirl but she's making a valiant effort to chat positively about a different topic – for this I am relieved. Ongoing sleep deprivation has eroded my emotional reserves and I think Lark instinctively knows it, even though she's not a mother yet. Writing these erotic stories has been a great distraction for her and she's earned a little extra money.

Nothing wrong with that.

'What about you Jordy – how did you lose your virginity?'

I smile at the memory, 'The underpass at high school with a boy called Stephen. We both wanted to lose our virginity and liked each other just enough to help each other out. It was more like a fumbling business transaction than anything else.'

'I had a boyfriend at fourteen. We'd been dating for six months.' Lark rolls her eyes and grins. 'I met him at a party. We went to a room with mattresses, full of snogging couples.' She shrugs. 'Losing your virginity seemed such an important thing back then. But I'm eternally glad it was him and I didn't lose my virginity to rape or coercion or indifference like some women I know.' She loads her plate in the dishwasher. 'Loss of virginity with your boyfriend doesn't make a good story though,' she considers. 'I have another idea in mind.'

Lark refocusses and gives me a hug. 'You're such a wonderful friend. I wish you were still in Sydney Jordy.'

'Sometimes I do too Lark. Perhaps I can convince Guil to get some work there.'

'Oooh yeah.' Lark sobers. 'I am so sorry to have had this major dilemma arrive with us on our holiday.' She points to her stomach.

'Hey! It's a wonderful gift and I am privileged to be the first person to know about it. Martin will sort himself, I'm sure.'

Lark purses her lips and nods. 'Is Guil having a late start?'

'Yes, the showers free.'

Lark slips into the shower and quietly dresses in a skirt and singlet top, watching Martin's sleeping body rise and fall under the sheet in their room. She won't wake him again; after all he was ill last night. She returns to the lounge room and curls up on the chair with another cup of tea, paper, pen and Jordy's laptop.

I'm feeling pretty savage, she thinks, but I have to do something to take my mind off all this trouble. First she jots down her rawness, her fears, her hopes, in a ragged way, underscoring each line several times. She puts that sheet aside. Then she writes ideas for the rest of their holiday – and also puts that sheet aside. Next she writes Loss of Virginity at the top of a fresh page and taps her teeth with the pen. What does she want to write?

Some of the wild events in her early teens where being a surfer girl meant everything perhaps is a place to start. She scrawls different ideas, random notes and phrases, writing and crossings out. She draws surfboards and waves along the edges while she thinks. By 8.45 she has the bones of her next story organised. Jordy and Celeste are getting ready to go out to meet a friend to go to the park. Lark opens the laptop and begins typing.

BIG TICKET

There we were in 1973, Michelle and Lisa, two young girls running wild. Away from our chronically entrenched alcoholic families, we found necessary relief and naive worldliness hanging out with the local surfie boys. That our surfie group lived an hour from any beach, in a river-side town, didn't seem to figure. They were so cool and exactly the sorts our parents would have freaked out about us being with. Undesirable delinquents were much worse company than boozing social climbing adults it seemed. Talk about double standards.

It was the year to change from Keyman jeans to stove-pipe Levi's, to try cigarettes and the drawback. We progressed from stealing little liqueur bottles in my parent's lounge room bar, to stealing our parent's loose change to buy bottles of Southern Comfort. In a strange duplicity, Dad cashed in his kid's insurance policies and emptied their piggybanks for beer money at the same time we took to botting money from kind folks on the street, saying we needed a bus fare or to phone home. There was always some sucker that would give money to two innocent young girls. When we'd get to the magic $30.00, we'd call it quits and then rush to buy a baggie of marijuana. All it cost back then, even if our consciences didn't lie down easy with our narcissistic pursuits.

I envied my best friend Michelle. Her parents were happy social alcoholics. They seemed a sort of normality to aspire to. My family buried Dad's alcoholism like a festering canker, under a band-aid of middle class conceit. Violent rows and physical abuse were the norm. The ground always shifted so my siblings and I didn't know what would come next. I mean, we left a schooner of beer and a tumbler of sherry for thirsty Santa every Christmas. Truly some perverted twist of our childish innocence in an alcoholic household. How sick was that.

Virgins we, Michelle and I carved out a different home. Any school period off, after school or on the weekends, this one dovetailed neatly into school and familial commitments. We craved to sit on a seedy carpet in a dingy house with these boys. We'd rock, stoned, shouting out the lyrics of David Bowie's Diamond Dogs or Space Oddity pounding us from tallboy sized speakers set at diagonal ends of the tiny lounge room.

House members and friends swirled in and out of the fug-filled room, contributing to the mess on the low coffee table. It was at all times littered with bongs made from Galliano bottles and garden hose sections, overloaded ashtrays, papers, cigarettes and Drum, half eaten munchies and forgotten drinks. Nothing else mattered for that time. It kept us sane enough to handle the mad fracture and frictions of our 'normal' life. Like chameleons, Michelle and I would pull on the illusion of good daughters on the way home on the bus.

One Saturday we arrived to see a six foot Twin Fin surfboard ploughed fins up like a space rocket, into the detritus on the coffee table. One of those big old Malibu boards. A buzz of excited expectancy pervaded the dingy lounge room. Two new surfie guys had just arrived from the 'mainland'. Anyone from the mainland was like, so cool, so different. Almost from a different species. They were 'free' – that meant not trapped in a small provincial town on an inward looking island. To Michelle and I these dudes shone with a possible escape ticket. Escape from our lives, escape from ourselves – any escape would do. Neither of us gave a moment's thought to who they might actually be as people, as long as they embodied the Big Ticket away.

The two newcomers – Clive and Domino, were tall and well built. Both were broad shouldered with long salt grizzled blonde hair. They were guffawing and talking to the in-house surfie boys, about five or six of them. Clive requested a big hammer.

'What's he going to do with a hammer, Lise?' asked Michelle in a small voice.

'Haven't got a clue,' I replied.

'You two shielas don't know nothing, ain't seen nothing, right Lisa, Mish,' barked Shane, the oldest surfie there.

'Okay,' we twittered, 'Sure Shane.'

Clive astounded us, by bashing the surfboard with the hammer. Repeated thumping splintered the fibre glass until a cavity a couple of fists wide was made. Greedy now, everyone's fingers pried away the shattered resin. The surfboard was chockablock full of hashish. All the boys shouted of glee.

'Wow. Farout!'

'On yer mate.'

'Cool, man.'

'Unreal, those pigs missed.'

Clive and Domiino received this adulation and backslapping magnanimously. Unlawful activities related to drugs gave instant status, especially when you weren't caught. Clive pulled out several bags of hash, passing one under appreciative noses. He crumbled some, breaking off a chunk for everyone.

'Look at the grain of it.'

'Oh smell, it's real strong. Not like that pissweak stuff from Bali last week'"

The boys rhapsodized with boisterous mumbling.

Soon every chillum and bong was alight. Tinfoil and old biros were bought for those who preferred a feistier hit. Cigarettes were shredded and several ten paper joints were put together with the skill of artisans. Those who could roll them and create a tamped, indented end were admired by all.

Michelle and I tried our hardest to keep up with the dope consumption of the surfie boys but never managed. This stuff was – wow – two or three puffs and we both fell back onto the grimy cushions around the table, off our faces. What little oxygen left in the dim room was down at floor level anyway. The rest became a bluish sweet smelling shrine to the God of hashish.

There passed a timeless interval with barely any conversation except nudges and the occasional grunt to pass on a joint or a bong. Everyone was whacked. I opened my eyes to see Michelle clagged upon her cushion. Next some music filtered in. Again some movement awoke me from the netherworld I drifted in.

A grumble had gone around, signifying that the munchies had hit boys' stomachs. They were going out, to dare someone to go to the shop. Being provoked into going munchie shopping was something that we girls were usually made to do. Standing in a shop stoned to your eyeballs, trying to remember orders, count money and relate to a shopkeeper was a truly nightmarish experience.

I struggled up into sitting position, took another toke passed my way and subsided back onto the cushion.

Blinking stupidly, a thought dawned. Hey, there's Clive, Domino, Michelle, the household dog flaked out and twitching from doggy dreams, or maybe its stoned state, plus me. Domino was pashing Michelle in a vague sort of way. Clive ogled me, though his eyes were so bloodshot and bulging and mine blurry, I couldn't be sure of his meaning. Clive now took a crackling suck, reducing a joint down to a finger burning roach as he inhaled and held. Holding onto a burning roach signified a tough man in surfie circles. Another great affectation to aspire too.

'Aarrgh,' he shuddered as some smoke billowed out of him. I picked helplessly at the frayed edge of the cushion. The hashish had robbed me of a brain, enslaving each thought. On the other side of the table, Domino groped under Michelle's Indian shirt. She rolled a look my way.

We'd talked about our virginity of course. We debated its virtue and our attitudes on 'going all the way', along with our progressive exploits with boys, on the phone and at school.

'What about you Lise? Whatja do with Steve in the underpass?' asked Michelle.

'Oh he just pashed me and gave me a love bite,' I replied. Every detail was shared.

'Ya not gonna let him are ya, he's not cool.'

'Na. Anyway you and Rodney were getting' pretty hot behind

the school gym I heard.'

'Yeah, but I dropped him. He's too pimply.'

'Well when are ya gonna do it?'

'As soon as. Being a virgin is the pits.'

'Have you done your biology homework yet? Geez my pierced ears are infected. That needle must've been rusty.'

We were desperate under the guise of cool, to give it away – to the fellows who appeared to have something we wanted. Naively we'd been conditioned to believe there might be some exchange for our virginity's value, even though it had become valueless to us. We felt our virginity, consciences, mental acumen and loving spirits were ours to bestow or give away now we were fourteen. Underage didn't matter with our hormones racing pell-mell towards reproduction. Michelle and I had already begun our periods. Such a long drop from twelve when pleasing your parents, doing well at school and a whole sense of self were still mainly intact.

Martin wanders out at about ten, looking pale and morose. Lark looks up briefly, unsure whether to stop or continue typing. He's shown only mild enthusiasm about her writing or her interest in doing it. Inwardly she shrugs, he can be like that with her creative endeavours, but at least he hasn't disapproved either. He makes a cup of coffee and puts a hunk of baguette and a banana on a plate. Jordy has left and Guil is singing in the shower. She's lost the thread of her writing so she saves the document and shuts the laptop. Keep it simple, she thinks, taking a deep breath.

'Jordy and Guil have rellies coming to stay, so we'll have to find move out for at least a week,' she says.

'Okay.' He clears his throat. 'They've been very good to let us stay so long. When?'

'Two days time.' She says in a rush. 'My new passport should arrive today or tomorrow. We could go and see Leisje like we planned, or just go to Holland?'

Martin considers while he chews, barely looking at her.

'As long as your passport arrives, that's possible. Otherwise we'll have to stay somewhere in France and wait for it.' After a pause he adds, 'if we've only a day left in Paris bar packing up tomorrow afternoon, is there anywhere you'd like to go?'

He flicks a look at her, swimming for the raft of normality like her.

'Can we go to musée de Cluny this afternoon? Maybe walk over the bridges and around the Arche De Triomphe tomorrow morning?'

Martin rubs his stubble. 'Okay. I have to go to the Bibliothèque Sainte-Geneviève on the Place du Panthéon. One of the other lecturers at Uni asked me to do some research for him. It's one of the most important libraries in Paris for books and manuscripts from the Middle Ages.' Lark looks at him curiously; it's the first she's heard of it. 'He texted me a few days ago,' Martin adds.

'Alright, why don't we go to the Musée de Cluny and you can shoot off to the Bibliothèque Sainte-Geneviève after that? I would love to see some of the medieval tapestries and illuminated manuscripts at Cluny. We can work out what to do while we are out. I've already sent a text to Leisje this morning in case that becomes the plan.'

Martin nods, finishing his coffee.

'How's the 'appy maman et père?' Guil comes in hauling a tee shirt over his head. Lark rolls her eyes. Such timing, such gentle Gallic humour – surely Jordy has told him about their trouble?

'Mate,' grunts Martin. Ah, the monosyllabic communication of the Aussie male, thinks Lark. 'Shower time.'

Lark opens the laptop again, needing to bury herself behind its lid to avoid too much scrutiny. Of course Guill doesn't notice.

'You are writing another histoire érotique?' he says, fishing out a cigarette and lighting it as Martin disappears into the bathroom.

'Fourth story Guil. It'll be about loss of virginity.'

'Ah, beaucoup de grands livres can be written about this. Many books.'

Guil goes to the kitchen, returning minutes later with coffee and the end of the baguette, with no banana, she notices.

'We're really very grateful to have been able to stay with you and Jordy,' says Lark. 'We might go to Amsterdam if my passport arrives soon. If not we'll hang about in Paris until it comes.'

Guil has a long pull on his coffee. 'It will be good for you two to have some time to work things out. It is a big adjustment to accept babies,' he says, taking a drag of his cigarette. 'I 'ave to go to work now but we can meet for a meal later – perhaps around nine thirty?'

'Sounds lovely Guil.' Lark agrees, grateful that under his jolly exterior he understands their situation.

Her eyes stray to the screen. Words and phrases formulate in her mind, while Guil smokes, chews and swallows. He gets up, collecting his phone, wallet, keys, trawls down the hall and returns with a packed bag.

Lark scribbles notes and types. She pauses to say 'Ciao,' before picking up speed when Guil leaves the flat.

'Get the towel man,' Domino mumbled to Clive, who post-toke looked as capable of moving as a block of cement. It seemed to be a repeated request between them. He swivelled himself round to pull out a faded beach towel from a beaten up silver framed back-pack. He bundled it up into a rough square and shoved it over the hole in the surfboard.

Domino half carried Michelle and positioned her on the surfboard. 'Nothing Else Matters,' by Metallica was playing on the sound system. I could see from the limp state Michelle was in, that the song was entirely apt. Her archetypal white blonde hair so loved by surfies, draped over the peaked end of the board and her blue eyes were bloodshot and vacant. Probably like me, Michelle's brain was taking a vacation.

There was no coy flirting at which she was an expert. Domino and Michelle got straight down to business with me, Clive and the dog as an audience.

He straddled her on the board. Enough clutter lay under the surfboard to keep it from tipping or fishtailing from their movement and weight. Michelle pulled her top up and he kneaded her little breasts out of her padded bra. Tissues she'd used to stuff the bra to create those breasts flew into the hazy air like sacrificial doves. Domino kissed her lips hard now, undoing his belt and fly so his thing was visible. He tried to also undo her levi's but they were grafted onto her legs. She shimmied, pulled and pushed until they were free of her buttocks. He pulled her legs up and peeled the jeans down to her ankles.

Clive appeared disinterested and was rolling another joint. The dog looked up blearily and smiled, I swear, panting with his big doggie tongue lolling about. I felt fascinated and repelled, uncomfortable with a sweaty feeling around my crutch. The thought struck me to crawl away somewhere, but being so stoned, lethargy defeated me. I watched the arcane rite. The surfboard had become our new altar to worship and offer up sacrifices to. We were to discuss this excitedly many times later – never the sex itself, but the heavy symbolism. We didn't realize until much later, that we'd been the sacrifices and that the worth of our virginity was just a fatuous lie from society to keep us out of trouble.

I'd seen Domino's dick erect in all the clothing kerfuffle. It seemed as wide as it was long, nestled in his pubic hair like a mushroom in the grass. Is that it I thought, Dad's great donger seen in the bathroom flashing unbidden into my mind.

He lunged at Michelle's snatch with his thing in his hand. There was some fumbling while Michelle stared at the macramé light-shade wide eyed. When he found the right hole, he pushed and poked, trying to bash down the hymen door. Domino was in a hurry now, breathing raggedly. Clive watched as he licked the edge of rolly papers. Michelle screamed and flailed as Domino got his cock inside her. He rubbed and ground himself against her pubic bone while she moaned, tears now weaving down her cheeks. Domino groaned and twitched. It was all over.

He pulled himself off her, sort of laughed and hitched up his pants, making sure his fly was up before accepting the now lit joint from Clive. Michelle, paler than I have ever seen her, staggered up into sitting position, pulled up her levi's and fled to the bathroom.

Faster than I could have believed, Clive was up from his

laidback slouch, to grab me. He rolled on top of me, pinning down my already torpid frame. The same procedure followed.

Clive gave me a sloppy wet-ashtray tongue kiss while groping under my top. I was completely paranoid about the other guys returning and wanted it to be over, fast, so offered no resistance. The towel on the surfboard had regained colour, now bright red with Michelle's blood, a sacrificial altar alright. Clive and I stood up, I pulled off my shoes and we divested ourselves of jeans. I lay down on the board, noting that Michelle;s virgin blood felt sticky on my bum. Clive pinned me with his weight once again. Though bigger than Domino, Clive was probably too stoned to manage a full erection. He fiddled around 'down there' for a moment – was he putting on a condom I wondered?

This is it, this is it, this is it – aargh. His penis had pierced me like a hot knife. I'd partially lost my hymen when I was eleven, riding a runaway horse, bouncing on the pommel of the saddle. This made it less painful to lose my virginity. Clive was so stoned, he took it slowly. He rested his goateed chin on my forehead and draped his weight over the rest of me. I couldn't have moved even if I'd known to. My legs just flapped along the sides in a state of shock. A multitude of sensations passed. I could see him bleary eyed up there above me. The door slammed as Domino left the room. I shut my eyes as a warm wet flood trickled out of me. Oh shit, I've wet myself.

'Oh no,' I moaned and clutched Clive's back. A girdle of shame embraced me. Clive oblivious, shuddered, let out a snort and jerked as he came. As his cock died inside me, he blinked in a glassy way. He aimed a kiss at my mouth with his smoker's breath again but received my cheek as I turned away. He tried to get off but only managed to roll onto the messy table then onto the floor with a stunned grunt, disturbing the dog, which yelped and ran away.

So that was our deflowering, our initiation into the gang. Before that we'd just been window dressing; now we were true surfie chicks or so we believed. We were yet to discover the narrow parameters entitled to us – holding the beach towel during the day at the beach and spreading your legs at night. It *eventually seemed narrower than our family and school life. By fifteen, Michelle and I had left that crowd behind us and by seventeen, we had left the island.*

It wasn't until a score of years later, after I had what I thought to be my first orgasm, that I realized I hadn't unwittingly pee-ed myself at fourteen as I lost my virginity.

Lark Connor

22

*I*t's after lunch by the time Lark and Martin get moving. Rather surprisingly, she finished her story. There are a couple of bits that could be reworked and polished but overall it's complete.

Very 'Puberty Blues' she notes, not sure if European readers might relate, in spite of the story's truths. Writing it has been cathartic; Lark feels calm and empty. If there's trouble with Martin, then bring it on. Let's get it resolved and over with, she thinks, looking at him hunched in a nearby armchair, glasses on, steadily texting and surfing the net, occasionally talking to her about destinations and travel plans. He looks raw and shocked pale. There are gaps where he sits there inert, biting his fingernails, blinking and sighing. She reminds herself again he was sick last night and manages not to demand clarity on his upset this morning, Though questions do queue for answers, she has pushed them away so she can write.

How fabulous, Lark's passport arrives, so while they are out at the Musée de Cluny, they decide to catch a train to Amsterdam tomorrow. Martin goes online and books tickets. Before he leaves her to do his colleague's research he puts his palm on her belly. He's been like a crystallis since this morning, almost entirely wrapped up in himself.

'It will all be okay Lark, I promise.' He searches her face. 'I'm still completely overwhelmed about the twins but I'm working on it.'

Lark reaches for his hand and looks at his nails bitten down to their quicks. 'That bad is it. Is that what got you this morning?'
He pulls his hand away. 'Kind of. I don't think even cigarettes could give me relief for this curveball.'

After packing up most of their stuff that evening, Lark, Martin, Jordy and Celeste meet Guil at Café Martin in Saint Fargeau. Lark draws Jordy aside to ask her about Marcelle while they eat and Martin and Guil drink wine.

'What, you didn't know? Oh, Lark, didn't he tell you?'

'No. I didn't know until a couple of days ago. He never wanted to discuss his past. We've been happy making our own world at Bondi.'

Jordy nods. 'Well at least you know now.' She gives Martin a severe look across the table but he is busy talking to Guil and doesn't notice.

'Jordy, has he seen her when he's stayed with you and Guil during those two trips here in the last few years?' Lark hates the wheedling tone in her voice.

'No. Perhaps a couple of times socially,' she thinks back. 'I don't think so. All he could talk about was you and seemed very happy.'

Jordy looks puzzled so Lark quickly says, 'Thanks Jordy.'

Jordy takes Lark's hand. 'Existence is throwing everything at you right now isn't it?'

'Sure is. But you know that old saying: When the going gets tough, the tough get going. It was Mum's motto and though it's an oldie, I still think it's a good homily.' She looks over at Martin, steadily drinking with Guil. If she's honest with herself, he's been withdrawn since coming back from London. He's in some unreachable place inside, she can feel it. The shock of finding out about twins is still reverberating between them and she senses that he's retreated further and battened down the hatches.

'Did he get his research all done?'

'No, he says he'll have to come back to Paris to do more.'

'Come and stay again when Guil's cousins leave. I love having you visit. Reminds me of flatting together and also of home,' says Jordy.

'Okay. I want to talk to you more about the baby thing too. I am so ignorant.'

Jordy laughs. 'I guessed that. We all figure it out though. Biology takes over whether we're ready for it or not.'

'Merde, the bottle is empty,' says Guil calling a waiter. 'Une autre bouteille, merci.'

With a wistful smile Jordy says, 'Guil has always liked his wine and recreational drugs. Where he works, there's a culture of it. The French like to imbibe, just like the Aussies – it's a national pastime for them. Even you and I had our time of binging, but we grew out of it.' Jordy looks wistful. 'I hope one day he'll grow out of it too.'

23

*E*arly the next morning, Martin and Lark pack the last of their things after a hurried breakfast. They say their goodbyes to Guil, Jordy and Celeste and walk their suitcases down to the metro at Saint Fargeau. Peak hour is a crush all the way on the jungle of trains they take to Gare Du Nord. They catch the sleek red and silver Thalys train from there. They'll arrive in Amsterdam at high speed in under four hours, stopping only at Lille and Brussels along the way.

'We keep our passports handy, but there are rarely checks nowadays. So much better than before where you had to show passports and go through customs in each country,' says Martin when they settle into their seats.

After the rush to get to the train, it's a relief to relax. Most commuters are on their devices; there's free Wi-Fi. Martin busies himself doing touristic research for Amsterdam on his phone, showing Lark maps and discussing places to visit. While he reads though the research notes he organised yesterday, Lark checks a text from Michael she hasn't had time to consider this morning. She sent 'Big Ticket' with an email to him yesterday, mentioning the 'Puberty Blues' angle and her travelling itinerary. She also queried if heterosexual stories were enough.

Lark

BIG TICKET is a shocker, fine story, perhaps more graphic than erotic, already been picked up. You're gaining a audience. Hetero is just fine. Keep the stories rolling. One every week or ten days is best. See if you can put something together on your travels.

Next article subs: Devotion
Same word count arrangement
Deadline: Monday 9/30/16 -10/4/16

Contact me any problems
Michael Lawson.

She leans back, watching the blur of Parisian suburbs giving way to areas of forest and countryside. She feels emotionally ravaged by the last couple of weeks. Yet the four stories she's written have burst out of her in spite of it all.

Her creativity thrives on pressure; she knows this from her design work. When there's not much work on, she languishes and produces little. Conversely when there are creative deadlines and demands mounting, more ideas erupt, more project ideas present themselves. So much so, she has trouble sleeping at these times. Are there more erotic tales to weave? She feels empty at the moment. The whole revelation of twins is still blowing her mind. She puts her palm on Martin's thigh, closes her eyes and let's herself drift.

Martin kisses the top of her head and wakes her when an attendant with a snack cart arrives.

'Coffee?'

'Yes please. And perhaps a packet of nuts and the fruit salad looks good too.

'Lark, its only eleven, we ate a couple of hours ago.'

'Hungry though.' She smiles at him through a noisy tummy rumble. 'See?'

'We're about half way there. I've worked out where Liesl lives near Beatrix Park. We can catch a taxi from Central Station. You said she texted arrangements for the key to her flat?'

'Yes, she won't be home until six from her job. She said we're welcome to hang out at her place or there are a few bikes near the front door we can take out for a ride this afternoon.'

'There is lots of public transport we can take to places too, once we dump our gear,' says Martin, opening the plastic lid on his coffee. He still looks bleak, but is trying to pull out of his inner cave.

When she finishes her coffee, Lark laces her fingers into his.

'Are you getting used to our twin juggernaut Martin? I'm still processing great chunks of disbelief myself, so I'm sure you must be too.'

'I'm overwhelmed. One baby scared me enough to turn into a monster and run away. Can you imagine what the thought of two does to me? Can you?' His eyes take on a sheen and his Adam's apple bobs while he tries to swallow his emotion. Tears aren't far away. 'So much trouble. We should never have come away. If we'd stayed home none of this would have happened.'

'You can't know that,' says Lark.

Martin takes several deep breaths to calm himself and asks, 'how long do you want to stay in Europe? Do you want to cut the holiday short and go home?'

'As long as I'm well, I can't see any reason to go home yet. We should stay as long as we can. Check the reciprocal arrangements in London at least. Maybe we could even have the twins overseas? They'd have dual citizenship then wouldn't they?'

'Slow down Lark!' Martin then surprises her saying, 'I've been doing an internet trawl on twins and twin births. Have you found out much yet?'

'Not much yet. Just a few baby conversations with Jordy.'

'Twin births are more complicated than single births,' he says. Already he's flicked on his phone and is thumbing screens until he finds what he's looking for. 'Here's a good one. We've got to bone up on the whole thing as soon as possible. There can even be complications this early. Anyway, have a read.' He passes her his phone.

She reads about pregnancy as an older woman. The vanishing twin syndrome and how pre-eclampsia can reduce the flow of blood to the placenta. Gestational diabetes, which can happen to any expecting mother. Amniocentesis and nuchal translucency scans to check for Downs syndrome and other problems. There seems to be far more intervention throughout twin pregnancies – lots more ultrasounds, prodding and poking. At birth there can also be a heap of complications from babies in the wrong position, low lying placentas, caesareans and prematurity. Epidurals and caesareans are recommended. Ugh!

'That little book you got for me says nothing about any of this,' says Lark.

'Hmm, I thought it would be enough info when I looked at it. Ignorant me, and twins are a different ball game to single babies.'

'Well it's a good thing I gave up the idea of a water birth in my younger days. Sounds like hospitals are the in thing for twin births, doesn't it?' She tries for humour, but is sobered by the information. Perhaps it would be sensible to go back home for the births.

She passes Martin's phone back to him and he gives her an intense look. 'I think an English speaking doctor and staff would be a good idea. Language complications would be hard for both of us.' He tears mindlessly at the paper coffee cup. 'I know what your answer will be so don't get upset, but are you sure you don't want to terminate the pregnancy Lark?'

'Absolutely not! You saw them Martin, they are almost fully formed, our baby twins.'

'Alright, alright!' Martin tears the cup to pieces. Thought I'd check one last time. Its going be a helluva ride for the next... 20 years. You know that?'

'I know. As long as we can keep it together, keep on loving each other, we can make it work.'

Famous last words, she thinks, staring at Martin, wondering who he really is. 'If you don't want to stick around and be their Daddy, I'm sure my mum will help me.'

'Yes she would, she's always trying to manipulate you. Perfect opportunity,' answers Martin, bitter.

'You bastard, you'll be happy to have her help if it enables you and I to juggle our lives as new parents,' says Lark. 'Who the hell are you Martin? I feel like I hardly know you. What would it matter to you if Mum supports me because you don't want too?'

'Sorry Lark. This is bringing out the worst in me.'

They fall silent, turned away from each other while the Thalys hurtles through Holland's flat countryside.

'I really am sorry. Let's try to be friends,' says Martin after a while, reaching for her hand.

She squeezes back, in recovery. For the last hour they take out their phones to share photos, send images and chat to friends and family, catch up on social media and the threads of their lives back in Sydney. Lark takes out her journal and jots down some ideas and embellishes the word 'devotion' in a Celtic design. It's a displacement activity for the chasm of anxiety she feels. Michael spreads a wide net of general writing themes, easy to fall through and create nothing. None of her ideas set off sparks so she puts her journal aside.

The country gives way to more built up areas and soon the train moves into the urban density of Amsterdam. They disembark into a milieu of people scurrying hither and thither. They know no Dutch, but many guards speak English and so are able to assist them. With the help of their directions and a map of the station, they find the right exit to take a Tesla taxi to Leisje's apartment in Rivierenbuurt, North Amsterdam.

They stop near a corner several minutes from Central Station. First impressions of Amsterdam from the car window are the canals, high pitched roofs on tall ordered buildings and bicycles everywhere being ridden or stacked in racks.

'We have to get the key from Leisje's neighbour Mrs. De Haas,' says Lark. 'She's elderly and always home except for market day,' she continues while they extract their cases from the boot and pay the driver. Two front doors open directly onto the street. One is adorned with Tibetan prayer flags, the other is plain with a small window box nearby. They knock on the plain door and wait for the old lady to answer the door, which opens as far as the security chain allows.

'Hello Mrs. de Haas. We are Leisje's friends Martin and Lark come to get her spare key. She left it with you for us.'

Mrs de Haas twiddles with her hearing aid, turning up the volume and reaches for her glasses hanging on a chain about her neck to examine them. She has a shock of white hair and sharp blue eyes.

'Yes, you fit the description, but you could be anybody. You are from Australia?' she says in accented English, suspicious eyes darting.

'Yes we are.' They stand patiently while she scrutinises them again.

'You have no Dutch?'

'Regretfully not,' says Lark.

'Passports please! I have to be sure. I can't give Leisje's key to the wrong people,' says Mrs. de Haas, as if quite often people knock on her door for keys.

'They find and hand over their passports through the chain. Alarmingly, she shuts the door and for a few minutes they wait until the door is opened and Mrs. de Haas returns their passports with Leisje's key.

'Welcome to Amsterdam,' she says.

'Thank you.'

They turn and let themselves into Leisje's place, relieved to have passed muster with Mrs. de Haas, who watches them enter before shutting her door. In the small vestibule there are a few bicycles, a closed door and a staircase, which they climb, the whiff of incense noticeable in the air. Martin takes the suitcases up to the next level, which is an open plan lounge room and kitchenette. Lark is already opening cupboards and the fridge, searching out bread, cheese and a few salad vegetables.

'One o'clock. I'm so hungry. Leisje said to help ourselves.' Martin silently joins Lark to make drinks, cuts the crusty rye bread and finds cutlery. Near a street facing window, they sit and eat at a small table covered with a batik tablecloth, aware of the residue of brittleness between them. Leisje's home has an eclectic range of furniture in bright primary colours. The walls on this level are festooned with prints of Vishnu, Krishna, Shiva and other deities, Lark can't name. The kitchen is a study in mandalas painted on the cupboards. Next to the table they eat at is a small shrine, with a few wilted flowers and incense sticks. In to corner next to the bookcase is an amp and electric guitar.

Martin and Lark are used to this kind of décor. There are a wide range of people that live at Bondi, a colourful contingency of them are into all sorts of new age, neo hippy lifestyles or spiritual quests. They've also had friends who have cultivated discipleships with masters or gurus just as other friends have stuck with traditional religions. Or none at all.

Martin gets up and looks at the music sitting on the stand next to the amp: Led Zeppelin, Deep Purple, ACDC, Black Sabbath, Nirvana. 'Looks like Leisje's into guitar riffs big time,' he says.

'She was a guru hopper when she lived in Sydney. There was a Master in Byron bay she was quite taken with. Loved rock 'n' roll too, and would travel out of her way to see any vintage bands.'

Lark takes their plates to the sink to rinse, tidying away the food. They explore the rest of the house, finding a small bedroom and bathroom on the next level.

On the bed there is a scribbled note: '*this is your room, love Leisje.*'

Above, with a dormier window and sloping walls is Leisje's bedroom. There are more spiritual posters, another shrine and enormous old speakers crowding her room. They carry their suitcases upstairs to the bedroom, eyeing each other uncertainly across the bed.

'Let's go for a bike ride, its so lovely outside,' says Lark, sidling out to the bathroom. Martin does the same and they descend through the house to the front door.

'Leisje says take any of her bikes. The key to the bike lock is hanging behind the front door. Ah, here it is.'

'Great, she's left us a map inside one of the bike helmets,' says Martin. 'We can bike around the area, maybe go to Beatrix Park. There's a pool there.'

'I'll go and get our swimmers out. It's hot enough.' Lark runs back upstairs while Martin looks at the map.

They spend the rest of the afternoon in Beatrix Park being lazy, riding the paths and swimming. Though ordered, the park soothes them and by late afternoon they've both recovered enough to smile at each other again. They collect some yoghurt, bread and salad vegetables on the way back to Leisje's place to shower off the chlorine. Lark notices a spot of blood on her underpants and wonders about bike riding but not enough to think about stopping. Leisje arrives home soon after, dumping her satchel on the floor to take Lark into a big bear hug.

'Hallo! So good to see you Lark! Are you staying in Amsterdam long?' asks Leisje. Hallo Martin?' She shakes his hand. Leisje is almost as tall as Martin with an open sunny face and dreadlocks to her waist, each dread tipped with coloured beads. She smells of sweat and mothballs.

'We'll stay a week or so,' says Martin.

'Your dreadlocks have grown so long,' says Lark. 'They were only as long as my hand when you left Sydney.'

Leisje laughs, 'I haven't cut my hair since then, what is it, three years since I came home?' It is an artwork don't you agree?'

'Sure is,' says Lark, laughing too.

'Ugh, I have to shower. Working at the refuse depot is such stinky work, but I get to drive a cute truck and pick up old furnitures and all kinds of stuff.'

'We bought a few things. We can get started on a meal.'

'Yes! Lovely! Are you still vegetarian Lark?

'Yes, we both are.'

'Me too!' Leisje laughs again. She takes the stairs two at a time and has a quick shower while Lark and Martin make a salad and an omelette.

'Oooh, a treat to have friends cooking. You must come and stay more often.' Leisje comes downstairs, her dreads wrapped in a towel. She's changed into a loose dress with a chain belt.

'So, you passed inspection with Mrs. de Haas?'

'Yes we did,' says Martin. 'She had to see our passports though.'

'Really?' laughs Leisje. 'She is a real friend and looks out for me.' She puts on music, some kind of Indian zither and wailing is the only way Lark can describe it. 'What have you been doing this afternoon?'

'We rode over to Beatrix Park and were very lazy,' says Lark, carrying plates and food to the table.

'Would you like to go out tonight to look around? We can take the metro into the Centruum for a walk or go to De Wallen, the red light district. Prostitution is legal here like cannabis. You still smoke?'

Martin does occasionally but I haven't for years,' says Lark.

'Me neither,' giggles Leisje. I live where I can have it anytime but I'm way over it!'

They clear up and catch a train to the Centruum. The night is warm but not humid like Sydney and it doesn't get dark until late. They visit De Oude Kerk, a church with gorgeous tall windows and small houses clinging to its walls in the red light district. Red neon lights glitter on the canal and street, as tourists and customers wander past lingerie clad women seated in windows, awaiting clients. To see prostitution sold in such a brazen manner unsettles Martin and Lark, yet the alternative practiced around the world – hidden and considered unsavoury, is just as thought provoking.

'The women have their own union and protect each other,' says Leisje as they walk. 'There are transsexuals operating here as well. We are used to this in Amsterdam. I was surprised how it is practiced in other places.' Leisje points of a particular display of three women posing provocatively almost like a shop mannequin display.

'We are lucky women Leisje,' says Lark, glad she has never taken the option of prostitution as these women have.

'Yes, we are.' Leisje looks grave for a moment before grinning again. 'Come on, we'll have an ice cream before we go home.'

'Are you two into any alternative stuff,' Leisje ventured on the train back to the flat.

'Not really. I did do a yoga class and some meditations in my twenties,' says Lark.

'I went through a period of reading about different modern spiritual leaders a while back,' says Martin. 'Interesting, but not really my thing.'

'Ah you've meditated Lark? I love to do this. I live near a meditation commune and visit every morning to do a meditation. Would you both like to come tomorrow?'

Martin gives Lark a quick bemused look, 'Okay, we'll try it, why not? Is there anything special we need to bring or do?'

'Great!' No, nothing to bring except yourselves. We'll have to get there by 7.30, okay?'

'Yes, that'll be fine.'

When they get to Leisje's apartment she retires to her room and soon the fragrance of incense curls around relaxing flute music from the top floor. Lark and Martin fall into their double bed, tired but keyed up from their day. Inevitably they join together in some revivifying sex; the need to connect and their subsequent orgasms wash away their troubles for a while.

24

"Time to get up,' says Leisje from their door. 'It's 6.45am. Lark can hear pigeons cooing on the window ledge before she turns on the shower. Martin takes over the bathroom and she trips downstairs to see Leisje sitting cross legged in front of her shrine murmuring to herself. She puts a bowl of petals in front of the buddha statue and lights more incense. Lark's stomach is growling.

'Howling,' says Martin, joining the women for a cup of tea and some fruit. They take the bikes and ride to the meditation centre.

'The meditations are held in a house where disciples live and worship,' says Leisje as they wait at traffic lights 'I visit every morning and sometimes on weekends. There are other meditations in the afternoons but I can't make those very often.'

'You're really into it then?' says Lark.

'Yes. I'd love to live at the centre like Theodor, my boyfriend. You'll meet him soon. The disciples worship a master who believes in personal freedom, lots of sex and pursuing the path to enlightenment in this life not the ever-after.'

'Here-after or heaven,' corrects Martin, ever the stickler for words.

'Sound's good,' says Lark, an agnostic, but open to other

people's ideas.

'When my Mother moved in with her boyfriend, she gave me the flat and I've become used to having my own space. I'm too selfish for communal living,' laughs Leisje.

They arrive at the meditation centre, a large house with a garden full of summer flowers. Four disciples including Theodore greet them. Theodore is tall and prematurely balding with a necklace of tattoos. He gives a cursory nod at Leisje's introductions, more interested in taking Leisje into a sumptuous hug and tongue kiss, feeling her butt as if he hasn't touched it in days. Zendra, a plump guy in a singlet & shorts explains the meditation to Lark and Martin, who both feel nervous but willing to try something new.

'The Transformatie meditatie is an active meditation going for one hour,' says Zendra, happy to speak in English for their benefit.

'Ah, so no sitting and watching your breath or third eye type of thing?' asks Martin.

'No, that's Rustige meditatie, a tranquil one later in the afternoons. If you like this style, you can come to this too,' says Zendra, smiling. 'The Transformatie meditatie is six ten minute stages. The first, we breathe out very fast, ha, ha, ha, like this, with feet apart,' he says. Second ten minutes we howl, like wolves, arrrwoooow, like this! Number three, we sing at any pitch, anything we want. Four is crying, screaming, shaking, letting out anger, rage, sadness. Five, we crawl or sit, and last of all, we dance with joy in our hearts.'

Martin looks at Lark like, what have we got into here and she nods with a roll of her eyes.

'We'll need you to fill in and sign this waiver form,' says Theodore, who has extracted himself from his passionate fondling with Leisje. You have no health issues?'

'No,' says Martin.

'I'm pregnant,' says Lark.

'That's not a health issue,' says Leisje. 'You didn't tell me. Congratulations! Just take it gently, follow your instincts in the meditation. Oh here.' She hands them blindfolds. 'We keep our eyes shut or blindfolded.'

They fill in the form, sign and are led to a large room, the floor covered in gym mats. They remove shoes while other disciples join them; Lark counts twenty people separating out across the space, some tying blindfolds on at the same time she and Martin tie on theirs.

The music begins. It's very loud and throbs with a heavy base. She can hear people panting all around her and joins in. Very soon her limp arms and hands stiffen into fists with her out breaths. This is so strange and hypnotic, she thinks, wondering how Martin is. She can hear him near her, his panting guttural, almost like a dog. The music changes just as Lark is feeling light headed. It is quiet by comparison, with high dwoop sounds overlaying and becoming faster, all but drowned out by wolf howls, shrieks and throaty screams. Lark feels silly for the first few minutes, making half hearted howls, but something takes over and soon she howls and screams with the best of them, feeling herself transform into what she considers her totem animal; a dingo.

It isn't very hard to move from howling to singing; Lark imagines she is a pop queen then an opera singer who has lost her ability to sing in tune. All around her she can hear people singing, babbling - some harsh and throaty, others soft and melodious. She finds her body following with its own dance patterns. She has forgotten Martin, Leisje, the twins, everyone and just exists for now, here, in the moment with herself.

Then she is crying when the music takes on deeper, melodic tones with cymbals ringing through it. Lark howls with tears. Her blindfold becomes wet. She wipes her nose with her hand. The pain of Martin's betrayal flowers in her mind. All the uncertainty she's suppressed hovers and hurts.

She drops to her knees when the music releases her into quiet ocean waves breaking, with harp weaving through it. She crawls and sits, bereft, part of her mind washed clean while the other part is incredulous. Minutes later, Lark gets to her feet, remembering that dance is last. The music is Indian techno pop and she gives it all she's got. She sways and turns, delirious and satiated.

The meditation finishes. Lark takes off her blindfold, meeting Martin's eyes next to her. 'That was...'

'Mind blowing,' croaks Martin, using the blindfold to mop sweat. 'Blown away.' He reaches for her hand. They focus on each other feeling a strengthened connection, exhaustion, exhilaration... astonishment. Leisje approaches them, tying up her dreads with her blindfold, her face red and sweaty.

'What do you think?' she asks, clear eyed and smiling.

'Amazing. I feel like I could blow away like a thistle,' says Lark.

'I feel like I am a big St. Bernard dog carrying such a load with me everyday, I am almost dragged under,' says Martin, focussing inward. 'The meditation let me throw off the burden.'

'Many feel that way. It is extremely powerful,' beams Leisje. 'Now I must rush home and get ready for work. You can stay and have some breakfast with Theodore and the others or come home.'

'We'll come home with you,' says Martin, not ready to face strangers after the experience they've been through.

'I'm drenched. I need a shower,' agrees Lark, collecting her shoes. They hurry out and bike back to the flat. Leisje takes a first shower and has a quick breakfast.

'Are you going to the Centruum today?' she asks, collecting keys and her phone.

'Yes.'

'I'll call you when I finish work and we can meet up.'

When she's closed the door, Martin says, 'I can't believe we just did that Lark'.

'I can't believe what it did,' says Lark, still floating in an exhausted bliss. They drink their tea and eye the posters of enlightened gurus with different eyes; they'll never be devotees, they both think. But who knows?

'What shall we do today?'

Martin picks up Leisje's electric guitar. He flicks on the amp, dropping the volume down low. He strums and does a few chord changes. 'Don't know. Make love? Go sightseeing around Centraal again after? We can just wander and there's a flea market called Waterloopleinmarkt you might like, lots of second hand clothes, books, and stuff...' he switches off the amp and puts the guitar on it's stand.

'Sounds perfect,' says Lark, a big grin spreading across her face. She leads him to bed.

After languid lovemaking upstairs, they spread out Leisje's map on the table to plot their day's activities. Amsterdam is compact and easy to get around on foot, bike or public transport. Alighting from the train later, they trace the course of Amsterdam's medieval city walls. The internet gives them a list of local vegetarian café's; the Terra Zen Centre is perfect for lunch. Dutch double salted licorice, a small obsession for Lark, is their next stop at Jacob Hooy & Co. They walk back through the Red Light District, as busy during the day as it is at night time.

The Erotic Museum with displays of erotica and sex through the ages is fascinating, especially to Lark. Some men are performing a street theatre mime outside. One man is dressed as a business man, while the others parade as Trans men who proposition the 'straight' guy. They do the performance so well, it is really funny. From sex to piety, they queue to view Oude Kirk's interior, admiring the vaulted wooden ceiling while sobered by the gravestones underfoot.

'Can we go to the flea market now?' Retail therapy beckons. Lark wants to buy some looser dresses now her tummy is pressing against her skirts.

'Okay.' Martin gets out his phone for directions to Waterloopleinmarkt.

An hour later, Lark has a simple A-line dress with primary coloured shapes and two paisley boho dresses in a bag. Great second hand bargains. She's also found two suspense novels in English for a few Euros each. Martin buys books and an antique amethyst necklace while she's been shopping.

'Turn around, I'll put it on, wife.'

'Hey, I'm not your wife yet. I love it Martin.'

'Well you're as good as, Mrs. Oswald. We've been in a defacto for three years.'

'Yes, but until we actually marry, I'll stick to Haylen. In fact, should we go for double barrelled – Haylen- Oswald?'

'Oswald- Haylen? Not fussed… perhaps one twin can have one surname and one the other?

'No, don't be stupid.' Lark's hand flutters to her curved tummy. Leisje calls to arrange a meet-up at 6pm as they bicker.

'How are you feeling after the meditation,' she asks when she meets them arm in arm with Theodore.

'Fantastic. We had no idea it would have such an effect on us.' Lark has been on a high all day and she can tell Martin has too. Leisje laughs.' Theodore nods in agreement. 'We can walk along the canals and go and have a meal at my favourite vegan café.'

'That sounds great. I am so hungry all the time,' says Lark.

'So you're pregnant Lark. Are you happy about this?' asks Leisje.

Lark gives Martin a quick look. 'We are getting used to the idea. What about you Leisje. Are you interested in having kids?'

'I come from a large family,' says Leisje. 'It has cured me of wanting children I think. Thirty six seems very old to start a family. Mum had six kids before she was thirty two.' Leisje smiles and swings her dreads. 'Besides, I'm too selfish.'

'Never say never Leisje,' says Theodore. I'm a forty three year old bisexual, yet I have three children.'

Martin and Lark turn to stare at him.

'Ah you want to know why I am Leisje's lover when I have a family? My ex wife and I divorced amicably and we share the children every other month.' Theodore frowns and stares across the canal. 'Children can be very hard wearing on relationships and these days adults are so self absorbed. It is sometimes too hard to adjust to the selflessness needed to raise children.'

Leisje squeezes Theodore's hand. Martin and Lark get a sense of some deep issues under his words but are at a loss as to what to say.

Theodore smiles. 'So it is good I give you my words of wisdom. It might help you later when you are sleep deprived and overwhelmed.'

The heat of the day is still bouncing up from the streets and stonework, but the canals give a sense of coolness to the Cenrtuum as they walk. At De Bolhoed cafe they find a table, order and chat. Lark looks around at the light green and orange interior and sees a cat asleep on a chair nearby, even though the café is full of patrons, how lovely!

Where are you from Theodore?' she asks. She can't resist and gets up to pat the cat as it yawns and stretches.

'I'm from Germany, but my father is Dutch. I worked as a lawyer for the hospitality industry in Dresden until I found our Master. When I came to the commune I met Leisje.'

'So you still work as a lawyer?' asks Martin.

'No I decided to have a break. It is very stressful work. Now I do massage at the meditation centre. It pays my bills.'

The waitress brings first drinks, then their meals a little later, taking their table number away.

'Our master believes in lots of sex.' Leisje says.

'Why is that when so many religions frown upon it? Historically sex has been the scourge of human existence since Adam and Eve, according to religions' asks Martin.

'Our master believes sex can be a transcendent force. The losing of inhibitions put in place by society is healing and necessary to reach self fulfilment,' Leisje answers. It is a pat phrase that Leisje has probably said before in answer to this question.

'A different angle I guess. A bloody entertaining one,' grins Martin.

'We're all made from sex,' says Lark with a rhetorical flourish. 'Why do we all get so screwed up about it?' She is already in love the café and the food when it arrives is wonderful.

'Our seventh chakra, the sex centre in most religions, is the most maligned,' answers Theodore, forking a samosa into his mouth. 'Take me, I am bisexual. Even today I can be in trouble for this in many places. Surely it is better to have tolerance for people's different preferences?'

'Yes, it is.' Lark and Martin agree, being fairly open minded, but know for many people it is difficult to agree with anything out of the norm.

'All your posters and incense Leisje... are you a follower of any in particular?' asks Martin. 'You don't mind me asking?'

Leisje laughs. 'I'm like a squirrel, I collect many of the old ideas of Eastern religions like Buddhism and Taoism. But I like the ideologies of many modern masters and gurus. A refuse worker who is a spiritual searcher, many think I am cuckoo!'

'I am more singular. I have been a devotee of our Master for many years,' says Theodore. 'And you, what's your poison? They say this in Australia?'

'Yes we do,' laughs Martin. We're not particularly spiritual, but we both think the Transformatie Meditatie is amazing.'

'You must come to some of the other meditations we run.'

'Yes we will,' says Lark, finishing her last mouthful and for once feeling her hunger satisfied.

25

Martin and Lark settle into a pattern; meditation, sex and sightseeing. They manage to put aside their initial reticence to breakfast with the disciples at the centre one morning. Polite queries are made about their spiritual status, nothing pushy.

'The disciples offer many different types of alternative therapies here. Olga here, does past life work and dream interpretation. Zig reads tarot, Frederique gives massage and rolfing, I offer chakra reading and so on,' says Zendra. We all earn money for the centre and ourselves by offering these services to others.'

It all sounds intriguing, but both agree the meditation is enough for now considering they see themselves as atheists.

'Just a moment,' says Lark the next day when they are about to leave the flat. 'Gotta write something down.' A drift of words murmur through her mind like bioluminescent organisms, bringing goosebumps to her arms.

In the back of her mind, Michael's story directive 'devotion' has been brewing. An idea has come to her in a spine tingling rush. Of course – the devotion of a new recruit to an alternative religion! It's a perfect setting for writing. Tangled in this inspiration is another idea Lark is trying to snare before it dissolves. She scrawls a couple of quick pages. They go out to the Van Gogh Museum, having visited the Rijksmuseum the afternoon before. Clouds are building and by evening, it's overcast. All Lark can see as they make their way back to the flat, are the swirls of Van Gogh's painted firmaments overlaying the Amsterdam sky.

On Saturday and Sunday it pours. Summer dissolves in the rain; the city is tinted in cool greys. Locals rush about with umbrellas and tourists seek refuge in museums. Other than a dash with Leisje to the organic markets on Saturday morning after meditation, Lark and Martin sequester themselves the flat while Leisje spends the weekend at the commune with Theodore. The deluge is a godsend for Lark. Her fevered imagination is concocting two stories at once.

'Perhaps the meditations are inspiring you,' suggests Martin, who is content to read and surf the net while she writes. But he does try to seduce her away from the laptop later in the afternoon and succeeds. They make love slowly for an hour or so, getting up as the light leaves the day to quell the hungry shrieks from Lark's stomach with some dinner.

She wakes during the night to chunks of story glimmering in her mind's eye and creeps down to the lounge room to type, delirious with new ideas.

OM

It took all Melissa's love, devotion and surrender to accept the therapist's finger's revolving deeply around her buttocks, ploughing into her glutes. Circling ever closer to her arsehole. Melissa slitted her eyes and practised her new mantra, 'Om ah de Blessing om...'

'Just let yourself be at one with your inner self,' murmured the greying therapist through his rather nasal breathing. Was it his exertion giving her the massage or the bird's eye view of her oiled up rump that made his breathing so ragged?

'Om ah de Blessing om,' Melissa chanted under her breath, trying to banish such thoughts while the therapist's stubby fingers circled and plunged in, despite her anus puckering in

protest. The therapist had made it clear that in the anus was centred much of humanity's stresses and he was gifted at giving release. His breathing grew louder and Melissa gritted her teeth as he delved. She tried to be at one with the cosmos and let go of her inner tensions.

There was an odour in the room that kept on overloading her sense of smell; like sweaty socks and old semen, not quite masked by the cloying aroma of scented candles. The massage table smelt like it had been embalmed in human juices long ago and the prickly white towel didn't quite cover the sour pong. That odour Melissa recalled, closely resembled the smell in the room where her conservative existence had undergone irrevocable change – the place where her new life had begun. What she had been doing for the previous twenty three years Melissa couldn't quite recall with fingers up her arse.

'Where nothing ever happens,' was the catchcry for the neighbourhood Melissa had lived in all her life. She'd attended a private girl's school enshrined in the same suburb and married well, to another product of the same area. Working for the local council as an Administrative Clerk gave her the steady promise of gradual promotion, good maternity leave and superannuation. 'Comfortable' was how she described her upbringing to her friends, 'comfortable and secure,' her marriage and work. Privately she likened sex with her husband as 'comfy' as a knee length skirt and blouse two times per week.

Over a latte one Saturday at the local café, her friend Emily gushed praise for a Psychic she had found online and scrawled the Psychic's web address on a piece of paper for Melissa. It lay forgotten in her handbag until a few weeks later when she was looking for her keys and it fluttered out onto the floor. Picking it up Melissa experienced the oddest thing, like an earthquake shuddering inside her mind. On a whim she looked up the web page and filled in the online form for an appointment, surprised by the action as it was entirely out of character for her.

The following Tuesday Melissa drove to a wealthy street in the Eastern Suburbs, parked and pressed the intercom in a gated wall of a mansion jutting into the blue sky above it. She was buzzed into a courtyard with a trickling water feature, tinkling mobiles and giant amethyst crystals scattered carelessly about. A tall man in his early thirties with short dreadlocks, a loose shirt, shorts and a nose ring greeted her.

'Hello, you must be Melissa Harvey. I am Jack Prendle,' Jack introduced himself and shook her hand, turning it over and tracing the lines on her palm.

'Yes, hello Jack,' replied Melissa pulling her hand away, uncertain. Now the experience was here, alarm bells at the edge of her comfortable life were jangling in a fury. Emily's been here and survived, she told herself, so I'll be fine.

'Come through,' said Jack.

Melissa followed him through a palatial formal lounge room scattered with large burgundy cushions all placed to take in the view of Sydney Harbour from the enormous picture windows. She noticed several incense sticks creating a scented fug before following Jack into a smaller room off the lounge room. It was fitted with more big cushions and a smell, like sex had been had there recently. Jack and Melissa sat down; Melissa tucked her legs in neatly on the cushion and looked at Jack.

He took her hand again and peered into her eyes. 'Is there anything you'd like to ask me – any questions you have Melissa?'

Melissa wondered what to ask. Emily had primed her a bit on how the session would go, but she really didn't have anything pressing that concerned her, so she answered, 'not really.'

Still holding her hand, Jack's eyelids fluttered as he said, 'I can see you'll go on a journey in the coming months.... but not one related to physical places. More like a journey of the heart and mind.'

'What does that mean?' queried Melissa, perplexed. She and Robert had talked about going on a cruise with her parents at Christmas but nothing was planned yet.

Jack looked at her and talked in a slow drone like she was a little stupid.' It means you'll be going through a growth period in your life. I can't tell you what that will be, but it will involve a group of people unknown to you now.'

Melissa gazed at him, wondering how he could possibly predict what was going to happen to her. 'How many children am I going to have?' she blurted, trying to steer the conversation towards something more tangible.

'Children... you won't have in the near future,' said Jack, turning her hand to peer at more lines. 'Your children will be created with someone you haven't met yet.'

'But I have a husband, Robert,' Melissa garbled, rather shocked.

'Your husband has a future that dovetails with yours much later,' Jack said obliquely, 'but there is someone else who will have a great and rewarding influence upon you.'

Melissa was astonished by Jack's comments. She flat out doubted his empathetic ability and wondered if he was just making it all up. Here was a total stranger challenging her predictable future. She decided then and there to listen and be polite but not take anything he said seriously. His monotonous voice continued to seduce her with words for a future that sounded so unlike her that she giggled and bit her lip. Yet the possibilities he suggested melted into her mind like the gift of unexpected rain in a drought. She went home bemused, feeling like a goldfish in a bowl looking out at another world.

A week later Emily invited her to an introductory talk by a new spiritual guide she'd heard about. Melissa accepted without once considering the drip feed of possibility the psychic had given her; normally she would have turned down the offer without a thought.

His Holiness Adrian Blessing had blown her away from the ponderous course of her life with his charismatic words, mesmeric blue eyes and languorous sexy gestures. At the end of the talk Melissa and Emily eagerly signed up to become his followers. Both proffered credit cards to pay the $250 donation to the devotee with the handy credit card processor at the door. They were given a folder with a new name each; an optional voucher to have His Holiness Adrian Blessing's face tattooed on their inner wrist at a city Tattooist and a new set of 'life' rules, the easiest of which was a change of wardrobe. All their clothing must be blue to mirror the Master, Adrian Blessing's eye colour and conveniently an expensive booth had been set up at the back of the hall with clothing of the right shades of blue. That evening Melissa arrived home in a highly charged state with several shopping bags and an attitude that flummoxed her tired husband. Three thousand dollars later, Melissa had signed up to do a month long retreat with Emily and His Holiness Adrian Blessing.

A fortnight passed and here she was, getting her every orifice cleansed and massaged for a month long submersion with His Holiness Adrian Blessing.

'Just lie for a moment, until you are ready to get up,' the therapist whispered. 'Perhaps I can book you in for some colonic irrigations afterwards?' he added as he dried his oily hands and put the lid back on the Vaseline jar.

Melissa lay there feeling like a leaf blower had scoured her lower colon. It was her second initiatory experience in the cult. The first one yesterday, had really turned her head. Arriving smartly turned out in a shapeless blue kaftan, she and thirty other new recruits sat in a circle giving their names like they were at kindergarten. A one hour meditation ensued, first with fifteen minutes of chanting, 'Om ah de Blessing om,' When soft flute music lead into the sound of bells tolling, everyone disrobed and swayed with dreamy expressions and eyes shut against each other's self conscious nudity.

Melissa had looked wide eyed across at Emily, who gazed back in the vaguest way. She didn't seem to mind suddenly being naked with a circle of strangers. The music changed to furious drumming for the last fifteen minutes. Amazingly Melissa was surrounded by human dogs and puppies on all fours, yapping, barking and sniffing each other's bottoms. A frown from the group leader prompted Melissa to become a dog too – shying away from a rather large shaggy dog in glasses who tried to mount her in the mêlée, while a shrill female dog with a blonde bob yapped at her furiously.

'But what was the point?' Melissa asked Emily over a glass of chilled grass juice later.

'I think His Holiness Adrian Blessing is so divine,' garbled Emily, 'perhaps it's to break down our inhibitions?' She was thoroughly enjoying herself with these new experiences. Having recently divorced, she was in a narcissistic freefall.

Yes, thought Melissa, you'd never see an adult pretending to be a dog in her neighbourhood. Perhaps it would lead to a breakdown in society if people did. She could see that Emily had already suspended reasonable thought.

Melissa got up from the massage table and wiped the excessive amount of Vaseline out of her butt-crack. She clothed herself in her indigo sarong. Today's class, Chakra Reading, promised to be a more spiritual experience she hoped. His Holiness Adrian Blessing was to attend the new devotees and she could feel the excitement building inside her at the thought of seeing him again in spite of her reservations.

Poor Robert, her husband had not understood her sudden need to 'go and find herself.'

'Melissa, you're already home here. You're not lost,' he'd told her after their comfortable missionary sex that night. He had looked so dear and mystified in the glow from the bedside lamp, that Melissa had felt remorseful. How could she explain the sudden canyon of change that yawned between them or her driving need to follow this path?

'I'm due a month's holiday so I'm going to do this retreat with Emily. I am sure that will be enough time for me to settle myself again, Robert,' she whispered back, not at all certain if that were true.

Melissa found Emily dressed in soft blue, eating a wilted sprout sandwich in the cafeteria. She grabbed herself a cold croissant and they made their way to the school camp hall which doubled as His Holiness Adrian Blessing's temple. Chimes rang and two sweaty devotees assigned as monitors stood at the doors to sign everyone into the hall for the Chakra class.

The new initiates filed in. There was His Holiness Adrian Blessing dressed in a deep blue robe, seated on the stage! Something not unlike a small orgasm shuddered through Melissa. She melted on seeing him and knew everyone in the room had the same reaction to his charisma from their mindlessly beatific expressions. His Holiness Adrian Blessing cast his gaze around at the gasping devotees, some of whom had fallen to their knees in breathless ecstasy. The monitors organised everyone, hauling up the fallen and propping them back into the orange bucket chairs. His Holiness Adrian Blessing gestured to the wings – a middle aged man and a large breasted woman, both dressed in blue shirts and soft trousers, came to stand beside him on the stage.

'Who are they?' Melissa asked Emily.

'They are the lieutenants of His Holiness,' Emily whispered back, not taking her eyes from His Holiness Adrian Blessing.

Music started up and the audience began to sway as one by some collective osmosis, but when the master put up his hand, it was instantly shut off. His Holiness Adrian Blessing folded his hands and bowed to the new devotees, who went wild with joy, spontaneous tears springing down many glad faces. He turned to the two other people beside him on the stage and nodded as the hall quietened.

'His Holiness Adrian Blessing has a sore throat today. He is unable to speak to you,' said the male lieutenant. The crowd sighed and shuddered with disappointment.

'But he has seen something evolving in myself and my partner here,' the woman pointed at the man with a gleam of jubilation in her eyes. 'His Holiness Adrian Blessing has understood that Shaun here and I, have reached enlightenment.'

All three on stage folded their hands and bowed as one to the new devotees, who erupted with cries of amazement. Melissa felt an overwhelming joy encompass her – this was why she was here despite her arsehole feeling so peculiar, so invaded.

Up on stage the lieutenants led His Holiness Adrian Blessing away. The music started up again underpinning the clapping and swaying until the enlightened lieutenants returned to the stage.

'For those who do not know me, I am known as Rosa. We will now begin the Chakra class,' the woman boomed across the hall. 'Please disrobe and hang your clothes on the school-bag *hooks by the door. Return to the centre to form a circle please.'*

Thirty people obeyed, staring self consciously at each other. The two monitors at the door scurried in, depositing a tin of blue poster paint and children's paintbrushes by every second initiate.

'Everyone, please observe this chart,' said Shaun, pointing to a chart at the side of the hall which showed a diagram of the chakras. 'For those of you unfamiliar with chakras, these are the seven energy centres in our body which energy flows though, interlinking with each other in the subtle body. Familiarise yourself with the chart please.'

Everyone dutifully took in the chart.

'Now one partner will paint circles where the chakras are on their partner and then the other will do the same. The first chakra, 'Understanding and Will', just above your heads, can just be imagined at this stage,' Rosa commanded. She smiled across at her enlightened partner as the devotees set to work.

Ten minutes later they all looked ridiculous, nude and covered in blue polka-dots and circles from forehead to genitals, where uncertainty had rendered some very drippy rings.

'Form a circle again please. Could the women now blindfold the men with the blindfolds provided,' was the next instruction.

Once accomplished, the women were asked to come in the centre of the circle. Melissa looked around at the group of ladies who were all sizes, ages and shapes. Most of the women were at a guess were between twenty and forty. The men, she thought, were older, maybe late twenties to one chap with sagging genitals who looked so old, she couldn't guess his age.

'Ladies, you can now freely touch the men and experience the energy radiating from their chakras,' suggested Shaun. 'There are no rules here. You can freely experience the energy with any of the males in the outer circle.'

There was a collective intake of breath from all the participants, followed by tittering and uncertain shifting in the group of women. Stranger and stranger, thought Melissa. Some rational part of her mind tried to interfere but she silenced it by mentally repeating her mantra, 'Om ah de Blessing om...'

'Come on ladies, don't be shy,' Rosa called to them from the stage.

Melissa turned to look at a couple of the more nicely developed men. The woman with the blonde bob that yapped at her in the dog meditation glared at the other woman and bared her teeth. She took a few steps to touch the podgy man with glasses who was clearly her partner, and gave a look of possessive zeal to everyone. The two lieutenants approached her and she left the hall with them and did not return.

The women left trailed their hands over the men. Melissa and Emily grinned at each other and made eyes about the two guys who were beautifully young and sculpted, with well endowed seventh chakras. For one man the attention was too much and his little darting penis blew its load over the hand of a petite woman with brown curly hair. She stood, struck with embarrassment and a monitor bought tissues over to them both.

'Alright ladies, please find your original partners and take off their blindfolds. The men can now blindfold the women and move to the centre of the circle,' ordered Shaun.

Melissa noticed that the men were eager and quickly got on with the job. The women were soon standing blinded and nervous.

'Now it's your turn gentlemen, to enjoy the chakra energy of the ladies,' said Shaun. 'Remember gentlemen, that there are chakras other than the seventh one.'

Melissa's partner hadn't been very thorough with her blindfold. By turning her head slightly she could see the men coming along her left side. She willed herself to stillness as she was groped by the older man, followed by several other fellows, whose sweaty hands focused more on her genitals than anywhere else. She was amused to see to her left, the spectacled shaggy-man rushing around feeling and touching every woman he could.

'Thank you ladies and gentlemen. Please remove the blindfolds and form a circle again. I'm sure you're all feeling much more in touch with your chakras now,' Rosa smiled from the stage. 'The latter part of the workshop deals with your spiritual merging,' she continued. 'His holiness Adrian Blessing believes it is important to remove inhibitions and strictures imposed by society. To affect this, he has carefully designed this one month retreat so that you'll return to your normal lives transformed and at peace.'

Melissa looked across at Emily and her shoulders jumped with excitement. Yes! This is why I'm here she thought, forgetting how peaceful her life was before the retreat.

'Look around you,' motioned Shaun, 'find a partner you feel a connection with.'

With some shuffling and mingling, choices were made; first-in-first-serve applied to the most attractive women and men partnering up quickly. Hesitating, Melissa was taken aback to see the older man standing in front of her elbowing other contenders away. More self assured, Emily fared better, managing to snare one of the lesser hunks. All eyes turned towards the two lieutenants, awaiting instructions. Around them the monitors were unrolling narrow foam prayer mats.

'Sit with your partner on the mats provided please. We will begin with chanting, 'Om ah de Blessing om.' As the energy takes you, begin to reach out and touch the chakras of your partner. That's right. Now branch out and touch freely. You are going to make love to this person in front of you, feeling their chakras blending with your own.' Rosa's voice took on a husky note. 'Feel the collective energy pouring from all of your chakras intermingling in this room.'

There was a furtive eagerness with some of the devotees who, taking the most literal interpretation, ignored the eyes upon them to snog and grope each other. Other participants looked uneasy at the lack of privacy but succumbed to the power of the collective, soon touching and handling their partners with greater and greater intimacy.

The shaggy man was mounting the brunette, his jelly rolls quivering with excitement. The guy with the biggest cock rubbed it repeatedly through the labia of his partner, a small redhead with tiny nipples. The two monitors shuffled through the busy participants, handing out condoms as the need arose.

Melissa noticed her friend Emily losing herself to a bout of cunnilingus. She wondered what her ex-partner Bill would think if he saw Emily now, especially as the hunk moved to spear her with his vigorous shaft. The school hall filled with groans and energetic grunts, all chakras forgotten, bar one.

She herself went through the motions with her older partner, kissing and feeling his body. His erection poked up from his greying pubic hair, but Melissa couldn't let go, even chanting her mantra. He didn't force her, despite a plump cowgirl gyrating and ululating on top of a surprised fellow right next to them.

The lieutenants paraded the hall, murmuring breathy encouragements to the tardier devotees just as if it were a game of pin-the-tail-on-the- donkey at a children's party.

'Yes a little further, yes that's the way, no – you've missed the G spot, getting warmer, yes that's it!' she heard Rosa say as she walked between the thirty orgiastic participants.

It was while some of the first couples grunted out their orgasms that Rosa touched Melissa on the shoulder. Looking up, she found Rosa's naked pendulous breasts billowing above her. 'You're to go with Shaun,' she murmured, a spot of sweat gleaming in her slight moustache. 'Take your clothing with you.'

Melissa got up and Rosa took her place. She took a firm grip of Melissa's partner and buried his head between her breasts.

I'm going to get thrown out, Melissa worried. She stepped around the screwing couples and those languishing post-coitally. Threesomes had sprung up in a few places; two standing men were screwing both sides of a pop-eyed woman wedged between them while another couple were at it doggie style with another female disciple lying underneath licked the proceedings with abandon. Two women in the corner had shunned the usual and been supplied by the monitors with a strap-on and were busy pleasuring each other with it.

'What's going to happen?' she questioned Shaun's back as she followed him.

'You've been chosen,' he threw back at her, 'to complete the Chakra workshop in the presence of the master It is a rare honour.'

Melissa's stomach turned over and she nearly wet herself. She was going to have sex with the guru himself! Shaun led her through the wings of the stage to a small green-room at the back of the hall. His Holiness Adrian Blessing sat with his feet up on a table sipping a post lunch chardonnay.

'Go and attend those that can't help themselves, will you,' he said to Shaun in his mellifluous voice.

Where was his sore throat? Melissa could detect no hoarseness at all. What was more, his blue robe was flung over the back of his chair. He was dressed in old denim shorts, a red shirt and old runners and looked quite normal. Melissa didn't know whether to be shocked or amused and it must have shown on her face.

'Not what you thought hey?' His Holiness Adrian Blessing looked at her and grinned. 'Now why are you not participating with enthusiasm? I am curious. Call it market research.' He leaned back and gave her an electric smile.

Melissa bunched her clothes against her belly, thinking of what to say. It wasn't the age of the man who had opted to partner her. Her husband flashed though her mind but she realised it wasn't some kind of filial piety for him either.

'Because,' she bit her lip. 'Because it looked like sex with him would be too com-fort-a-ble,' she stressed the syllables.' The epiphany hit her like a mallet: she knew in that moment that 'comfortable' had become an anathema to her.

Adrian Blessing burst out laughing. 'Never judge a book by its cover,' he answered. 'You may just get a surprise. That disciple is an old guru-hopper from way back and if anyone knows all the sexual tricks in the world it's him. Now please, get dressed and have a glass of wine with me and maybe we can have some fun later.'

Lark Connor

Martin reads 'Om' while Lark they eat lunch, chuckling at all the right places.

'You're showing a cynical streak, but I love it.'

'Don't you remember the gossip we've heard over the years? Friends who have become involved with this guru or sect, or 'awakened' one?' She uses her fingers to accentuate the words.

'Yes I do.' He looks thoughtful. 'Perhaps women discuss the salacious details more than men.'

'I guess. But I think women talk more deeply about life anyway.' She laughs. 'Despite the great experience we're having with this daily meditation, my mind boggles at what perhaps a Tantra meditation with a pro-sex guru might mean.'

He gives her a kiss on the nose as she chews. 'Your wild imagination at work again?'

'Yes. Reality can be even stranger than fiction though, can't it? Look at what's happening in our lives for starters.'

The other story brimming in her mind comes from a comment of Theodore's and the trans seduction street performance they saw outside the Erotic Museum at the Centruum. Rich pickings, she thinks and she begins typing at speed to capture the story threads in her mind.

Lark is so preoccupied she doesn't realise Martin is also lost in thought.

'Some research I organised through inter-library exchange with Geneva has come though to Paris. They will only keep it there for 48 hours if I don't confirm my claim for it. Sorry Lark, but I'll have to go back to Paris.'

'Really?' Lark looks up from typing to see Martin peering at his phone, glasses on.

'Why don't you stay another couple of days with Leisje. When I get back we can go to Christiania in Denmark like Theodore suggested? Or perhaps Sweden then? I'll just take my backpack.' He says it as if it's already decided he's going.

'You have to go back to Paris now?' Lark, returning from the creative vault with her fingers paused over the keyboard, is slow to grasp his words.

'Yes, just a couple of days.'

'Where will you stay?'

'I've already sent a text to Remi and Adelyn to see if I can sleep on their lounge for the night. If I go early Tuesday morning I can be back the following evening. I'll be free of that commitment then.'

A ghost of anxiety flutters in Lark's mind but she shrugs it away. They've been having such a marvellous time. Martin's anxious flit about the pregnancy is behind them now and the meditations have helped them both with the enormity of twin parenting.

'Okay.' She resumes typing. 'Go for it.'

They've just had a particularly satisfying fuck after she sends the story to Michael and she's feeling fully charged and magnanimous. If she can just get the introduction done by the evening and the weather clears up tomorrow morning, they can trawl Noordermarkt for more clothes, trinkets and presents after the meditation. If the rain clears they can go sightseeing again for the afternoon. Now she's sent 'Om,' to Michael, the only hurry she feels is to get the next story down while it bubbles in her mind. The Sydney Mardi Gras will be a perfect backdrop, Lark imagines, lost in thought again. An hour later, with her research from the internet, she's ready to begin.

SHADI GRAS

'Argh!' he groaned, 'not happening.' Sam's head drooped on my shoulder as he shuddered out his orgasm.

He reached for a roll of kitchen paper, wedging it between his elbow and ribs to tear a ragged sheet off with one hand. His other hand held his wilting penis. Nestled in a spray of gelatinous come, it looked like a pink snowball with dubious white icing on a children's cake. He used the sheet to wipe his spray from my belly and mopped up his dwindled rod.

While he bent and reached for his pants, I stood legs apart, undies forgotten on the floor, with my ankles entwined in the stainless steel shelving of the cool-room. Been here before with him, but I can't stop myself coming back for more, I thought.

My partial arousal was screaming for some hard cock thrusting into me. I could feel my sex gnashing its drooling teeth. I shuddered with frustration and took a deep breath to squelch it as he straightened to buckle his belt.

'It's okay,' I whispered, wanting above all else to mollify Sam's insecurities about his poor performance.

'It's a problem of mine,' he told me on our first unsuccessful screw, 'just so you know I'm still hot for you anyway.'

What a deadly hook that was. Hell, I liked him, so like many times before, I'd just go and masturbate in the staff toilets in a few minutes. I'd try next time to conquer his premature ejaculation.

At least I knew I could satisfy myself...

I drew in the chill from the metal shelving, gazing at the passive vegetables and foodstuffs around me. In that clever way of all women that draw a longbow on an unrealised ambition with a guy, I dissembled:

'You're so hot Sam,' I lied.

He pursed his lips and tied on his apron, giving a dubious grunt. I avoided his morose glare as I pulled up my undies and flicked down my miniskirt. He followed me out of the cool-room to the steamy kitchen where some eggplant and saffron curry bubbled on the stovetop and carrot cakes sat forgotten on the *bench nearby.*

I'd been working at the vegetarian restaurant in Taylor Square for six months over summer as a cake cook. Admiration for the chef – Sam had bloomed into lust. He was tall with a great ass, saturnine good looks and curly dark hair. Man, he could chop vegetables so fast steam almost came off his blade. His cooking was sublime. From my cake assembly bench I could perve on him while he sliced and diced, whipping up heavenly food on the other side of the kitchen.

'Oh!' Lark throws herself back in the chair and rolls her head to ease the stiffness seeping into her neck after typing most of the day. The light is dwindling out of the day even though it's barely 4pm. Everything in the flat seems overbright and luminous after hours at the keyboard.

'Cup of tea Martin?' she calls up the stairs where he went a while ago.

'Yeah, thanks.' He clatters down the stairs a few moments later taking off his glasses. 'Reading a novel is such a luxury.' He waves one of the books they found at the market.

'About time to cook dinner is it?'

'Yes please,' says Lark.

'Got to get a bit more finished?'

'Yes, a few more paragraphs. I'll try to get it finished tonight or tomorrow morning.'

We were the first to arrive at the restaurant, beginning the early afternoon shift. Consequently we spent many hours alone together. Sam was my Spanish friend's old partner and he'd already had a couple of kids with her, so I knew he was up to the task. I doubt she would have tolerated a guy who couldn't get it up. I was reluctant to talk to her about having the hots for her ex – she could go off like an incendiary bomb if she didn't like what was said to her. Despite the fact that she and Sam hadn't been together for years, she was the sort to be possessive even with her ex-partners.

Everyday Sam and I sweated together to create entrées, main courses and desserts for the restaurant's clientele. Sam planned alluring menus to entice the customers while I put my creative talents to work making a marvellous array of cakes, all covered with artistic icings and frostings.

'How's this icing Sam?' I asked him sometimes. We'd stop and share the beaters, discussing the icing between licks as a distraction from the heat billowing in the open windows and the sound of the traffic snarling past a few floors below.

That was how it had begun several weeks before. We had gotten silly with a bowl of kahlua frosting and ended up naked in the cool-room sucking it off each other before the other staff arrived.

Today it seemed there wasn't enough magnetism to ignite Sam's limp dick. I had just returned from the toilet where I'd thrashed my clit and cunt with my vibrator, when the other staff began to arrive.

Lula, our maitre de always blew in first with a gust of lesbian glory. Even more so today, as it was the Sydney Gay Mardi Gras parade today. Her bright purple hair was gelled up stiff with gold glitter and small rosettes. Rather than her usual nondescript sundress, Lula was dressed in a glittery green g-string and an conical pointed orange brassiere with gold wire coiled around the breasts. On her feet were steel capped boots.

'Hi darl,' she boomed, her voice smouldering and deep. She fluttered her heavy false eyelashes at me.

'You look fabulous Lula,' I replied, giving her air kisses. 'Are you going to serve tonight like that?'

'Why not? I'll be missing the parade working here,' grumbled Lula, reaching with a pointed pink fingernail to flick a drop of sweat off my top lip. 'Besides, the committee's decided to allow businesses to have floats in the parade and we girls aren't happy about that.' Lula frowned but it cleared instantly. 'Now the post-parade party, that'll be just so cool.' She winked as she stowed her bag and tied on an apron around her naked waist.

'Have you two been busy?' she enquired.

I rolled my eyes and she smirked. 'Sam...' I said with the

thumbs down sign.

'Oh darl,' Lula knew all about my affair with the cook. 'Give him up! Time to come over to the other side,' she teased, wiggling her breasts at me in belly-dance fashion. 'Why bother with guys who deny you pleasure because they can't keep it up? Or guys who can but think it's their sweet right to come first and leave you hanging?' She harrumphed and began to twirl one of my curls. 'I'd have you in orgasmic heaven in minutes.'

She was just flirting with me. She knew I was straight, but it didn't stop her trying it on.

'Maybe one day I'll shock you and try it Lula,' I said giving a provocative swish of my tongue. 'Lots of selfish guys out there don't know any better, it's all too true.' I sighed and wiped my sweaty hands on my apron.

I'd lived in Darlinghurst for three years after dropping out of art school and blowing down from the north coast. In that time my sexual education had expanded to accept that what people did in their own lives was their own business, whether straight or gay. I reckoned that as long as it was consensual and wasn't violent, it was okay by me. It was an enriching awareness. I had several gay friends and really enjoyed them, just as I knew some straight people who were real pricks.

Lula watched my tongue and licked her lips. 'I'm first in line darl,' she purred.

I laughed and moved over to the tall windows while Lula automatically began folding serviettes into snowy cones. There was still time enough to get two cakes out of the oven to ice and decorate and from the restaurant it was a great view of Taylor Square where the parade would come up Oxford Street.

The blue afternoon languished in the heat past the windows. Sydney Gay Mardi Gras banners lazed on the breeze all the way down Oxford Street. There was still some traffic skulking up from Hyde Park but I could see traffic police putting metal barriers right down Oxford Street to keep the spectators out of the way of the parade.

The street would empty of traffic soon and spectators would take up positions for the big event. On the shops and telegraph

'Dinner's ready,' says Martin, coming over and squeezing Lark's shoulders.

'Oh, I could do with more of that. Dinner smells yummy.'

Lark rolls her shoulders, before getting up to run upstairs to the bathroom. She picks up a box of matches from near the stove and lights an incense stick from Laeitje's shrine on her return. Martin raises an eyebrow but continues to serve the stir fry and smoothies he's just made.

'Mmm, yum.' Lark eats fast, suddenly ravenous. These babies make her so hungry. 'We've been here how long? A week? So I've still got another twelve days before I have to see Dr. Fournier again.'

'Yes, the appointment's on the 7th October.'

'Can we go to Hamburg for a couple of days then onto Denmark, Sweden and maybe Norway before we go back to Paris for the appointment?

'Sure we can.'

'Are you happy Martin?'

'Yes, though it will be good to get this research out of the way.'

'Are you still enjoying the meditations?'

'Yeah. There's something about it that is quite unique. It shakes up a lot of stuff, but in a good clean way. What about you?'

'Yes, I'm still enjoying it too, though I don't think I'll ever be a devotee.'

'Same here. We could get the CD and do it back at Bondi. Not too loudly though,' Martin laughs.

'There might be a centre in Australia somewhere.'

They finish dinner. Looking out at the steady rain puts them off venturing out, despite an earlier idea to try out the Sunday night Rustige Meditatie, at the centre.

Martin picks up the electric guitar again and plays some simple songs with the volume turned down. Lark drifts about the lounge room picking up things of Leisje's and turning them over in her hands while she thinks about her story.

'Any more blood?' asks Martin.

'A speck here and there but no clots.'

'Well I'm relieved about that, given how vigorous the meditation is.'

Lark snorts. 'Not to mention our sex life Martin. I actually feel fully charged, brimming with energy. Horny as hell.'

'Even now after a full day working on your stories?'

Lark smiles and sidles up to Martin, insinuating fingers around his neck. 'Yes you old rocker. Feel like going upstairs?'

'Again? Mmm, sounds delicious. I'll just compose a riff for my fans first.'

'Should be pink,' Lula observed the white serviettes with disapproval. She scanned the bookings folder. 'It's going to be so busy tonight. There'll be clients coming in early. They've booked the seats near the window so they've got the best view for the parade. 'Now grab that bag of streamers and balloons we got last week and let's get this place looking more festive. Go get that chef of yours to help,' Lula commanded as she fanned herself with a menu.

Sam walked out to greet Lula and grinned at her attire. He knew to make allowances for the day. He and Lula consulted on the night's menu as I returned to the kitchen to take cakes out of the oven and continue with icing four I'd cooked earlier.

Half an hour later the drinks waiter arrived dressed in a singlet, shorts and thongs with his formal shirt on a hanger over his shoulder.

'Gawd it's hot enough to fry eggs on the pavement out there,' Paul said, taking the plugs out of his ears and wrapping the cord around his walkman. 'You're not going to serve like that are you Lula?' He ogled her big bottom.

'Yessiree darl,' Lula drawled, reaching her arms up and

rubbing herself against him. Paul lost colour and backed away to safety behind the bar. We had a game of balloon tag until Paul got paranoid about his glasses and liqueur bottles. We all thought it funny how much time Paul spent shining and arranging those bottles. Even when it was frantic in the kitchen, he steadfastly refused to leave his allotted job to help.

'It'll be pumping here tonight,' Toby the kitchen hand said as he came though to the kitchen. 'Hi Marni.'

A wiry compact guy, Toby had that bleached look of most surfers, but loved to wear a cap over his wispy blonde hair. Only I knew he was prematurely balding despite only being in his twenties. He raised his cap just enough to wipe his sweaty forehead. His was the worst job working over the hot sinks and dishwasher.

'Hi Toby, howz the surf at Bondi today?

'Flat as glass,' he replied mournfully, tying on his apron. 'Oh by the way,' he fished in his pocket and pulled out a battered wallet. "Here's that twenty I owe you.' Toby was an eternal bott but always paid me back so I didn't mind too much.

'Thanks Toby,' I washed my hands and took my wallet out of my bag to stow the twenty dollar note.

'Finished with that?' Toby picked up one of my discarded icing bowls and ran his finger around it, taking it out with him to talk to Paul. I shoved my wallet away and pushed my bag back under the bench.

At 6pm our waitress Suze came in. She usually arrived with her flatmate Russell, who also waited our tables. Tonight she had a stranger with her.

'Russell couldn't make it, said to say sorry. He was up half the night throwing up. Food poisoning I think,' she gushed, looking from Lula to Sam. 'This is Jake, a friend of Russell's. He's waited tables at Cornrow in the city and Laurel's Cafe.'

Sam held his knife poised. 'How long did you work at Laurel's?'

'Nine months last year,' replied Jake, flicking his dark fringe out of his tawny coloured eyes. 'Ring and check with the chef Maurice if you want.' Lula went out to make the call and came *back with a positive response.*

'Get yourself an apron and familiarise yourself with the menu Jake,' Lula said briskly. 'Thanks for coming in. Suze? Can you organise the buffet carts and both of you can set tables. It's gonna be flat out tonight, starting in an hour.'

There was something quite mesmerising about Jake's eyes. Combined with chiselled cheekbones that rippled as he spoke, a trim figure and a small goatee, he turned me on, no doubt about it. I guessed from the logo on his tee shirt and those honed muscles of his that he was a gym junkie. When I met his eyes though, his slid away. Perhaps he had a girlfriend already.

The next hour got busy. I took a quick look at the street from the restaurant window before we opened. Sunset was still an hour away but the shadows were like long strands of liquorice along Oxford Street. There were hundreds of people already in position at the barriers. Buildings were already lit up with pink and blue neon and transformed into confections. Placards and banners had been put up to celebrate the Mardi Gras and to remind people of the political aspects of the parade – to give gay people more rights and respect in society. The Sydney Gay Mardi Gras had begun only a few years earlier, but 1983 looked like it was going to be a ripper.

At seven we opened the doors and very quickly the restaurant filled. Lula was in her element as many of the patrons dressed outrageously for the occasion. We opened the large restaurant windows facing Taylor Square at 8pm. Some of the clientele had paid extra to sit out on the awning to watch the parade. They clambered though with their wine glasses, food temporarily forgotten. Everyone else crowded around the windows to watch in a state of high excitement while Lula, Suze, Jake and Paul were busy serving and clearing tables.

'What a hoot!' said Toby, shutting off the commercial dishwasher to stare out at the spectacle coming up the wide street. I took a stool to the sink to look too. Sam came up behind me and rubbed himself against me as we watched.

There was an enormous crowd of enthusiastic spectators, ten or twenty deep as far down the street as I could see. After the giant banner with 'Sydney Gay Mardi Gras' splashed across it, carried by six of the most beautiful gays dressed in sequinned G-strings and winged boots, came a float blaring music, made to look like an Olympian temple with older guys simulating sex with young men. All their bodies were painted with gold and the leafy wreaths in their hair glowed with green tinsel. On the next float twenty moustachioed guys in leather S & M gear danced and writhed in formation. Gay mermen lounged on the next one, their tails draping along the edge of a sea castle ruled by a wide-chested Poseidon painted with turquoise sequins, who wielded his trident with lewd gestures.

'Oh it looks so cool!' I marvelled.

Watching this spectacle while Sam rubbed up against me made it all the more exciting. There were so many beautiful guys honed to their best, gyrating next to the floats. Having such fun.

The next dancers strutted by with the most fabulous peacock displays rising up from their backs, matched with iridescent bird masks. Holding a banner about homophobia, two semi-naked guys marched next, painted to look as if they'd been beaten.

'There they are! I've heard about them,' said Sam over my shoulder. 'Look!'

A float with bearded men dressed in nun's habits arrived with a painted gothic sign that read, 'Sisters of Perpetual Indulgence.' The nuns looked so naughty, showing their bare stilettoed legs and blowing kisses. The crowds cheered them on.

'Freaking hilarious, they'll upset the establishment!' said Sam.

We could hear their religious chant as they came into Taylor Square and passed by the cafe.

More synchronised dancers came next with exotic bejewelled butterfly wings and studded crotch pouches. Decorated floats and dancers with extraordinary costumes in all manner of undress continued to stream up Oxford Street to the enthusiastic applause and wolf whistles of the spectators. In the kitchen we could hear our guests roaring their approval from the restaurant and awning.

As the last of the parade passed into the junction of South Dowling Street, I turned to Sam and kissed him, more aroused than I knew what to do with, but I knew it was back to work any minute. And it was.

In a flurry Suze and Jake came through with plates and new orders. The rest of the evening passed in a blur of activity for us all. The restaurant took on a celebratory party atmosphere. I don't think Paul out at the bar had ever had to work so hard. We were all very relieved when last customers left at midnight.

Lula, Suze and Jake took the laundry cart out into the restaurant and cleared the tablecloths, serviettes and the worst excesses of consumption. All the decorations could stay until tomorrow. We cleared up, put foodstuffs away and set up the restaurant for tomorrow's lunch. Toby and Paul made doggie-bags to take home. Finally we converged in the kitchen to wind down.

'Did good guys!' drawled Lula, linking arms with her partner Marjorie, who usually arrived as Lula finished work. She looked like Lula's twin in a g-string, brassiere and Doc Martins, but with green hair gelled up with glitter. 'Now it's time to go partying, yippee!' Lula hooted as she left.

It was 1.15am and time for us all to go. 'Wanna to come to my place for the night?' I asked Sam.

'No, Marni, I'm knackered.'

'Okay,' I was pretty tired too. I plucked my bag out from under the cake bench and blew kisses to everyone. 'See you tomorrow.'

Lark rubs the sleep out of her eyes and squints at the pale sun shining through grey scudding clouds. After making love again last night, she'd stayed up late writing more of her story which she'd read to Martin somewhere before midnight. Suggestions he made spun webs in Lark's mind as she slept.

'Come on, we'll be late for the meditation.' She nudges Martin awake and wanders out to shower, feeling a little sore but satisfied after sex twice yesterday. Martin stumbles in, has a piss and gets in the shower too. From the look of him, he's ready to make love again but Lark takes him between thumb and

forefinger and points his stiffy down. 'We've gotta go soon.'
'Alright, alright,' mumbles Martin.

They cycle through the wet streets with minutes to spare, chain the bikes, chuck off their shoes and do the meditation. Afterwards they bike back with Leisje, who showers, has breakfast and leaves for work.

As planned, they catch the train into Noordermarkt, snagging a few more bargains. Lark has to restrain herself; the markets are full of marvellous things. She's in love with Amsterdam and what it has to offer. They walk along the canal and visit Anne Frank House, which Martin booked online the day before. It is a sobering experience and leaves them both thoughtful for the rest of the day.

'Such a different time and circumstance,' says Martin. His grandma had fled Italy to live in England just before the Second World War started; he recalls her anecdotes and sympathises with Anne Frank.

They arrive home before Leisje and Lark puts aside her ruminations about Anne Frank to finish what she now considers her frivolous story. Such a different time and circumstance indeed.

Outside a breeze ruffled the banners along Oxford Street and dried my sweat, allowing me to forget the cooking grime I was covered in. There were many groups of semi-naked revellers in outlandish costumes still out and about. The makeup on many faces looked smeared and tawdry but they looked happy and full of mischief. I walked down the side street past the East Sydney Technical College on my way to Darlinghurst where I shared a fusty old apartment with two friends. Most of the lights were on in the block; we were all young night-owls, especially tonight. I fished for my key in my bag, found it, but also found an absence; my wallet wasn't there.

'Shit,' I muttered, 'what a bore.' I rechecked my bag with some silly hope it might magically appear. Then I remembered Toby giving me the twenty dollars and cursed him, though I knew it wasn't his fault. Somehow my wallet had fallen out. My wallet

was back at the restaurant under the cake counter. Muttering, I turned round and headed back. I needed money to catch a bus down to Bondi early in the morning for a swim before work.

I slipped past a couple of snogging guys at the restaurant entrance and up the stairs to let myself in. Sam and I both had keys for the early shift. I shut the door, unaware of rustling sounds coming from the kitchen because the noisy old air-con unit near the door blocked a lot of sound.

As I rounded the door to the darkened kitchen I was stopped in my tracks. There was Sam, his naked body bathed in a pink and blue neon glow from lights outside, passionately kissing an equally naked Jake. I was so shocked that I stood there frozen into the shadowy spot near the bar area. Unable to move, unable to stop watching the guy I had the hots for in the arms of another – man.

Jake ran his hands down Sam's chest and hips. He proceeded to lick his way down to Sam's erect shaft, it pulsating with anticipation. Sam moaned and swayed against the stainless steel bench behind him as Jake took his cock into his mouth. He ran his teeth down to Sam's bulging balls and nipped them hard. Sam buckled and shuddered. I could see Sam was ready to blow. I knew how quickly that happened. But Jake pulled his mouth away and plunged his hand into a bowl on the bench. He grabbed a handful of ice-cubes and mashed them onto Sam's engorged cock. He collected more ice-cubes and ran them over Sam's shocked face and down to his nipples.

'Naughty boy, none of that,' said Jake. Sam's erection visibly wilted. 'My turn now,' he commanded, pulling Sam's head down to shove his own cock deep into Sam's gagging mouth.

I should go.... The thought slowly bubbled up through the shocked molasses of my mind. I was in turmoil, barely comprehending what I was seeing. Sam was a straight 'vanilla' man, yet here he was... Some threads of outrage writhed like tentacles of a jellyfish on the outer reaches of my mind but I just couldn't grasp them. The immediate sensuality I watched was as shocking as it was mesmerising.

Jake pulled his cock roughly from Sam's mouth. Sam looked

up at Jake like a supplicant to a new shrine.

'Up boyo, time to take it like a man,' Jake murmured. Pulling Sam to his naked feet and swivelling him. Sam looked over his shoulder at Jake. I caught his look of apprehension and compliance from my dim hiding place. Jake picked up a wooden spoon from the bench. With one hand massaging Sam's shaft, he began to stroke and softly smack Sam's buttocks with the spoon. I knew it was absurd but outrage bubbled in my mind. Jake was using my best mixing spoon!

When Jake was sure Sam had been lulled by this mild flagellation, he pushed him to lean over the bench. Sam's knuckles gripped the bench hard as Jake beat him while he masturbated. Sam grunted at each blow. Even in the neon glow, red spoon welts were easy to see appearing. Just at the point when my frozen mind began to rally and I wanted to barge in to stop them, Jake stopped. Sam gasped gutturally, his whole body quivering in shock.

'I really should go.' I ordered myself. Yet I just couldn't stop watching. Perhaps it was the nature of the evening. All that Mardi Gras titillation had inured me to this voyeurism.

'Spread,' ordered Jake, pushing his knees between Sam's. He spat on his hand and ran it down Sam's butt-crack, inserting his thumb in Sam's anus, almost sampling its pleasure it seemed to me in my deranged state of mind. Jake pinched Sam's balls and then guided his shaft into Sam's anus while biting down on Sam's shoulders.

They fucked hard for a few minutes, grunting like fighting stallions until Jake withdrew and commanded Sam to fuck him. When Sam entered Jake, I knew without a doubt that his vanilla days were over. Sam was utterly consumed by this experience. Even more, he hadn't prematurely come like he did with me.

The thought cut like a kitchen knife. A sob rose in my throat and I clamped my hand over my mouth. I stumbled away through the restaurant, my wallet forgotten. As I reached the door to the exit, I heard them both reach a crescendo of frenzied grunting as they bellowed out their orgasms, shouts entwined.

27

'Time for meditation again.' Leisje sings this morning while she showers. Martin bolts through next, followed by Lark. Martin is finishing breakfast when Lark comes downstairs.

'I'll be back tomorrow late afternoon.' He hugs and kisses her, picks up his backpack and is gone. Lark and Leisje follow soon after, biking over to the centre in the early sunshine.

When she returns to the flat and Leisje has gone to work, Lark checks her emails, texts and various social media. There is a missive from Michael again:

Lark, I've given 'Om' a quick read, it's hilarious. Sure to attract some interest. Style is improving.
Here's the next title I'm looking for:

Next article subs: Till death do us part
Same word count arrangement
Deadline: Monday 10/4/16 -10/11/16

Contact me any problems
Michael Lawson

She texts back to him.

Michael I've written an extra story, will I send it in? Lark

Yes of course, Michael texts back a few minutes later.

Lark opens up her new story and checks it, altering a few typos, editing and rephrasing a few lines here and there and signs it. She presses send, and slumps in the chair. What a marathon that was. Martin will be in France by now. She feels drained for the first time. All this writing, meditating and sightseeing and sex; she decides to have go back to bed for a nap.

She wakes up just before 1pm and fixes herself a sandwich and a juice. A handful of nuts next, with an apple. If she goes into the Centruum this afternoon, she can find something to see or go to another market. She decides to attend the orgiastic needs of her cervix, which swirls up, pressing. With the Amsterdam guide book in her hand she goes back to the bedroom to pleasure herself. She rubs the line of light bruises on the insides of her thighs from where Martin nipped her yesterday. With fingers and a fantasy, she brings herself to a groaning climax.

Afterwards she browses the guidebook, realising when she looks up, their bedroom is a mess. She makes the bed and tidies their clothes away into the cases. She folds up Martin's fleece jacket and holds it to her nose to take in his smell – she misses him already. She decides to put it on; wanting to envelope herself in something of his even though it is a mild day. In one pocket is a carabiner clip from their suitcases. In the other, a metro ticket from Paris which she draws out. With it there is a fold of pale pink notepaper, tied to the ticket with a strand of pink hair. Lark looks at it in her hand, a horrible prescience beating in her mind. She carefully slides the note away from the ticket, unfolds and reads it.

Martin
I need you, its urgent. Come back to Paris. Can we get together soon? 33 0624 994 281 Love Marcelle xxx

She reads the words again. Fifteen words. A tectonic plate grinding up in a molten lava flow. It reaches her toes, her heart, her mind and she screams, hurling off the jacket as if it is poisonous.

'Fucking bastard, fucking shit.' He's been fooling around, still playing a double game with me and his ex. A shower of needles pierce her perceptions. Lark shakes with rage, with hurt, with humiliation. She hurtles down the stairs to find her phone, punches in his number. No answer. Like last time he ran.

'Fuck! It's like before. He's bolted, this time back to Paris to see Marcelle. Well I'm not going to take it with patience and forgiveness this time. A women scorned, yeah. Hell hath no fury...' Lark screams in rage. 'What can I do, what can I do?' She paces the lounge room, guts churning, teeth grinding.

Go confront him, but how do I find where he is? Her mind is working, pistons pumping.

Yes, ask Jordy for Marcelle's address. No, don't want to trouble her. She races back upstairs. With the eyes of a forensic pathologist, she examines everything in Martin's case. I'm going to get Martin out of Marcelle's clutches. I love him – still. He is the father of our twins. Double worth it.

Nothing. No further clues in his case or contents. She unscrews the note she threw on the floor. The phone number. She jabs the number into her phone.

'Bonjour, ceci est Marcelle, laisser un message après le bip , je vous rappellerai.
'Hello, this is Marcelle, leave a message after the beep, I'll call you back.'

Lark hangs up and screams. A fucking answer phone. She tears at her hair, consumed with frustration, then feels remorseful and runs her hands over her tummy hoping the adrenalin rupturing in her mind isn't upsetting the babies.

Agh! What can I do, what can I do? The pain knifing her mind is intolerable. She sits on the bed, tries Martin's and Marcelle's numbers again. She finds finds herself reaching for her backpack and stuffing clothes and other necessities into it.

'I'll go to Paris and confront him. What can I tell Leisje?' she gasps through tears.

She phones Leisje at work and waits for departmental shuffling to locate her friend before she convinces herself it's a mad plan and she should wait until Martin returns. What if he doesn't come back? asks an evil whisper. What if he's been planning this all along? What if he was with her when he ran away? Shrieks of uncertainty trampoline her thoughts into more of a horror show.

'Hi Leisje, Martin's left some of his research books behind and I'll have to take them to Paris,' she manages to blurt. A crap excuse but all she can think of.

'Okay, can't you scan and send them or something?'

'No, there are two books and notes. He left in such a hurry this morning. I'll leave our cases here if that's okay and give the key to Mrs de Haas?'

'Just keep the key until you come back Lark. You have somewhere to stay tonight?'

She hasn't even thought about this detail. 'Yes I have, thanks Leisje. See you tomorrow.'

She tries Martin and Marcelle's numbers again with no luck. 'Argh.' She hurls the phone at their bed

She picks it up again and calls the Thalys office to book herself a ticket to Paris.

Pressing her temples, she concentrates on re-packing, heaving out the mad assemblage she stuffed into her backpack earlier. She goes to the toilet and changes into a comfortable dress and sandals.

'Just get this done,' she mutters, buckling her backpack on and gritting her teeth against the tears. She closes up the flat, relieved to keep the key and not face Mrs. De Haas. Less than an hour later she is on the next Thalys to Paris.

Lark recalls the train ride much later as hellish. Tissues are something shock doesn't think of so she uses her only tee shirt every time the tears stream down her face, unable to face the buffet car to buy some. She continues to try Martin and

Marcelle's phone numbers. She accelerates from disbelief to self recrimination, loathing to rage. Examining her last three years with Martin, she tries and fails to find clues. Ah the futility of her well meaning devotion; she disparages herself with bitterness. Suspicions crowd like gleeful ravens, to be dispersed with will when, between tears she remembers her unborn babies.

At 5.10pm as the Thalys is nearing Gare du Nord, Marcelle answers her phone.

'This is Lark, Marcelle.' Lark breathes hard. 'Is Martin staying with you?'

Marcelle pauses before answering. 'Er, yes. He will be home by 6pm he said.'

'Let him know I am arriving in Paris very soon. Please give me your address.'

'Really? You want to come 'ere?'

'Yes I do.'

There is a pause, she can hear Marcelle breathing. 'Okay.' Marcelle gives her the address.

Lark hangs up on her, unable to bear listening to her sultry voice any longer. 'Pink haired witch,' she spits into her tee shirt as more tears flow. What if Marcelle's baby is Martin's too? Lark folds over and hugs herself as the horrifying idea sweeps through her. She forces herself upright before other passengers do more than glance at her discomposure.

Lark strides through Gare du Nord, a tempest of rage focussed inward. She finds a taxi rank and caring little for the expense, zips across Paris in peak hour traffic. She alights and pays outside a nondescript high-rise with many apartments in Goncourt, not far from Belleville. Shouldering her pack, she presses the intercom for flat 14 and catches the lift to the third floor when Marcelle buzzes her through. The door is open and Martin is waiting for her.

They look at each other as if eons have past since they last kissed.

'What's going on Martin?' Lark shouts, blotchy and deranged. She feels like hurling her backpack at him, knocking him over, scratching and biting. Punishing him. Perhaps she'll save that for the bitch Marcelle.

'Lark, it's not what you think.'

'Really? Then what is this about?' She throws the crinkled piece of pink paper at him, dingo teeth snarling. He stoops and picks up the piece of evidence, glances at it and faces Lark again.

'Come inside and I'll explain.' Martin looks grim, his voice grave.

Lark wants to brawl right there on the doorstep, but follows him into the apartment, needing answers. Marcelle is waiting in the lounge room and stands, looking unnerved for the first time since Lark has known her. The flat reeks of clove cigarettes and sandalwood and is decked out with simple décor in minimalist colours. Martin stands next to Lark and reaches for her hand. She flinches and doesn't reciprocate, feeling the urge to slap him.

'Stuff you,' she mutters, thinking, I can go home and have the twins and never see him again. Tears spring down her face again at the thought.

'So you're with Marcelle now?' It's an agony to say.

'No, I'm not. I'm your partner, not hers,' says Martin. 'Lark, look at us, we don't look much like we're related do we? But we're twins, fraternal twins like you're carrying. Marcelle looks like our Mum and I look like Dad.'

Lark scrutinises them, her suspicion raging full pelt. Her artist's eye sees subtle similarities; the shape of their jaws, the curve of their eyelids and mouth shape. She hasn't noticed this before, having never seen them standing side by side. She draws a jagged breath, confused and still alight with scalding suspicion.

'But you said... you were with her.' She looks at Martin.

'So I was. As her brother.'

'We are twins,' repeats Marcelle. My real name is Michelle Oswald, same surname as Martins.'

'But I thought she was your wife. Martin you told me...' Lark is confused and reeling. a whisper flutters below her outrage, impossible to acknowledge.

'I said I lived with her and we owned a house together. We did, in Manly.'

'It's very complicated,' says Marcelle, fluttering her hands and grasping them before her.

'I'll tell you,' says Martin, sighing. 'We were born in England and emigrated to Australia when we were six, 1982 that was.' Martin looks at Lark, who still looks utterly molten with rage.

'Our twins Martin, what about them? I don't know if I can stand a history lesson from you,' she sneers. 'I'm not one of your students.' She sucks in a breath. 'Why haven't you told me this before? I'll tell you right now, I have never felt so much like hitting someone.' Tears scald her cheeks and she slaps them away.

Martin puts up his hands out in an attempt to calm Lark. 'Please, try to hear us out. I'm sorry. I understand your feelings.'

'You can't possibly understand my feelings Martin. I'm carrying our children but I'm finding out you're just a deceitful liar.'

A small moan escapes Martin's lips. He pulls himself together though and starts speaking again, while Marcelle hovers, holding an unlit cigarette. 'Mum and Dad thought a job offer in Australia for Dad in his early forty's was a win-win situation because he'd been retrenched and couldn't get work in London.' Martin looks from Marcelle, who nods, to Lark. 'We moved to Scotland Island in the Pittwater Estuary in Sydney. Dad worked as the ferry operator until we were fifteen. Mum stayed at home and looked after us. By then we were attending Pittwater High School.'

'I went there too,' Lark says, feeling even more bewildered.

Neither Martin nor Marcelle spark any memory from high school. She remembers little from those years anyway.

Marcelle takes up the story, shedding most of her French accent. 'Mum really missed England and her Italian mother, our Nona, so they decided to return to England. Martin refused to go. He was really happy in Australia and didn't want to leave, did you?'

'No, I didn't. The rest of the family packed, sold up and returned to England, leaving me in a boarding house to finish high school.'

Lark frowns and shakes her head. None of this is ringing any bells at all and she is feeling overwhelmed. Such a tempest of adrenalin and emotion has been storming through her the last few hours, a small part of her is amazed she can comprehend anything at all.

'It tore our family apart. Mum gained England and her aging mother but lost her son. I bore the brunt of that,' says Marcelle, her mouth the sharp line of bitter memory. 'I couldn't handle it. I'd lost my twin brother and I became Mum's grief councillor – enough to screw any young teenager's head up. I flunked my GCE A Levels and got in with a bad crowd of people. All the time I was firing off letters to Martin. I wanted him to come and fix things. To rescue me.'

She snatches up her lighter, but a slight look from Martin stops her.

'I was too wrapped up in my own stuff,' says Martin. 'Sure, I missed Marcelle, after all she is my twin... but I was independent, had a great set of mates and we were having lots of fun.' He shrugs. 'seemed so important at 18.'

'So I went AWOL, got into a lot of drugs and chaos. I reinvented myself as a languorous French girl; I'd topped year ten French before we left Australia.' Marcelle strikes a pose and looked at Lark to see if all this was sinking in. She sighs. 'I met Guil in my early twenties. A group of us, including Guil, decided on a hair brained, booze spawned idea to go to Australia to find my lost brother.'

'Okay, Stop.' Lark puts up her hands as if to ward their story off. While she thinks, they can all hear tinny French television playing in the next apartment. 'That's making sense – I think. But what about this sham marriage - the living together in Manly stuff Martin? Why all the secrecy - even from me? I mean – ouch... triple ouch. The sister in Canada? Does she exist?' She turns to Marcelle. 'Why do you keep asking me if I remember you Marcelle?'

Marcelle begins to answer but Martin cuts her off. 'I know Lark. I'm sorry. 'You're right, no sister in Canada, just one, Marcelle, in France.' He continues, 'I'd moved from Scotland Island to Sydney mainland long before. I was boarding in a place run by a very strict Mormon couple. When Marcelle found me, it was easier to say Marcelle was my fiancé when she visited than to tell them truth they probably wouldn't have believed,' says Martin.

'I was into very skimpy clothes back then, boob tubes and the tiniest of shorts. They nearly asphyxiated when they saw me.' Marcelle's eyebrows lift and she tosses her pink hair. 'Guil had met Jordy in a city nightclub by then but returned to Paris. I think he'd already made up his mind to be with her even then. I met you with Jordy one night out, remember?' asks Martin.

'We've discussed that and I barely remember it. You know my memory isn't the best. It was years later when we got together,' says Lark. She bites her lip, still barely comprehending the whirlwind of their history.

'We stayed in Sydney and bought a house with our inheritance when Mum and Dad died within months of each other. They were old parents to begin with and had a bad car accident. Dad died instantly. Mum lasted six weeks longer. When we bought the house, we continued our 'married' persona, partly for a dare and partly for convenience.'

'But I have some skeletons in my closet,' says Marcelle, pointing to her head. You really don't remember me do you Lark?' Marcelle asks.

Lark reaches back in her mind but draws a blank. She shakes her head 'no.' She still hasn't comprehended Marcelle as not-an-enemy and is scrambling to take in their twin history.

'The island Lark. Do you remember the house we used to visit with those delinquent surfie boys?' Lark's eyes widen and her breath catches as Marcelle continues. 'Do you remember those two surfers bringing their boards over on the ferry? Do you remember one of the boards being full of blocks of hash?'

'Yes I do,' Lark gasps, choking her words out. Something awful is about to be revealed, she can sense it. How can Marcelle know about that? She's about to blurt that she only wrote about this chunk of what she'd taken as an imagined embellishment of a vague memory, the other week, but she says nothing.

'I'm your bestie Michelle from that time Lark, before I left to go back to England.'

'No!' Lark is shocked to the core and staggers backward until she reaches the couch where she falls, shaking her head.

'Yes Lark. Look at me again. Look closely. My hair was white blonde back then. I had zits and crooked teeth. I was much plumper. An English plum ripe for plucking.'

Marcelle pulls back her pink hair and Lark sees the ghost of the girl she once knew. Her mouth drops open with shock.

'No! I don't believe it. How can I have forgotten? Blanked you out of my mind?'

'It's true Lark,' says Martin. 'I remembered you from high school when I met you with Jordy that time but you didn't remember me. Any wonder – I was just another weedy pimply boy until late high school when I shot up into a man. Michelle and I were secretive about being twins even then. We liked the idea that we knew something no-one else did,' he continues.

A collision of memories assaults Lark with the force of a petrol tanker. Her mouth hangs open as she tries to grasp something from this newly opened memory vault. High school was a rubbish experience with only one aim: to get the marks to get into university. She'd jettisoned those years within months of completing Year 12, friends and all, never looking back or contacting anyone from that time. Or so she thought.

'I remember you had a brother but never met him. You told me he was a pesky nerd and had as little to do with him as you could,' whispers Lark. 'That was you Martin?'

'The one and only.'

'There's more Lark,' says Marcelle, watching her with steady grey eyes. 'You remember the boys with the surfboard and the hashish,' Marcelle says again, fingers running along the seam of her shirt.

Lark shuts her eyes. She is about to hear something which she doesn't want to hear, she knows it.

'What they did to me. Sure I was keyed up to lose my virginity and stoned to the eyeballs, like you were. But not that way. Not by two guys. You couldn't help. You were stoned out of your mind too and just got punched aside when you tried to help me. Lay there while it was happening then crawled away to hide near those big speakers.'

Lark releases a guttural moan.

'I thought it was just something I imagined,' she whispers with horror. It can't be a memory. No, it can't be – really?' She looks at Marcelle, aghast.

The lid is off and the vault bares its sordid forgotten secrets. She'd crawled away and drowned out her friend's crying, listening to, 'Nothing Else Matters,' as it looped over and over, blaring from the speakers. She tried but couldn't save her friend. Marcelle nods a tight nod and both of them begin to shake and cry as they gaze at each other, the years stripping away.

'You and I swore not to tell anyone and I was already good at secrets,' says Marcelle, between tears. 'Twins often are, as you have just heard. You and I weren't supposed to be at that house. You took the ferry back to the mainland and I walked home. We stopped being friendly after that. You found your first boyfriend not long after and I could only watch your normal beginnings of womanhood from afar.'

A distant bitter twist distorts Marcelle's face while Lark wallows on the border of old memories, trying to gather shreds of the reality flowering in front of her.

'I'd look in the mirror and I didn't look any different to all our friends at school but the whiff of bong breath hung around my most intimate self and it took years to eradicate.'

'You remember all that?' asks Lark, squirming inside, sorrow for her lost friend, for their spoiled innocence, for her brushing it all aside in the whirl of growing up. She felt inside her backpack for the damp tee shirt to wipe the tears from her face.

'Like it was yesterday.' Marcelle picks up her lighter and lights her clove cigarette, inhaling deeply. 'You have a slight scar from the surfie's skull ring where it hit you. It's just on the edge of your jaw.' Marcelle blows smoke away as she reaches out and brushes her fingers on Lark's face, pressing on the faded scar.

Lark touches the scar too, disbelieving, yet knowing Marcelle is telling the truth. Martin finds a box of tissues, pulling out wads to dry their tears.

'As a result I have explored many different forms of self damage, sexual persuasions and bitter armour. Rape and upheaval makes it very hard to settle and accept a normal relationship.'

'I know, no I don't know, can only imagine,' Lark stutters. She can only envisage the long road women tread after rape to find psychological, emotional and physical restitution. She feels a stab of shame at writing her story, 'Big Ticket.' But how could she have known? She'd buried the experience so deep it barely surfaced, even in dreams. Of all her stories, it was one of the ones that Martin didn't read; perhaps if he had, he might have recognised something of what she'd divulged.

She looks from Martin to Marcelle, seeing their similarites as obvious now. Her freaked out emotional abyss within is still open, but has lost much of its raw panic. The fear that Marcelle's baby is Martin's has dissolved.

On the arm of the couch, Martin sits, watching his sister and lover, sympathetic to the upheaval they are going through. Especially Lark. He touches her shoulder and she bends her damp face into his hand, still angry with his artifice, but exhausted.

'I didn't know you were Marcelle's best friend then. Pubescent boys have their own concerns. When she told me ten years later what had happened, I vowed I'd find those two lowlifes. Coming from the island, it wasn't hard to trace a couple of the old members of that surfie house. It was amusing to see them — straight, short haired with families of their own. Shit scared that their past was going to drag up unsavoury details they'd perpetrated and so relieved when the axe fell elsewhere.' Martin flexes his hands, forming fists. 'From there I traced one of the men to Bali, only to find he'd died of a smack overdose a year before. The other one has been more slippery to locate, but I'm fairly sure he's living in Western Australia. I haven't finished my threads of research on him yet.' He looks grim. 'If I'd known about those guys when all this happened I'd have crushed them into dust.' Martin punches a fist into his open hand with an uncharacteristic grinding motion.

Silence drapes its soft eiderdown over the three of them, each lost in a web of intrigues over twenty year's old. Marcelle gets up and with a clatter of cups, makes tea in the kitchen. When she returns, Martin and Lark are still a performance art of stillness. The simple ritual of serving tea breaks the silence.

Lark wilts further into the couch. She arrived so revved up for confrontation. The story she concocted from Marcelle's note and the actual reality are so disparate. They are like two film negatives of the same picture that are impossible to align. She'll need a great deal of time to process all of it. She puts down her tea, stands in a wobbly way and reaches out to Marcelle, pulling her into a careful hug.

'Marcelle... Michelle, I missed you so much for years when you left for England. I just had to blank your leaving, it was too painful, even though it appeared I didn't care. I'm sorry I couldn't help you – so sorry. We wrote on and off didn't we?'

'But we lost touch,' whispers Marcelle.

'I just blanked it all out, particularly that part of the hash surfboard memory. It was more like a ghastly black story I imagined. They look at each other and cry again. Lark offers a hand to Martin and pulls him into their embrace.

'I've doubted you so much the last few weeks Martin,' snuffles Lark. They pull apart and grab more tissues as they resettle on the couch and chairs. 'I still don't get why you never told me.'

Martin thinks for a moment, biting his lip. 'Old habits die hard Lark, and old secrets bide their time. Michelle and I built a wall around ourselves and created our own world full of secrets when we were kids. We all have stories tucked away from prying eyes, family and friends, even our own eyes.'

Lark nods. She knows all too well, Martin is right; so many elements of her new stories come directly from her private stash. At least she knows Martin and Marcelle's truth now.

'But if you knew we were friends why didn't you tell me you were Michelle's sister? Lark blurts, another revelation crashing through her mind

'I don't know. I guess I thought you'd both had a falling out way back then. Neither of you mentioned each other ever.' Martin shrugs. 'No point trying to resurrect what's dead and buried. It didn't matter... we've been so happy together Lark.'

'And that's why you've been so freaked out about the twins Martin?' says Lark, changing track, the thought bubbling up to make some kind of sense.

'Yes. I don't want to bring twins into the world with parents that are less than committed. Our parents were, until they returned to England, following whims that jeopardised our stability. It wan't so much an issue for me 'coz I was already 18, but it really affected Michelle. Commitment to parenting has to be more than that for me. You understand?' Martin looked at her with a charged seriousness.

'I do now,' says Lark, awed, yet relieved they are communicating about it at such a deep level. 'We have enough love and compatibility between us to be good parents for them Martin. She sits again and collects her tea. 'Endurance as well. Perhaps I'm naïve but I think you know that too, in spite of your history, in spite of your fear.'

Martin lets out a sigh. 'I've been having a deep think these last weeks, especially this last one in Amsterdam. We've only known about the twins for a bit over a week, right? Leisje taking us to that meditation every morning has helped shake out my anxieties and release some of them. I can be a dedicated dad. I'm ready now. And I believe we can go the distance.' With a tentative smile, he adds, 'Bring it on.'

Still teary, Lark chokes as she launches herself at him, bestowing kisses. 'Oh Martin, I understand now.' She looks over at Marcelle smoking while she toys with her teacup.

'What about your pregnancy Marcelle? Is that why you wanted Martin here?' There is a quick look between Martin and his sister and then Marcelle nods. They've been discussing it, she can tell. 'Ah, the research. Am I right? Is that why you came back to Paris?'

Martin looks sheepish. 'Yes. I don't want Marcelle to go off and have another termination, especially after all the hard thinking I've been doing about our pregnancy. Our twins. I needed to confront my own stuff from the past and the termination barrow I was pushing, before I could talk to her.'

'Sorry Lark, to freak you out so much. I also have had many

doubts this pregnancy. I needed to talk to Martin.'

Lark gives them both a searching look. 'Believe me Marcelle, I understand. We've been going through so much soul searching too. We women are assigned a womb, but the choices that come with it are not easy.' She rubs her forehead with the palm of her hand.

'Who is the dad Marcelle? Just tell me if it's none of my business. I can be a nosy dingo sometimes.'

Marcelle stubs out her second cigarette with a grim twist.

'Alejandro is a Spanish bisexual friend of mine. I have an occasional thing with him when he visits Paris. He stayed with me for a few weeks. I might be amoral by most standards but I have one rule: one at a time, for reasons you know about.'

Lark winces, still raw from their barrage of knowledge.

'We have already talked about it and Marcelle has contacted Alejandro. He is not adverse to the idea of being a father, but will probably be an occasional dad. Having talked to him myself, I don't think we can expect much more, though strangely, his Catholic roots took centre stage and he was very against a termination,' says Martin.

'What about you Marcelle? Do you want to be a mother?'
Marcelle flutters her hand. 'I don't know I'd make a good mother. I have become very selfish as I've become older.' She stares into middle distance at some invisible image of herself holding her own child. 'Being a single mother can be hard too, I see it often.'

'Not wanting to pop your jaded bubble Marcelle, but you are great with Celeste. Much more a natural than me.'

Marcelle gives Lark a wistful smile. 'Perhaps.'

'Alejandro is coming back to Paris to talk it over with Marcelle. He'll be here in a few days.' Martin reaches out to Lark again and she takes his hand and places it on her belly. They have been through the ringer today and come out the other side of their astonishing story. She has a lot to think about.

All Lark's vital functions, stalled because of the high stress make themselves known with a surge. 'Where is your toilet Marcelle and do you have anything I can eat? These babies and I are starving.'

28

'That's as far as we got reconciling our intertwined histories and coming to terms with the event of your arrivals,' Lark says, gazing from the slate blue Pacific out the window to the three expectant young faces sitting opposite her and Marcelle.

'Your father Alejandro, who you look so very like Josh, arrived a few days later. A kind, bear of a man, who rode his moped up from Madrid. He suited me just fine and convinced me to have you,' says Marcelle, looking at her son.

'Martin and Alejandro hit it off and we became excited that we could have a joint pregnancy, birth and be new parents together. They went out on the moped to get some wine to celebrate. They were run down by a truck near Belleville Station and killed instantly.'

The sadness is still there even after eighteen years, thinks Lark, and always will be. She looks at her twins Kirra and Clancy, all grown up now, looking like both Martin and herself, but like themselves as well.

'After a terrible period of turmoil and sadness, Lark and I banded together and returned to Sydney to have you all. We were very lucky to have Lark's mum to help and all your births were problem free,' says Marcelle.

'I didn't manage to write the story for the agency for a couple of years after Paris and your births. Michael's article criteria; 'Till death do us part,' was just too close to those terrible events.' Lark looks at her daughter Kira, who has been an avid writer since she was ten.

She reaches out for Marcelle's hand. 'Since then I've continued to freelance for the agency while Marcelle took over the fashion boutique in Mosman.'

'Somewhere along the way we became middle aged lesbians, successfully co-parenting you three without your dads.' Marcelle nods at them and smiles. 'We know you've all wondered about your beginnings since you were tiny and why you have two mothers but no fathers. Now you're all eighteen, the real story of your conceptions and the events that created our unusual little family can be shared.'